Other books in the Alexis Davenport series:

Dangerous Reflections (Book One)

Twisted Reflections (Book Two)

Desperate Reflections

The Adventures of Alexis Davenport, Book Three

Shay West

Booktrope Editions
Seattle, WA 2014

Cover Design by Shari Ryan

PRINT ISBN: 978-1-62015-535-6

EPUB ISBN: 978-1-62015-542-4

Acknowledgments

There are a lot of people to be included in this section:

Thanks to A.M. Donovan for entering a contest to name this book. I think *Desperate Reflections* sums up the emotions in this book better than I could have ever imagined.

Thanks to Jeff and Lisa Hollar for entering a second contest geared toward finding a point in time for the final showdown between Alex and Drifter. And while I tweaked the idea a little, the pair of them still came up with the time and place.

Thanks to Michelle Tracey for giving her local library paperback copies of the first book of the series, *Dangerous Reflections*. Because of your gift, many people have enjoyed the book, and there's no greater gift than the gift of adventure!

This final book of Alexis Davenport is for the fans. She wouldn't have made it this far in her adventures without you!

Chapter 1

ALEXIS DAVENPORT CHEWED on her nails while she waited for her best friend, Jennifer McDonald, to show up at the house. She tried to distract herself by checking her Facebook but her mind kept replaying her last trip through the mirror. She'd never experienced anything like it. Seeing herself and the girl whose body she would inhabit, floating in the void, being jerked rudely back into her own body.

What happened?

For the hundredth time, the question flashed through her mind. And for the hundredth time her mind drew a blank.

When the doorbell rang, she nearly tossed her computer on the floor in her haste. She ran to the front door and opened it so quickly Jennifer squealed in fright.

"Geez, Alex! Give me a heart attack why don't ya."

"Sorry," Alex said as she grabbed Jenn by the arm and yanked her into the house.

"Leave my arm attached, please and thank you."

Alex ignored Jenn as she ran back to her room. She slammed the door behind them, knowing her mother wouldn't hear. She was at work and wouldn't be home for hours yet.

"Okay, something has really got you spooked. Something happened didn't it?"

Alex turned and faced her best friend in the whole world, the only person who knew her secret. She hadn't planned on telling anyone about her ability to travel back in time. But when Jenn had walked in on her while her spirit was gone, Alex didn't have any choice but to tell her. It had been a relief, really. She finally had someone she could confide in and someone who could help try to figure out the ins and outs of this special gift.

Through trial and error, Alex had figured out that she was a Traveler, someone who could travel back in time using mirrors or any reflective surface. The first time her reflection in the mirror had changed to that of a young woman from Ireland, she had been sure she was losing her mind. Or suffering from an inoperable brain tumor.

When she realized her gift meant that her life was in danger, she almost wished she *did* have a brain tumor. An evil Traveler was going back in time, trying to change history and it was up to Alex to stop him. She had no idea why he was going back or what his ultimate plan was. To her, it didn't really matter. When the Traveler went back in time, she had no choice but to follow.

Only the last time she had traveled, something had happened before she could complete the transfer of her spirit to the Mongol girl she had seen in the mirror. She had been trapped in the void and had been pulled back into her own body before the transition could be completed.

"So are you going to tell me what happened or stare at me all day?"

Jenn's question pulled Alex back to reality. She told Jenn what had happened, wincing as her friend yanked her journal out to write down every word of Alex's account. Jenn swore she was going to write a book someday and make a million dollars when some big Hollywood producer asked for the movie rights. Alex was afraid someone would find the journal, have her committed to an asylum somewhere on a remote island or high atop a mountain and leave her in a white room for the rest of her life.

"Oh, man. Just when we thought we had everything figured out..." Jenn shook her head. "Did Sean or his Master say anything about this?" Jenn flipped through the journal, trying to find the spot where she had detailed Alex's meeting another Traveler like herself, someone else working on the side of good.

Alex shook her head. "I've been over every detail of the trip to Scotland and I got nothing!" She flung herself face down on her bed, ignoring Jenn's annoyed snort as the jostling caused her to muss the page.

"I can't find anything either."

"I am so tempted to tell mom or Aunt Karen or someone else about this. Things are getting out of control. I'm not sure I can deal with this by myself much longer."

"By yourself? What am I, sliced bread?"

"You know what I mean. Seems like something an adult should be aware of, ya know?"

"I don't know, Alex. The only reason I believed you was because I found you standing there in the bathroom like a corpse." Jenn shivered. "Do you really think your mom would believe you?"

Alex groaned. "Probably not."

"What about telling the boys?"

"Paul and Simon? I don't know, Jenn. What good can they do?"

"I don't know. Just seems like a better idea to tell them than an adult. At least they have imaginations and would probably buy it."

"Maybe we should just keep this between the two of us."

"Yeah, maybe that's best." Jenn cleared her throat. "So, what have you decided to do about Drake?"

Alex wanted to put her hands over her ears and pretend she hadn't heard Jenn's question. She didn't want to get into another fight about her boyfriend. Or maybe soon-to-be-ex-boyfriend.

Am I really going to break up with him?

"I have been a little distracted by the mirror stuff." Alex said, hoping Jenn bought the excuse.

When her reply was met with stony silence, Alex dared to look up at her best friend, hoping she hadn't made her angry. Alex was tired of fighting about her changing feelings for Drake. When she saw Jenn staring at a page of the journal with her face pale as a sheet, Alex jumped to her knees and snapped her fingers in front of Jenn's nose.

"Jenn, what is it?"

Jenn shook her head and squealed so loudly that Alex gasped in fright. "Alex, oh my *gawd*, I can't believe that we never thought of this before. It's been right there in front of us the whole time!" Jenn giggled and jumped up and down while seated cross-legged on Alex's bed.

"Would you mind filling me in?"

"We are serious idiots for not thinking of this sooner. I mean it, Alex. Serious. Idiots."

Alex grabbed the journal from Jenn's clenched fists, forcing the girl to look up and into her face. "What are you talking about?"

"Sean and Gavin, Alex. What time do they live in?" Jenn stared at her smugly.

She sighed. "I really don't think we have time for games. If you have something to tell me, just spill your guts already!"

Jenn merely blinked a few times and refused to say another word. Alex clenched her jaw.

"The 80s. Happy now?"

"And what century? The 80s can refer to 1580, 1280..."

"Nineteen eighty. And if you don't tell me what the hell you are so excited about I swear, I'll..." Alex gasped, her heart skipping a couple beats. She broke out in a cold sweat and her mind went completely blank, refusing to latch onto what she was certain had been Jenn's point.

"So the super genius finally gets it!" Jenn grabbed Alex by her upper arms and shook her while she whooped and shouted so loudly Alex wanted to clamp her hands over her ears. Instead, both girls jumped up and down on their knees, screaming and laughing at the same time.

When she could breathe again, Alex grabbed her laptop while Jenn called her mom and asked if she could spend the day at Alex's. Alex barely heard her as she opened a window in Google, fingers shaking so badly she could barely type the words.

Sean and Gavin could be alive in my time!

Chapter 2

MAX PODER TOOK a deep drag off his cigar and blew it out slowly, watching the smoke swirling toward the shelf that held a myriad of old photographs. The old black and whites were his most prized possession. He spent many an hour gazing at the faces, though he hardly needed to. He had them memorized.

Staring at the faces of his ancestors usually filled him with pride and a peace that nothing could shake. But not today. Max sighed and snubbed out his cigar in the large crystal ashtray sitting on his desk. He picked up the phone and dialed. When the voice answered he said, "Get to my office."

Max waited with his fingers steepled under his chin. When he heard raping at the door he answered, "Come in."

Lane Stygian strode into the office, his face his usual mask of stone. Max wished he hadn't trained the man to hide his emotions so well. He pointed to a chair and smiled as Lane sat down. Max watched his student for a time. Lane merely stared back.

"Lane, my boy, we have ourselves a situation." Max used Drifter's given name knowing full well the man hated to be called Lane. He preferred Stygian or the name his comrades had given him: Drifter.

"Yes, sir," Drifter answered.

"It needs to be handled most delicately."

"Agreed, sir."

Max sighed, knowing he wouldn't get any more than one word answers. "Perhaps it's best you not travel for a while, until I can find a way to get rid of the...ahem...*problem*."

"Any other orders for me, *sir*?"

Max smiled. Finally, the man's stony façade was beginning to crack. "As a matter of fact, I do. While you might not be able to travel for a time, that's no reason that my plan must come to a halt. There's one important thing you can be doing that doesn't require you to travel."

"And what would that be?" Drifter sat up straight in his chair.

"I need you to do some research." Max leaned forward as he revealed his plan and the part Drifter was to play.

He laughed aloud at the naked hunger in Drifter's eyes as he saluted. Max dismissed his man and leaned back in his chair, relighting his cigar and pouring himself a glass of bourbon. While his plan would still move forward, there was the little matter of Mark witnessing Drifter's traveling. He had come up with the explanation that Drifter had a medical condition. But Mark was smart and Max knew the man didn't believe a word of it.

How could he have been so careless?

Max threw the glass against the wall, growling in fury. Everything depended on Drifter's success in changing the past. Not only had he been thwarted at every attempt by a specially gifted Traveler—and a *girl* no less—Drifter now had to worry about a fellow soldier finding out his secret.

And ruining all of Max's plans.

He walked to the shelf and grabbed a picture that was hidden behind all of the others, dusting it on the sleeve of his uniform. He gazed into the dark eyes he knew so well. His heart swelled with pride as his thumb gently traced along the insignia of the Schutzstaffel: Adolf Hitler's infamous SS.

I will succeed in my plans to bring honor and glory back to our family once again.

Chapter 3

ALEX LOOKED UP as the bell rang and shoved her books in her backpack. As she walked down the hall to meet Mr. Edwards, she tried to calm her nerves. Today was her first tutoring session and she had no idea how to tutor a large group. She tried to help her friends with their homework but most of the time she just let them copy her, knowing they would pay the price in the end when they didn't do well on their tests.

She was also distracted by thoughts of Sean and Gavin. She desperately wanted to locate the pair. She would finally have someone who could Travel to help her in the here and now. Alex hoped the three of them could find a way to defeat the evil Traveler.

You have to find Sean and Gavin first, Alex.

As she got closer to the room, she heard rowdy voices and the sound of chairs scraping against the floor. Taking a deep breath, Alex opened the door. When she saw who was in the chair closest to the door, she wanted to turn tail and leave.

Beau Johnson, the hottest guy in school, sat grinning from ear-to-ear. When he spotted Alex, he whispered something to the boy behind him and they broke out into laughter.

Could my life get any worse?

"Let's settle down. I've asked Alex to help. If you want to continue playing sports, and make it to your senior year, I suggest you take this seriously."

Alex smiled gratefully at Mr. Edwards as the class quieted down.

"Now, I've chatted with the other teachers and we have a plan for the semester. We'll be hitting all subjects so I hope you are as good with science and math as you are with history. Here you go."

He handed Alex a stack of papers.

She flipped through the pages, breathing a sigh of relief. Most of the stuff was fairly easy. She grinned as the students in the room groaned and whispered to each other, none having a clue what most of the material was covering.

"Let's break into groups. I'll lead one and Alex can lead the other. Any questions?" Mr. Edwards looked over the top of his glasses as though daring anyone to speak. "Fine. Starting on this side of the room, you'll be in group number one, you're in number two, you're in number one..."

Alex counted in her head quickly trying to see which group Beau would end up in. *Why does it matter? You don't even know what group you're in charge of!*

"Okay, I'll take group one and you take group two, Alex. We'll go over the first page today."

She wanted to groan when she saw Beau heading in her direction. She swallowed against the dryness in her throat and fought the urge to smooth her hair. As the students took their seats, she read through the first page of the packet Mr. Edwards had given them, relief washing over her as she read the familiar information. The students would be going over the history of the United States beginning with its discovery.

I could do this in my sleep.

Alex wondered if she could force the mirror to change so she could go back to visit those early years in American history. She often tried to visualize what the country must have looked like back then, so wild and new and free. *Not to mention dangerous.*

"Are we going to sit here all day or are you going to help us?"

Alex blushed and looked up at a tall girl with a surly expression on her face. She was slouched down in her chair and tapped her pencil on the desk.

"Just getting my brain ready to discuss history."

"Don't you have any books or anything?" the girl asked.

Alex cleared her throat. "Well, no. I don't need them."

"Told you she thinks she's better than everyone else."

Alex turned to the voice. Another girl, someone she had seen hanging out with Catelyn Montgomery, the meanest girl in school and Alex's mortal enemy, looked at Alex with a sneer.

"I never said I was better than anyone else. I can't help it if I'm good in school. History's my thing. I don't need a book for what we're doing today. Now, who can tell me what you've gone over last week?"

No one said anything. Alex's anger rose when she noticed that six of the people in her group had their phones out and two others had earbuds in their ears. The rest looked at the clock or their watches and rolled their eyes.

"Did any of you even go to class last week? Do you have Alzheimer's and can't remember?" Alex asked.

"Look, Alex, we know you were forced into doing this. Why don't you just be cool and let us hang out while we're here. You wanna be cool don't you?" Beau asked, smirking at her.

"I'm not here to hang out. I'm here to tutor you so you can pass your classes. Doesn't it worry you that you won't be allowed to play ball if you fail?"

Beau blew her off. "Are you kidding me? Do you really think the athletic coaches would kick us off the team? It's a scare tactic."

She clenched her jaw against her first instinct to respond. She had been in this argument with Beau before and he obviously didn't see the need of an education. *Why should I care if they just sit on their asses and fail?*

As she sat watching the students staring at their phones, bobbing their heads in time to the music they were listening to, or with their heads on their desks, her rage exploded. Part of her knew that much of her anger was due to her Traveling but there was nothing she could do to stop it. Alex stood and grabbed the phones out of the hands of two students closest to her while at the same time kicking the chair of a student who was sleeping. She didn't care that the other group led by Mr. Edwards was now staring at her like she was insane.

"You want to play with this crap? Fine. Do it out there." She pointed to the hall. "As long as you're in here, you'll put the damn phones away and pay attention. You want to fail? Then do it somewhere else. For any of you that want to pass you classes so you don't get held back like some moron, feel free to stay.

"I'm taking time out of my busy schedule to help you guys. I really couldn't care less if you pass or not. Instead of being rude, lazy, jerks, how about you show a little respect and maybe put forth a little effort? With my help, you may pass your classes. Mr. Edwards asked me to help because I'm good at history and he knows I can help you. So how about giving me a chance before blowing me off?" Her breath came in gasps and she felt the heat in her face but she stood her ground. She tossed the phones in the laps of the students she took them from and waited for anyone to get up. When they all stayed put, she sat back down and faced her group.

"Now, once again and I'll say it slowly so you can understand me: What. Did. You. Do. Last. Week?"

Chapter 4

ALEX RUSHED HOME from school, eager to tell her mom about what happened in her tutoring session, but more so to get on the computer and see whether or not she could find any information on Sean or Gavin. She had searched for information on Sean but it was impossible to search through them all. He would be in his forties and Alex wasn't sure she would even recognize him from a picture. Today she planned on searching for Gavin. His name was unique enough that she thought she would have better luck and his appearance wasn't likely to have changed that much.

"How was your first day as a teacher?" Alex's mom, Patricia, teased.

Alex rolled her eyes. "I wasn't a teacher, Mom. It started out horrid but ended up being pretty good, actually." Alex told her mom about her outburst at the behavior of the students she was supposed to be helping.

"You know, I'm starting to wonder if all this technology isn't hurting you kids. Everywhere I look, you guys have your noses plastered to your gadgets. Just yesterday there were two girls in the store and they never spoke one word to another. Just kept plucking away at their phones." Patricia shook her head.

"We just like to keep in touch with our friends, Mom. It's not that big a deal."

"It was big enough that you lost your temper when it was interfering with your responsibilities."

Alex refused to admit her mom may be right. "Anyway, I got a handle on things. I'm going to start on my homework."

"Okay, I'll holler when dinner's done."

Alex shut the door to her room, grabbed her computer, and hopped on her bed, wiggling around until she was comfortable. She opened her browser and her Facebook page popped up. She wanted to search for information on Gavin, but she couldn't resist the urge to check her newsfeed to see what her friends were up to. *Mom would say I'm addicted or something.*

Jenn wasn't online to chat with so she scrolled aimlessly through her newsfeed. Just when she had decided that there was nothing much going on and that the information of Gavin wasn't going to be found amongst Grumpy Cat memes, idiot status updates, and the endless parade of inspirational pictures, she saw a recent post from Drake.

Alex sighed when she realized she hadn't given him a single thought all day. She clicked his name, curious what he had been up to even though a large part of her really didn't care. His wall was full of posts about the first theater production of the year and updates from Spotify. Gavin's face flashed through her brain.

Just as she was about to open a new window in her browser, she spotted something that made her breath catch in her throat. She scrolled down to get a better look. His status had changed from "in a relationship" to "single".

Why didn't he tell me?

Tears sprang to her eyes as she thought about what she should do. She hadn't changed her status yet. *Maybe I should. It would serve him right.* Alex went to her profile and changed her relationship status to single. She hoped he saw it and realized what a jerk he was for not even having the decency to talk to her about it. She grabbed her phone and texted Jenn, seething as she punched the buttons.

-Why do you care? You wanted to break up with him anyway.

-That's not the point. He should have told me.

-You have barely spoken a word to him in months. What did you expect?

-You just don't understand.

Alex tossed the phone on her bed face down, refusing to look as it vibrated at Jenn's response. With shaking hands, she went into her friends list and found Drake's name. She clicked on the Friends link and hesitated with her pointer over the Unfriend option.

Just do it Alex. It saves you having to actually speak to the guy. He's obviously moved on. Time for you to do the same.

She clicked the Unfriend option and closed out her Facebook window. She opened up a new browser window to search for Gavin's name, her fingers hitting the keys on her laptop so hard she feared they would pop off. Alex scrolled down through the list of names hoping one would stand out at her. There were a few advertising funeral homes, some LinkedIn profiles, even some on Facebook. She aimlessly clicked links, her frustration rising when the men she saw on the pages were clearly not Sean's Master.

Alex tried looking up Gavin's name and pairing it with the word Scotland thinking that would narrow the search. She sighed and scrolled down the list. After a few minutes, she shook her head, realizing she had scrolled down the entire list without actually reading any of the links. Alex groaned and moved her mouse back to the top of the page, determined to pay more attention this time around.

It's Drake's fault.

She was still fuming over his relationship status change and wanted to send him a text or perhaps call him and confront him about it. She only felt a little guilty at how angry she was. After all, she was the one that had ignored him for so long, trying to figure out why she was feeling that way about him. He was a great guy, nice, attentive, into theater, had a brain and could actually carry on a conversation, not to mention how hot he was.

So why didn't she want him anymore?

Alex chewed her lip. If she could figure out why she was avoiding Drake, maybe she could make it go away and they could start over. *But do I really want to?* She missed the dinners, movies, and date nights at Banana's Fun Park. Alex flushed when she realized how much she would miss the kissing and the necking.

Beau's face filled her mind and she gulped at the rush of heat that filled her face. It didn't matter how mean he was or that he had dated the girl that had made her life a living hell, Alex couldn't help but wonder what it would be like to kiss him or to feel his hand on her leg.

And there are those guys back in the past.

She closed her eyes. While she had been in the bodies of the girls in the past, there had been a man in each time period, someone who had made her toes curl and her heart beat so hard she feared it would burst from her chest. Each one had been different and yet there was something familiar about them, something that each one shared that made her wonder if she'd known them her whole life. *But that's impossible.*

Alex knew she was looking for something like that and she just didn't feel it with Drake. *I don't feel it with Beau either.*

"Oh for heaven's sake, Alex, stop fussing over boys. You have more important work to do," she mumbled to herself.

She methodically clicked on each link on her computer, switching between web and photo searches, hoping one of the photos would be of Sean's Master looking all handsome and dashing and Scottish. The more she searched, the more desperate she became, nearly crying when a link led to another dead end. The thought of having someone to talk to who had her same gift, someone who could advise her, was overwhelming. She didn't hold out the hope that her Traveling days were over. She didn't want to face the evil Traveler again. Alex shivered and hugged her arms across her chest. She knew she'd been lucky during the previous encounters and had barely escaped with her life from several of them. She didn't want to die.

I need to find Sean and Gavin!

Chapter 5

"SO IT'S OFFICIAL, huh?" Jennifer asked.

Alex nodded. She nibbled on her sandwich so she wouldn't have to answer right away. "Maybe it's for the best. I mean, it's not like I planned on marrying the guy or anything."

"That's true. It's so weird imagining our parents marrying so young. I mean, the last thing I want is to be tied down and start having kids."

"You? Have kids? I can't picture it."

"I don't know. That's what girls are supposed to do, right?"

"Not unless you want to."

"What about you, Alex? You want kids?"

Alex sighed. "I haven't thought about it. There's so much to do before I get to that point: get through high school, college, meet someone I actually want to marry..."

"If you wait till you do all that stuff, you'll be like thirty before you have kids. Geez, that's so *old!*"

"I know, right? Maybe I just won't have kids and focus on my career."

Jenn shoved a cookie in her mouth. "That sounds like a good plan. Kids are so much work and way too expensive." She swallowed. "Hey, did you have any luck searching for Sean or Gavin?"

"Not at all. I think I just need to figure out how to group words together to search better, that's all. I can't give up."

"They're out there somewhere. Too bad Scotland is so far away. If they lived here in the States, we could maybe just go for a visit."

"Oh man, that would be so awesome! Mom will never let me go to Scotland."

"I doubt mine would either. But hey, worse comes to worse, you can always go next year when you turn eighteen."

Alex groaned. "I hope I am done with this whole Traveling thing long before I turn eighteen."

The bell rang and the girls parted ways, planning to meet after school to ride together to the local university's theater. They had a new professor this year, Ms. Ashton, and she wanted the students to rehearse in the larger theater the university had whenever they could. She said it helped them with their projection of their voices so they would reach all the way to the back of the theater.

Alex had advanced biology and her tutoring session that afternoon. And while she was looking forward to her biology class, she was dreading the tutoring. She hoped the students would remember what had happened at their first session and behave themselves. She didn't want to have to take phones away again today.

She walked into the tutoring classroom and was relieved to see only a handful of students. While she was listening to her biology teacher chattering about dominant and recessive traits, she had thought of a fun activity to help the students study for their history material. While she waited for the rest of her group to show up, Alex drew pairs of rectangles on the white board, drawing horizontal lines across one of the pair.

The students filed in and sat near the white board, a few taking out their phones. Alex crossed her arms and raised an eyebrow and the students rolled their eyes, placing their phones in their backpacks.

"I thought we were here for history, not art class," Beau said.

Alex ignored the laughter and took a deep breath, trying to slow her galloping heart. She grabbed her notes for the material she received from the history teachers and turned to face her group.

"I thought we would try something different today. Rather than me sit up here and rephrase what you already learned, I thought I would share a study method with you guys that I use for all my classes."

"Why would we want to learn that for?" one student asked.

"So you can pass the history class, for one. Secondly, you can use this for your other classes. It's easy and if you do it the right way—"

"You said 'do it'. Bet you've never 'done it', have you?" Beau high-fived a student sitting next to him.

Blood rushed to Alex's face and she swallowed hard against the lump forming in her throat. The laughter of the group washed over her and she fought the urge to flee the room. Suddenly, the faces of the girls she had traveled into flashed through her mind. They all smiled at her and their eyes had an intensity to them as though urging her to do something.

"If you mean studying and passing my classes like a big girl, then yes, I've 'done it'. Now if you're done making juvenile jokes, I'll show you guys how to get through the rest of high school."

Alex let her lips stretch into a half-smile as she silently thanked the personalities of the girls with whom she had shared a body. It was strange, like she carried them with her even though they had been long dead, ghosts from history past. All of the women had been strong, each in their own way, and had had to deal with various hardships and danger.

Those girls have made me stronger.

She knew she never would have been able to take the taunting when she had first come to Grand Junction. When Beau's ex-girlfriend, Catelyn, had teased her, Alex had run and hid in the bathroom more than once. She had spent many a night crying over the cruelty of the head cheerleader and her horrid friends.

"If you guys want to pass this class and any others you might be close to failing, you need to have a way to find out what you don't know. How many of you answer the questions in the back of the chapters you read?" Alex nodded when not one of them raised their hands. "I bet you just sort of flip through your notes and maybe read the chapters, right?" A few of the students nodded, but all of them stayed silent. "And how many of you begin studying the night before the test?" Most of the students nodded this time.

"The only way to prepare for an exam is to study such that you are constantly quizzing yourself from day one rather than waiting. You really think it's easy to cram weeks' worth of info into your brain in just one night? Seriously. Not a good idea." Alex turned to the white board and pointed to the rectangles.

"I've drawn examples of 3 x 5 cards. You can easily use these to re-write your notes or the chapters you have to read and have a portable way to quiz yourselves as you study. You do a question on one side and write the answer on the other. Let me show you what I mean."

Alex spent the next hour showing the students how to take their notes and write the notecards. She had them practice, correcting them when they tried to put too much information on one side or when they had too broad of a question.

"Now, I want you to get some notecards this week and write your history notes on them like I showed you. I'll check them next week and have you guys break into groups so you can quiz each other before your first test."

The students groaned and complained as they put their books away but no one questioned her instructions. As she was erasing her writing on the white board, Mr. Edwards approached her.

"I overheard what you were teaching them today. Great idea, Alex. If they have the means to study, they can do better in all their classes."

Alex blushed. "Thanks, Mr. Edwards. I thought it would be more helpful than me just reciting their material to them over again."

"Have you considered what your schedule will be next year?"

"Not really."

"You should consider taking some classes over at the university. You've already taken all the advanced placement classes we offer here. The college classes would be more challenging and you could start getting college credits." Mr. Edwards gave her a side-long glance. "You *are* planning on going to college aren't you?"

"Of course. Just hadn't really thought about where."

"Well, you have a university right here in your own backyard. And if you begin taking classes, you'll get the feel for college life before you dive in with both feet after graduation."

Alex nodded. "I'll talk to mom about it. Thanks, Mr. Edwards!" She waved as she left the classroom on her way to meet Jenn.

Jenn was waiting at her locker, phone in hand, fingers furiously moving over the surface. *Probably texting James.*

"Took you long enough," Jenn said without glancing up from her phone.

"I was talking with Mr. Edwards about maybe taking some courses at the college next year."

"Seriously? Why do that to yourself your senior year? Take a couple of lounge periods and take it easy, why don't ya?" she said as they made their way out of the building.

Alex shrugged. "I don't know. Seems like a waste of time. I mean, if taking some classes gets me that much closer to a history degree, why not?"

"I love you, Alex, but you are seriously the biggest nerd I've ever known."

Alex punched Jenn in the arm as they walked to Jenn's car. "I can't help it if I actually enjoy school. Maybe it's because it comes easy for me."

"Rub it in why don't ya?"

"Hey, I can't help it if I'm academically inclined," Alex said.

"At least we're friends and I can take advantage of your large melon."

"Oh, so you're just using me for my brain, is that it?" Alex said.

"Of course," Jenn said with a grin as she slipped into the driver's seat.

Jenn turned up the radio and the two sang along as they drove the few blocks to the college. Alex had tried to talk Jenn into leaving her car at the high school and just walking over to the college, but Jenn enjoyed driving too much and the thought of walking back to the car after dark wasn't too appealing.

"What if we get mugged or something?" Jenn had asked when Alex teased her about driving a few blocks.

"There are plenty of other students who walk back. If we're all together, I seriously doubt anyone will mess with us."

"Well, you can walk. I prefer driving."

As the girls walked to the theater building on campus, Alex sensed Jenn wanting to ask her something and she had a feeling she knew what Jenn wanted to bring up. Alex's stomach coiled into knots.

"How long has it been since you've seen Drake?"

"Why does it matter?" Alex said, trying to do the math in her head. She didn't want to admit that it had been so long since she'd seen Drake that she couldn't remember exactly when they had seen each other last.

"Well, at least he's moved on, right?"

"I guess."

Jenn stopped before she opened the door. "Don't tell me you're feeling bad all of a sudden. Every time I brought him up, you just blew me off."

"I'm not feeling bad about not wanting to see him anymore. I'm mad that I had to find out about it on Facebook."

"Since you refused to even speak to him..." Jenn said, looking away.

"You're right, is that what you want to hear? You're right and I'm wrong and everything is as it should be. So let's just get in there and get this over with." Alex pushed past Jenn and opened the door.

Ms. Ashton was near the stage handing out packets that contained the parts and lines for the try-outs. She refused to give parts to anyone that didn't come to the try-outs. Just because someone starred in one play didn't mean they would automatically be in the next one.

"Our first play this year will be Rehearsal For Murder. This will be unlike anything you've ever done before. Try-outs will be next week so you don't have much time to learn the lines of the character you want to play."

Alex tuned out Ms. Ashton as she flipped through the packet. It gave her something to do other than staring at Drake and the girl hanging on his arm. Alex thought her name was Andrea or Angela or something like that. When Drake's new girlfriend smirked when she saw Alex watching them, Alex fumed and refused to give them the time of day.

"This looks like it's gonna be a fun play, Alex. Too bad we're in it and will know whodunit," Jenn said.

Alex mumbled incoherently and continued flipping through the packet, hardly noticing anything about the characters.

"You're not fooling me ya know."

Alex shoved Jenn and smiled.

"Hey guys!"

Alex looked up and grinned. "Hey, Amy." She didn't have any classes with Amy this year and she missed seeing her friend.

"I read this book over the summer. You guys, this play will be the coolest ever!" Amy clapped her hands.

Amy chatted about what she did over the summer, her classes, and her budding relationship with Paul. Alex was happy for them both. Jennifer, Amy, Paul, and Simon had been the only ones that had spoken to her when she had first moved to town just before her freshman year. She had been so worried about making friends but the four of them had made it so easy.

Alex stole glances at Drake and the new girl while pretending to be enthralled with Amy's description of her family vacation to Yellowstone National park. Drake tried so hard not to look at Alex that he might as well have been screaming her name.

You'd think I would care more about being dumped by my first boyfriend.

She wasn't happy about the status change on Facebook that announced their break-up but if she was honest, Alex had to admit that she wasn't even really that upset about it.

"So can you come, Alex?"

"Huh, what?"

"You didn't hear one word I said, did you?"

"Sorry, Amy. I was concentrating on reading the parts," Alex said, knowing Amy didn't believe her.

"I was inviting you to come to Banana's Fun Park for my birthday tomorrow."

Alex groaned. "I wish I could but I gotta work tomorrow after school." Sometimes Alex wished she didn't work at her aunt's clothing stores. However, it was nice having spending money.

"You can't ask for the night off?" Amy begged.

"I was the one that picked this schedule so I feel bad asking for the night off."

"Well, it sucks that it's the weekend of my birthday. Looks like rehearsals are over. Gotta run!"

Alex hurried after Amy, unwilling to spend another minute stealing glances at Drake and afraid he would want to speak to her. Her heart rate slowed as they got further from the theater.

"You can't avoid him forever you know," Jenn said.

Alex sighed. "I can sure try."

Chapter 6

DRIFTER WALKED with a brisk pace, hand flicking to his head in brusque salutes when he approached a senior officer. He ignored the wide eyes and quick side-steps of those in his way as he barreled across the tarmac, heading back to the barracks.

He couldn't remember ever being this angry. It took every ounce of will power not to grab the nearest man and squeeze the life out of him. When these fantasies filled his mind, the man always had Mark's face.

"Where you headed, Stygian?"

Drifter refused to look at Mark. The infernal man matched his quick pace. "Barracks."

"Having more issues with your 'condition'?"

Drifter remained silent, refusing to rise to the bait.

"This chat was nice. We'll have to do it again sometime."

Lane Stygian made his way to the barracks, fury flowing through his veins. He wished Master would send the meddling man to some far corner of the globe on a fake intel mission. *How can I complete my mission with Mark looking over my shoulder?*

Drifter opened the door to the barracks so forcefully he nearly tore it from the hinges. He stalked to his trunk and grabbed his laptop. He may not be able to travel back in time but he could still move forward on Master's plan. If he was to be successful, Drifter knew he would have to spend some time on the internet looking for the research article Master wanted him to find and spend even more time memorizing the contents.

As he waited for the laptop to start up, Drifter grinned, the eerie blue light from the computer illuminating his maniacal grin.

*   *   *

Mark watched Lane Stygian walk into the barracks. He curled his hands into fists. If he didn't need to report to a debriefing in ten minutes, he'd follow the man to see what he was up to. He'd never forget the day he walked in on Lane lying on his bed, eyes staring at the bunk above, body cold as ice. The story Stygian and Max Poder had cooked up about Lane having some sort of affliction sounded even more ridiculous now than it did when they had first said it.

The only affliction Mark knew that caused a body to go cold like that was death.

As he made his way to the debriefing, Mark vowed to keep an eye on Stygian and find out more about his mysterious affliction.

Chapter 7

"WHAT DO YOU MEAN you didn't do the assignment I gave you?" Alex glared at Beau, trying to ignore how sexy he looked when his blonde hair fell over his forehead.

"Come on, Alex. I've explained this to you before. I am going to be a professional football player and don't need to worry about school. The lame assignment you gave us is just a waste of time."

Alex gulped as Beau moved closer. *He smells so good!* He smiled down at her and her heart skipped a beat. She hoped her face wasn't turning red. She wasn't one of those girls that looked good when she blushed.

The moment was ruined as the rest of the students filed into the classroom. They split into their two groups and Alex asked for their note cards she'd asked them to make over the weekend. Only four students had them. She pinched the bridge of her nose and sighed loudly. She gathered the note cards and motioned the students to come with her to the far corner of the room.

"Do you want us all to follow you?"

Alex turned and faced the students who hadn't done their note cards and she bit back a smile at their uncertainty. Some were standing while the others were sitting and looking confused. "I only need the ones who actually did their assignment. You guys are on your own for the day."

Alex bit her lip at the indignant snorts and comments that followed her.

The afternoon flew by as Alex took turns quizzing the students with their note cards. They couldn't quite get through all the questions without having to look at the answer but Alex was pleased with their progress.

"If you guys keep this up, you'll pass your classes for sure," she said.

Alex hurriedly shoved her books in her bag and trotted out the door. Her stomach was fluttery and just a bit nauseous. She replayed her Driver's Education book in her head, trying to remember everything she had been studying. For the first time since Jenn's revelation that Sean and Gavin may be alive in the present, Alex wasn't thinking of locating the pair, nor why she had returned so abruptly before saving anyone from the past. She wasn't even thinking about Beau and how good he smelled, how he drove her crazy and not necessarily in a good way.

Her focus was on obtaining her driving permit.

She'd studied until she was sure she could recite the book by heart. Her Aunt Karen even let her read a little when not waiting on customers at the store. Her friends encouraged her and yet teased her as only best friends can do since she was the only one who didn't have her license yet. Alex was bummed that she had to have the permit for a year and that she had to keep careful logs of her driving time with a licensed adult.

At least I'll get it before I'm thirty! Alex jumped as her phone vibrated in her back pocket, and smiled when she saw the text message from Jenn: -Good luck on your test!

In seconds, her phone vibrated again, this time with words of encouragement from Amy. Alex smiled when Simon and Paul sent similar messages, although their texts were more sarcastic than supportive.

Her heart filled to bursting with happiness, she rounded a corner and stopped dead in her tracks.

Drake and his new girlfriend were standing by the lockers and they were locked in a passionate embrace. The pair didn't notice her approaching. *What the heck do I do now?*

Alex took a deep breath and stared at the phone in her hands, pushing buttons as though she were texting or checking her Facebook status. She refused to glance at Drake and his new girlfriend macking on each other. Her face flushed and her hands shook so badly she hoped she wouldn't drop her phone. She swore the kissing noises got louder as she walked by but she ignored them and bolted out the door, still staring at her phone as though engrossed in the best conversation she'd ever had.

Her mom was waiting in the parking lot. Alex tossed her bag in the back seat of the Blazer and scrambled into the front seat. The uncomfortable encounter in the hallway stole some of the excitement at the prospect of getting her permit.

"You seem distracted, Lexi. What's up?"

Alex smiled at her mom's pet name for her. "Just having trouble with some of the kids in the tutoring group."

"Are they giving you a hard time?"

"Yup. But if they fail, it won't be because I didn't try to help."

Alex was dismayed at the line at the DMV and hoped she would even be able to take the test. After choosing a number and taking a seat, Alex stared out the window, her mind wandering back to her last trip through the mirror, which made her think of Sean and Gavin. She wished she truly did have Internet on her phone so she could kill time doing Google searches for the Scottish pair.

"Karen invited us over for dinner this weekend. Mark's back in town for a while."

"It must be hard for her to have him gone so much."

"I'm sure it is. At least she has the stores to keep her busy."

Alex nodded. "That's true. Still, to only see him a couple times a year. Not sure I could do it."

"Karen knew what she was marrying into. Mark was in the military when they met and he was very honest with her about what he wanted as far as his career and family."

"It was his idea not to have kids?"

"It was both, I think. Karen never showed any interest in having kids and Mark never mentioned wanting them as far as I know."

"Why didn't you ever have more?"

"Because I stopped after having the perfect daughter."

Alex smiled as her mom hugged her. The words made her feel special even though she knew she wasn't perfect. She'd always wondered what it would be like to have a sibling. A big brother, or little sister perhaps. Her other friends had brothers and sisters and they assured her it wasn't all it was cracked up to be, although none of them would give their siblings away.

"Number 243."

"That's us, Alex."

Alex shook her head. "So soon?" She peered around the room and was surprised to find that many of the chairs were now empty.

Alex rubbed her sweaty palms on her jeans and made her way to the front desk. She waited impatiently while the clerk took down the information, marveling at how quickly the woman's fingers tracked over the keys.

The woman handed Alex the test packet and pointed to a partitioned desk. There were several other people there, heads bent, hands moving over the keyboard furiously. She found an empty spot and opened the program on the computer. When the answer to the first question came quickly and easily to mind, Alex relaxed and finished her text before many of the others that had been there before her.

"So how do you think you did?" her mom asked.

"I think I passed. I feel like I knew everything."

"Knowing you, you aced it."

When the nice lady called her back up, Alex walked to the counter on wobbly legs. The woman had a smile on her face which put Alex at ease.

"You passed with flying colors, young lady. Congratulations." She handed Alex a packet. "Here's what you need to know before getting your license. Read through that and make sure you give the driving log sheet to your mom. Now, if you'll step over here, we'll get your picture."

Alex cradled her learner's permit as she followed her mom out to the car. She wanted to hold it forever.

"You should put that in your purse, Lexi, so you don't lose it. They charge for that, you know."

Alex put the permit in her wallet. She walked to the passenger side and stopped abruptly when she ran into her mom.

"Mom, what are you doing?"

"You may as well start your driving hours now. Besides, it will be nice to be chauffeured around for a change." Patricia tossed the keys to Alex.

Alex trotted around to the driver's seat. The seat was a little too far back for her feet to reach the pedals so she moved it forward until she felt comfortable.

"Make sure to check your mirrors."

"I know, I know." Alex adjusted the rearview mirror and glanced in the side mirrors.

"What do you say we go out to dinner to celebrate? Your choice, my treat."

Alex pursed her lips. "Uncle Nubs?"

"Sounds good. Drive on, Jeeves."

Alex giggled as her mom fluffed and primped her hair. She put the car in reverse and glanced once more in the rearview to check that the coast was clear.

She gasped when she saw an unfamiliar face staring back at her.

Chapter 8

"WHAT'S WRONG, ALEX?"

"Nothing. Someone just ran behind me." Alex tried to keep her voice steady as she stared at the image in the rearview mirror.

She didn't have the same out-of-body feeling she usually got when she spotted someone else in the reflection. Alex squinted, trying to get a good look at the woman. Her eyes were bright blue and ringed with dark circles. Alex couldn't see any more of the strange girl than that.

"Is there a reason we're just sitting here?"

Alex shook her head and the woman vanished. She backed out slowly, heart still racing from the encounter. She didn't have the urge to touch the mirror like she usually did and there wasn't that impending sense of doom weighing her down.

Who is she?

Alex tried to focus on her mom's chatter but all she could see was the woman's tired eyes. Every time Alex glanced in the rearview mirror, she willed the woman to return and step back so Alex could see what she was wearing. It might give her an idea of what the evil Traveler had planned.

At the restaurant, the pair ordered fried green tomatoes as their appetizer. Alex picked up the menu and tried to focus on picking something for dinner, but her mind was on the woman. When the waiter returned to take their order, Alex hurriedly picked one of the hamburgers, hoping it was good.

"You seem distracted."

Alex looked up at her mom. "Just been a long day."

The pair sat in silence and waited for their fried green tomatoes to arrive. The first time her mom had ordered them, Alex hadn't wanted to even try it. She had wrinkled her nose and tried a tiny bite. And was hooked.

Alex forgot about the woman in the mirror until her phone buzzed in her back pocket. Knowing how her mom felt about cell phone usage at the table, Alex excused herself and went to the restroom. She locked herself into the stall and grabbed her phone from her pocket. Jenn's text demanded to know how she did on the test.

Alex's fingers flew over the keys, telling her best friend she passed with flying colors and that she had also seen another woman in the rearview mirror.

-What did she look like?

-Only saw her eyes

-That's not helpful

-Nothing I can do about it

-I have to write something down in the book

-She had blue eyes and looked tired

-That's better than nothing. U find Sean or Gavin?

-No. Will try again tonight

-Text me if U find anything

-K

Alex exited the stall and stood in front of the large mirror hanging over the twin sinks. She leaned forward, hoping her reflection would change to that of the woman she had seen earlier. Despite the danger, Alex knew the woman had to be in trouble. *I'm the only one who can help her.*

She jumped when the door opened on her right. Alex blushed and grabbed some towels, pretending she had just washed her hands. She made her way back to the table and found that dinner had arrived. Her stomach was all fluttery and killed her appetite. It worried her that she was so eager to travel back in time again. The evil Traveler had nearly killed her several times. Next time they met, she might not be so lucky.

Am I turning into an adrenalin junky?

On the drive home Alex had a hard time keeping her eyes on the road. They kept darting to the mirrors, hoping for a glimpse of the woman. She hurried to her room as soon as they got home, eager to start searching for Sean and Gavin again. Alex refused to admit that the two might have been killed by the evil Traveler.

They have to be alive! I can't do this on my own.

* * *

Drifter hurriedly placed the sliver of mirror in his pocket as men filed in the barracks. He forced the pleasantries past clenched teeth, wanting nothing more than to be left alone.

He pointedly ignored the men by turning to face the wall. Rage boiled inside, making him feel like a tea kettle. The urge to hurt someone, to kill someone was hard to fight.

Despite Master's warning, Drifter took the piece of glass out of his pocket and watched it shimmer in the light. He concentrated on his reflection, willing it to change to that of another man, a man who also wore a uniform, a man his Master wanted desperately to help.

Drifter stared at the man in the mirror and smiled.

Chapter 9

ALEX TYPED FURIOUSLY on the keys, growing more frustrated by the minute. Every Gavin or Sean she found wasn't the ones she was looking for. Fear forced bile up through her throat as her tummy flipped-flopped. She refused to listen to the voice in her head insisting that Gavin and Sean were dead.

If they were dead, it meant she might be next.

Her phone buzzed. She picked it up and swiped her finger across the screen.

-Any luck?

-No. Ready to give up

-Just keep looking. Can I help?

-U don't know what they look like

-Good point

Alex looked back to her computer screen. She bit her lip, wondering what she should do. If she was seeing someone in the mirror, it meant the evil Traveler was about to head back in time to cause mischief. But she didn't feel the same as she had when seeing another girl's face instead of her own. At those times, she felt out of control, as though someone were forcing her to stare into the mirror. She couldn't take her eyes off the stranger's reflection even if she'd wanted to.

This time had been different. She had been able to focus on her mom asking her questions, was able to glance away and back again.

What does it mean?

She stared at her computer screen, wondering what she should do. Searching for Gavin and Sean was proving a worthless waste of time. *I could go back in time again and ask them about what happened on the way home tonight.* Jenn's idea flashed through her mind. Alex wasn't sure she could travel back in time to find out who the strange girl was in the rearview mirror. When she had done it to visit Gavin and Sean, she knew enough details about Sean to hone in on him in the right time period.

How can I find someone just by their eyes?

Alex decided to search for Gavin and Sean a few more minutes before attempting to locate the woman in the past. She scrolled through pages of pictures of people named Gavin and Sean together in the same photo. Her eyed grew heavy.

Her breath caught in her throat. *It's them!* Alex clicked on the picture, palms sweating and heart racing. The webpage opened and she stared at the picture at the top of the article. Alex scrolled down to read the post, hoping it would have some way to contact the pair.

There!

Alex clicked on the blue link. It led her to a blog titled Traveling Twosome. She laughed out loud when she realized they were authors writing about their adventures through time. *Jenn's gonna be pissed.* She clicked on the Contact Us link at the top of the website.

What the heck do I say?

She twirled a piece of hair in her hands while she stared at the white box where she was supposed to type in her message. From the look of things, the two were doing quite well with the writing thing. Alex was afraid to post too much information in case they had an assistant that answered their messages. The last thing she wanted to do was draw unwanted attention to herself or to them.

She took a deep breath and began typing: Hey guys, it's Alex. Hope you remember me. I came to see you ages ago to do some research on ancient Egypt, namely King Tut and his wife. You were so much help that I thought I would ask for it again. Please contact me as soon as possible.

Alex put in her full name, email address, and hit send before she could change her mind. There was nothing in the message that would indicate that she was anything other than someone in need of their writing expertise.

She glanced at the clock. It was just past ten thirty. She knew she should get some sleep as she had an early shift at the store tomorrow but her mind was whirling. Alex knew it would be awhile before she could get to sleep.

Try the mirror thing.

Alex went to her bathroom and grabbed her hand-held mirror. She adjusted the pillows behind her back and settled back, holding the mirror in front of her face. Her breathing deepened as her gaze unfocused. She conjured the image of the strange woman's eyes in her mind, willing the mirror to change to the woman.

After a few minutes Alex tossed the mirror off to the side. A pair of tired blue eyes just wasn't enough to go on to zero in on the woman from the past.

Maybe I'll see her again in a larger mirror.

*   *   *

The alarm blared. Alex groaned and reached out to hit the snooze button. She snuggled down in the covers.

"You better not have hit snooze young lady."

Alex threw a pillow at the door. She sighed loudly and dragged herself from the sanctuary of the bed, hoping a hot shower would wake her up. Before she went to have breakfast, she checked her email, disappointed when she saw an empty inbox.

"I don't know why you insist on staying up so late when you know you have to work early the next day."

Alex mumbled at her mom as she reached for the cereal.

"I'll be in the men's store today so you're on your own with the women's spring inventory," Patricia said.

She didn't mind doing inventory. If she could choose, she'd rather be in the back than working the floor. For some reason, Alex didn't feel comfortable talking to costumers and working so hard to make a sale. Most of the women who shopped in Uptown Girl were snooty and looked down their noses at Alex and her aunt. It drove Alex up the wall.

"Doesn't it bother you when those women treat you like you are some sort of inferior human being?" Alex asked her aunt.

"Not at all. One thing you'll learn as you get older, Alex, it's that you can't control what other people think of you or even how they treat you. I am nice to them regardless and that's all I can do. If I let their behavior change me, they win."

Alex thought her aunt was being a pushover. When she heard the stuck-up tone of voice from customers, Alex wanted to tell them to go shop somewhere else. But she held her tongue and plastered a smile on her face. Causing a scene would cost her aunt business and Alex didn't want to do that.

She yawned as she opened box after box, sorting the folded clothing onto the large cart and hanging the other garments on the rolling rack. She lost count several times and was forced to start over, trying to make her sleep-fogged mind focus on the task at hand. While she enjoyed being in the back of the store, she didn't want to get behind and end up having to stay past the end of her shift. She was eager to get back home to see if Gavin and Sean had contacted her.

"Why don't you grab some lunch for us, Alex?"

"Okay, Aunt Karen. Where should I go?"

"How about something to go from that Fifties diner down the street? Here's some cash. Grab something for your mom too."

Alex pocketed the money and grabbed her purse. The sun was shining and it warmed her skin. She picked up the pace, feeling more alert with each passing step. The diner was empty so their order was finished quickly. She made her way back to work, opening the door to Downtown Boy to drop off her mom's lunch.

Her mom was behind the counter, ringing up a tall man wearing jeans paired with a dark suit jacket. Alex didn't get the look. She thought guys should either wear a suit or casual, not both. Her mom's cheeks were flushed and she giggled at something the man said. Alex watched as the stranger took his time grabbing his bag from her mom's hand, his hand lingering a little too long on her mom's slender fingers.

"I brought lunch," Alex said loudly, stepping up to the counter, trying to put herself between the fancy man and her mom.

"Oh, is it lunch time already?" Patricia asked.

"Yup. Here you go." Alex handed her mom the Styrofoam container.

"Would you care to share lunch with me, Bruce?"

They're on a first name basis?

"I'd love to but I have to get back out to the job site. Maybe I could come back and take you to lunch sometime." Bruce stammered and stared at his shoes.

Patricia cleared her throat. "Well, ummm...that's really nice of you to ask." She glanced at Alex. "I'll let you know, okay?"

"That sounds good. I'll see you soon. Well, not really soon, I mean, I shouldn't need any more clothes really soon since I just bought some..."

Alex stared at Bruce. He was carrying on like a middle-schooler asking his first girl out on a date. *He's a grown man!* She felt sorry for the guy. Her mom wouldn't dare go out with a guy that blathered on like that.

"I have Monday off. We could do lunch then."

Alex choked on her soda.

"Are you okay, Alex?"

She barely felt her mom pounding her on her back. She was still reeling from hearing her mom ask this doofus out on a date.

What is she thinking?

While her mom walked Bruce to the door, Alex stared at the man's back, willing him to leave and never come back. He had no business nosing around her mother like some love-sick teenager.

"What's with that guy?" Alex asked when her mom returned.

"What do you mean?"

"Oh, come on! He's a dork, mom. What's he thinking, asking you out like that?" Alex's anger grew as she noticed that her mom was wearing make-up. She couldn't even remember the last time her mom had worn make-up.

She did when dad was around.

As always, thoughts of her father sent her blood pressure soaring and her mood deflating. She had never forgiven him for walking out on her and her mom. He had served her mom with divorce papers on Christmas and had given up custody of Alex. He didn't even want visitation. Most days, Alex refused to think about the man. When his face or name popped into her brain, she squashed it before it could take over and make her miserable.

"We're both single, Alex. Grown up people go on dates too. And Bruce is *not* a dork."

Alex ignored the tone in her mom's voice that normally warned she was being pushed too far. "Don't you think it's a little too soon to be seeing someone?"

"It's been years since the divorce, Alex."

"What do you even know about this guy?"

"His wife died five years ago, his kids are grown and out of the house, he owns a successful winery in Palisade, he loves to camp and hunt, his favorite movie is Star Trek: Wrath of Kahn, he likes country music—"

"Okay, okay, I get the point." Alex turned and walked out of the store.

"Alex, wait!"

She ignored her mother's voice. Alex opened the door to Uptown Girl so hard that she nearly ripped a customer's arm off as she exited the store. Ignoring the woman's indignant gasp, she stomped into the back of the store, more to escape having to deal with customers than because she really wanted to finish the inventory.

Her hands shook as she held the clipboard. *I can't believe it!* She lost count of the new pastel tank tops. She threw the clipboard across the room, salty tears of anger trickling down her cheeks. She grabbed her phone out of her back pocket and sent a text message to Jenn.

-Why are you so upset?

-Seriously? How would you feel if your mom was dating someone?

-I don't know. Kind of weirded out, I guess

-Exactly

-What's he like?

-Total dork. Can't believe mom even likes him

-That sucks. Sorry

-Yeah. Last thing I need is a new dad

Alex locked the phone before ramming it back into her pocket. She fetched the corkboard, forcing her mind to focus despite her whirling thoughts so she could finish inventory and leave. Although it meant a ride home with her mom in the same car. She groaned.

At the end of her shift, Alex waved good-bye to her aunt and stalked out of the store, still fuming about the man that had flirted with her mom. She sat on a bench outside Downtown Boy and waited for her mom to meet her. The two walked to the car in silence, which suited Alex just fine. She didn't want to hear any more about Bruce the Dork.

I wonder if Sean and Gavin got back to me? The thought made her heart race and she forgot all about her mom dating.

When she got back to her room, she shut the door and grabbed her laptop. She tried to calm her nerves as she logged in to her email. A gasp escaped when she saw an email from Sean and Gavin. Her finger hesitated over the button, scared it would be some spam reply from an automated site or that they would say they didn't remember her and for her to leave them alone.

Alex took a deep breath and opened the email, nearly weeping in relief at what she read:

Dearest Alex,

Sean is right beside me as a write this and is as ecstatic as I am. I almost didn't believe it was possible. But looking back now, it seems so obvious. I should have realized the possibility of contacting you in the present. I apologize for the oversight and causing you undue stress. Sean hasn't encountered the evil Traveler since the one trip to Egypt. That is enough for me to say that this man is somehow tied to you and you alone. Sean and I are going to be in the US next month for a science fiction convention. We will extend the trip so we can spend some time visiting with you. Please write us back at this private email address so that we can communicate freely. If you travel again, please be careful. I have a bad feeling about this Traveler.

All our best,
Sean and Gavin

Alex held her hands to her mouth and giggled with relief. She couldn't believe that she would be seeing the pair in a month. She copied the email address they gave into a new message and wrote back to them, making sure to include her address so they could get a hotel nearby.

As soon as she hit send, she sent a text message to Jenn and told her to get on Facebook so they could chat. Alex was tempted to call her best friend and tell her the news in person but she was afraid of her mom hearing the conversation. Other than Sean and Gavin, Jenn was the only one who knew her secret of being able to travel back in time.

And she intended to keep it that way.

Alex yawned, her body exhausted after the long day at work. She thought the relief at having reached Sean and Gavin had a lot to do with how tired she was. She felt as though a great weight had been lifted off her shoulders. A small part of her felt guilty of putting the two men in harm's way but she needed their help. Gavin was a Master and Sean had been traveling longer than she had. Their knowledge and aide could save her.

Chapter 10

ALEX AWOKE to the sound of her mother's laughter echoing down the hallway. She put the pillow over her head, willing the noise to stop so she could go back to sleep. This was her only day to sleep in since she worked every Saturday morning at the store. She opened one eye, stared at her alarm clock, and blinked a few times to clear her vision.

It's barely eight o'clock!

As she rolled out of bed, she wondered who in the world her mom could possibly be talking to at this hour. Alex doubted her aunt was awake this early. She tiptoed over to the door but couldn't hear anything with it closed. She opened it slowly, holding her breath as it creaked ever so slightly.

Her mom laughed, a deep, throaty laugh that Alex hadn't heard in years. It was one she had reserved for her dad when he was being particularly charming. It was the kind of laugh a woman saved for someone special.

She's talking to him.

Alex couldn't even bring herself to say his name, even in her mind. The words were still too muffled to make out. She shut the door, her face flushing in anger. In her excitement of finding Sean and Gavin, she had forgotten about her mom's love interest. She brushed her teeth furiously, contemplating barging into her mom's room and demanding to know who she was talking to, perhaps shouting at her for waking her up so early on her only day to sleep in.

Her buzzing phone stopped her from doing something that would result in a grounding. She swiped the phone and saw a text from Jenn, asking if she could come over to catch up on the time travel notebook. Alex sighed, not really certain she wanted company and yet not wanting to be alone while her mom giggled and carried on like a teenager.

While she waited for Jenn to arrive, she ate a quick breakfast, fury rising when her mom continued to sit in her room chatting on the phone. *Like she has something to hide.* Alex rolled her eyes.

She heard Jenn's car screech into the driveway, as was her usual entrance. The girl didn't know the meaning of slowing down before hitting the brakes.

"Is your mom still asleep?"

"No. Just in her room talking to the dork from yesterday."

Jenn cleared her throat. "Sounds like she's pretty serious about the guy."

"She can be serious about him all she wants. I refuse to have anything to do with him."

"He can't be *that* bad, Alex."

"Mom and I don't need anyone. We're fine on our own." Alex shoved open her door, hoping her mom had overheard the two talking in the hallway.

While Jenn situated herself on the messy bed, Alex carried her laptop over to her small white desk. She wanted to see if Sean or Gavin had contacted her. She sighed in disappointment when she saw that her inbox was empty.

"Okay, I'm ready. Tell me everything about the girl in the mirror and what happened with Sean and Gavin. Send me the email so I'll have it word-for-word."

"I already told you everything about the girl." Alex forwarded the email from Sean and Gavin to Jenn's email address.

"Did you try to make the mirror change?"

"Yeah, and it didn't work. I don't have enough information to go on."

Jenn breathed out a frustrated sigh. "That's not very helpful."

"I can't help it. I tried. Hopefully she'll show up again and I can get a better look at her."

"It's so weird hearing you say you hope she comes back. It wasn't too long ago that you wished the mirror would never change again."

"Guess I'm getting used to it. And I don't want that evil Traveler to do something to hurt her."

"Me neither. Well, since there isn't new information for the book, want to practice our lines?"

Alex groaned. She hadn't even looked at her lines since Ms. Edwards handed them out. "Sure, but I haven't even looked at mine."

"We have plenty of time. Besides, you can memorize them quickly."

The girls worked on their lines until lunchtime. Alex was so engrossed in her character that she didn't hear when her mother got off the phone or when she called them for lunch. It was only when she rapped loudly on the door that Alex shook herself out of her character's head.

Her mom opened the door. "You girls hungry?"

"Starving. We've been going over these lines for hours," Jenn groaned.

"I have turkey wraps and some chips out on the patio."

"Thanks, mom." Alex wanted to confront her mom about who she was talking to that morning but decided to wait so as not to embarrass Jenn.

After Jenn left that afternoon, Alex took a deep breath to calm her nerves. She didn't want to fight with her mother but she couldn't let her make the biggest mistake of her life.

"So who were you talking to this morning?" Alex was proud that her voice barely quivered.

Patricia cleared her throat and blushed. "Bruce called to set up our date."

"Seems sort of rude to call that early when some people in the house were trying to sleep."

"I'm sorry if I woke you. I didn't think I was being that loud."

"Well, you were. Why do you have to see him anyway? We don't need anyone."

"Funny, I don't remember disallowing *you* to date someone." Patricia stood with her hands on her hips.

"That's different."

"No, it isn't. I'm sorry that you don't like the idea, but I *am* a grown up and *don't* need your permission to see someone. But I'd rather you try to understand."

"Oh, I understand all right. You're in a hurry to replace my father with a new one. Well, I'm not interested!"

"Now you listen here, young lady. I'm not trying to find a substitute father. I want to find an adult male that I can spend some time with. I'm lonely, Alex. Sorry if that offends you."

Alex recoiled at the anger growing in her mom's voice. "You can see him all you want. Just keep me out of it." She stormed off and slammed her door, wincing a little when the large mirror hanging in the wall shimmied a little from the force.

She huffed as she threw herself on her bed, wanting to text Jenn and yet wanting to be alone at the same time. She wanted to post on Facebook and Twitter about the unfairness of her life and yet she didn't want anything to do with anyone. It was a strange mixture of emotions that confused her and only added to her anger and frustration.

Why does mom need someone other than me?

The thought of her mom seeing a man made her stomach clench. Another man wouldn't be her dad. Even though he had walked out on them years ago, he was the only man she had ever seen her mom with. It would be too weird to watch her kiss someone else.

A timid knock at the door interrupted her whirling thoughts. When she didn't answer, her mom opened the door slowly.

"Can I come in?"

"A little late to ask since you already did."

"Alright, Alex, I get that you are upset, but I'm still your mother and I won't allow you to talk to me like that."

Alex glared at the legs of her computer desk. She refused to get up off her bed and look at her mom.

"What is it about Bruce that bothers you so much?"

"Everything. You don't need some guy in your life."

"I know I don't *need* a man. But they are kind of nice to spend time with now and again. Believe it or not, Alex, you'll understand some day." Patricia sat on the edge of Alex's bed.

"Whatever you say."

"I've invited him for dinner tonight. I suggest you be on your best behavior. I'd hate to send you to your room in front of our guest like a child."

"I'd rather not be here. Can I go to Jenn's instead?"

"No, you may not. You will conduct yourself like an adult or you'll be sent to your room. I'm going to the store in a little bit. I expect you to be here when I get home."

Alex threw her pillow at the door after her mom left, angry tears spilling down her cheeks. She grabbed her computer and tried to lose herself in an endless parade of status updates, pins, and tweets. As each moment brought the inevitable dinner closer, Alex was more and more tempted to leave the house and risk her mother's wrath. Sitting through dinner with her mom and Bruce was going to be worse than death at the hands of the evil Traveler.

But Alex knew that if she left the house she'd be grounded until she was eighteen and would never be allowed to get her driver's license.

And yet the temptation was still there.

She refused to leave her room when she heard her mom return. Music drifted through the house. It was her mom's favorite Pandora station playing a mixture of oldies. Once upon a time, when her parents had been happy, they danced to this music in their tiny home. She would wiggle her way between them and all three would dance around the living room.

I bet Bruce doesn't even like this music.

Part of her felt a little guilty for not helping her mom with dinner or setting the table but she ignored that tiny voice in her head and chatted with her friends on Facebook instead. When the doorbell rang, she rolled her eyes, knowing Bruce the Dork would be making a fool of himself.

Her door opened moments later.

"Our guest is relaxing outside on the patio. I expect you to come join us in a few minutes."

Alex rolled her eyes and refused to answer. She tried to find something important she needed to do, something related to homework or consoling a dying friend or someone that needed her kidney in the next three seconds so that she could put off going outside as long as possible.

Knowing she was pushing her mom's limits, Alex slid off the bed and shuffled to the kitchen. Her mom and Bruce were sitting under the covered patio, laughing and drinking tall glasses of iced tea. Alex grabbed a glass out of the cupboard and poured her own glass of tea. She could focus on it and sip it when she was about to say something that would get her shipped out of the country or to the nearest convent.

"Here she is. Finished with your homework?"

Alex didn't miss the edge in her mother's voice. "All done."

Patricia turned to Bruce. "She's such a good student."

"My oldest was always good at school. The youngest, not so much."

Alex mumbled something as she sat down on the bench next to the patio table. She could feel her mom's eyes on her and refused to glance toward the pair. She might have to sit out here and play nice but she wasn't going to sit at the same table with them.

She ignored the small talk between her mom and Bruce and watched the birds gathered around the feeders in the large back yard. She had learned the names of all the ones that frequented their yard: finches, starlings, sparrows, red-winged black birds, pigeons and doves. The sun had gone behind the red stone mountains of the Monument hours ago, leaving the back yard shrouded in shadows.

"Mind helping with dinner, Alex?"

She sighed loudly and plunked her glass on the table next to the bench. She schlumped into the house, refusing to look at Bruce.

"You are pushing it, young lady."

"I'm not going to fall all over the guy like you are. I don't like him."

"You don't even know him!"

"And that's the way I like it."

Alex grabbed the plastic patio plates and bowls out of the cabinet and loaded them onto a tray. Silverware and a full bowl of salad soon followed. She risked a glance in her mother's direction and a stab of guilt wormed its way into her gut. Her mom's face was red and Alex could see her throat working as though she was trying to fight tears.

She carried the tray outside and held the door with her foot. Bruce jumped up and took the tray from Alex's hands. She grunted something that she hoped sounded like "thank you".

She was spared any small talk while they loaded their plates with food. Bruce complimented everything and wrung his hands nervously. For a moment, Alex felt sorry for the guy.

"Bruce has invited us to his winery next weekend."

Alex pasted on what she hoped was a smile. "I'll be busy with rehearsals next weekend."

"Surely you can spare a few hours to tour the winery?"

Despite the warning in her mom's voice, Alex answered, "Sorry, mom. Our first play is only a month away. Besides, I'm working at the store Saturday and Sunday."

"It's okay. Some other time," Bruce said.

Alex looked up at Bruce and hated the feeling of relief at his words. She didn't want to feel grateful to him, even if he was helping her to avoid spending more time with him.

She stared at her plate while her mom and Bruce ate and chatted. As soon as she was done, Alex got up from the table and brought her plate into the house. She took her time loading her dirty dishes into the dishwasher, watching her mom through the window. When she gave no indication that she even knew her daughter wasn't sitting at the table, Alex wandered into the living room to watch some television.

Her heart rate sped up when she heard the back door open, readying itself for a confrontation. When none was forthcoming, Alex calmed a little. She heard her mom putting leftovers in the fridge and loading the dishwasher. The door to the patio opened again and she was left alone.

Alex flicked through channels and settled on a program on the History channel about the taming of the West. When the show was over, she went to her room, not really tired but unwilling to stay in the living room in case her mom and Bruce decided they wanted to come inside.

As she lay in the dark listening to her mom's laughter, Alex wondered again what she saw in the guy.

Why does she need someone? Aren't I enough?

Chapter 11

THE NEXT MONTH flew by for Alex. Between rehearsals, working at the store, tutoring, and driving lessons, the days ran into one another in an endless stream. The girl she had seen in the rearview mirror hadn't made another appearance and for that Alex was grateful. She had too much on her plate and couldn't deal with a trip back through time right now.

"I can't believe they will be here tomorrow! Has it really been a month already?" Jenn asked while they ate lunch outside.

The weather would soon be turning cold so Alex cherished these moments in the warmth of the sun.

"I know, right?"

"And you meant it when you said I could come with you?"

"For the hundredth time, yes. You can come with me."

"Do you think they'll mind if I take notes? For the book?"

"I don't know. I guess not."

"Well, I have to write all this down. I'm telling you, Alex, there's money to be made. People love time travel stuff."

"Let's get through high school before you turn us into famous authors, okay?"

Jenn sighed. "If we are rich and famous, we won't need high school."

"I plan on finishing. And going to college."

"Seriously? Even if we make millions in book sales and movies, you'll still go to college?"

"Of course! Why wouldn't I?"

Jenn looked at Alex like she had grown a second head. "You wouldn't need to, that's the point."

"Running a famous museum has been a dream of mine since I was a kid. Nothing will change that."

Jenn shrugged. "Suit yourself. I will spend my days traveling the world and hanging out with famous people."

The two finished their lunch and headed back to class. Simon, Paul, and Amy had gone back in earlier, leaving the two girls alone to discuss the impending visit by Sean and Gavin. Alex couldn't focus on her class work. Even her acting was suffering. She flubbed through well enough so that she didn't ruin every rehearsal but she wished she could force her nerves to slow down and get back to normal.

After her last class, she headed to the restroom before going to the tutoring session. For some of the students, the tutoring was paying off. They had passed their first exams of the semester and gained a little confidence in their ability to do something other than run, or throw a ball.

As for the others, Alex wanted to wash her hands of them. They refused to listen to her study tips, never participated in the quiz sessions, didn't do the note cards. Rather than spend her time trying to reach them, Alex focused her time on those students who were trying to do better.

She stared at her reflection in the mirror while she put on lip gloss. Suddenly, her reflection shifted to that of the tired woman she had seen in the rearview mirror of the Blazer.

The woman was dressed in a nurse's uniform. It looked old to Alex. She had blonde hair and the same bright blue eyes Alex remembered from the last visit. Her uniform was buttoned to the top and closed with a pin that had a red cross in the middle. The woman's eyes widened and her mouth moved quickly as she backed away, crossing herself in Catholic fashion.

Alex shook her head and the image shifted back to that of her own face. She turned and leaned against the counter, trying to figure out what was happening. In the past, when the reflection changed, she had been drawn to touch the mirror. With this woman, it was different. Alex remained in complete control of herself.

What is happening?

Rather than worry about it, she pushed the oddity to the back of her mind. Sean and Gavin would be here tomorrow and she would ask them about this. She grabbed her phone out of her back pocket and hurriedly sent a text to Jenn. Alex rushed off to the tutoring classroom, flushing a little when she saw she was the only one who hadn't yet arrived.

She tried to push the distractions aside so she could focus on helping the students for their next round of exams, but her mind kept returning to the nurse. The uniform looked familiar and Alex wanted to get her hands on a computer so she could look up pictures of old nurse uniforms.

Alex rushed to meet Jenn when the class was over so they could head over to rehearsals. She wondered how she was going to remember any lines with the strange woman's face taking up every spare inch of space in her brain.

"I can't believe you saw her again!" Jenn said breathlessly as they walked to the university.

"I know! I hope Gavin and Sean can tell me why this time is so different. No weird vibes or anything. The normalness is freaking me out."

"Only you could say something like that and have it totally make sense."

The pair walked into the theater, feeling out of place on the college campus. They felt so small and young, like everyone knew they didn't belong.

"Is it just me or are college guys super hot?"

Alex rolled her eyes. "You have a boyfriend, remember?"

"Doesn't mean I can't look."

"It actually sorta does."

"Well, what about you? You're "Little Miss Single." You should go for an older guy."

"No, thank you. I'm good being by myself," Alex said sharply.

"Why the attitude?"

Alex sighed. "Sorry. I'm just touchy about the subject."

"You didn't used to be."

"It's this thing with my mom and Bruce." Alex put as much acid into her voice as she could when she said his name.

"I still don't see what the big deal is. Your mom's a big girl and your dad left a long time ago, Alex. Maybe you should give the guy a chance."

"Mom and I don't need a man around. What's the point? So he can drink and be a jerk and leave us?" Alex was surprised to hear the hitch in her voice.

"Alex, not every guy is like that."

"Yeah, well you never know for sure, do you? Why take the chance? I'd rather be single and have my heart intact than trust it with someone who can break it."

Jenn reached out and gripped Alex's elbow in sympathy. "You'll change your mind someday."

"Doubt it."

Any further talk was interrupted as Ms. Ashton walked onto the stage in a flurry of drama. She called the students to the stage to do the second act of Rehearsal for Murder. Alex groaned. She was in the second act which meant she had to somehow remember her lines despite her turmoil of emotions.

The afternoon passed quickly. Alex was amazed at how well she did. Her lines had somehow flowed as naturally as breathing. She relaxed and let herself get lost in the character she played. It was much the same as traveling back in time. Her spirit took over the body of another girl and she got to be a different person for a short time, though with real danger involved. On stage, the biggest danger was forgetting your lines or tripping over place markers.

She was even able to ignore Drake. Her gut barely twisted when she had to interact with him on stage, and when he kissed his new girlfriend, she didn't really care.

There was a strange car in the driveway when she got home. She said good-bye to Jenn, wishing she could ask her friend to hang out but she knew her mom wouldn't be happy about an unannounced guest. The last thing she wanted to do was be in the same house with Bruce.

Alex walked quickly to her room and almost made it when her mom yelled at her from the kitchen. She turned and walked back down the hallway.

"You're on your own for dinner tonight. There's some soup and cheese and bread to make a grilled cheese sandwich."

Alex gaped at her mom. She was wearing some of the new clothing from the store and had obviously spent the afternoon curling her hair. Her face was radiant as she walked Bruce to the front door. Alex followed them and peered through the front window. Bruce opened the passenger door to his car then closed it gently after her mom climbed gracefully inside.

As she fixed herself a simple dinner, Alex wondered why her mom had left her behind. She was relieved that she wouldn't be forced to endure an uncomfortable dinner trying to make small talk with a man she didn't care anything about, and yet being left behind didn't make her feel any better.

She didn't have any homework so she sat down to watch some TV, wondering if Sean and Gavin were in town yet or if they would arrive later tonight. They had her cell number and said they would text when they arrived at their hotel, regardless of the hour. Alex checked that her phone was on vibrate. It was against the rules for her to have her phone on at night so the last thing she needed was to have it ring in the wee hours of the morning. It would be difficult to explain to her mom the necessity of having the phone on to receive a text from two strange men.

She checked her phone every few minutes despite the fact there was no vibration indicating an incoming text or phone call. The pair hadn't been able to give her an estimated time of arrival since they were driving from Denver rather than flying. They planned to meet during Alex's lunch hour. She was terrified she would get caught. That someone who knew her or her mom would see her out with Jenn and two older men and tell on her. She would be grounded for sure.

Alex knew she had to risk it. She couldn't do this on her own. Jenn was a good friend but Alex needed someone who had her same gift of time travel, someone who knew more than she did about how it all worked. The evil Traveler was up to something and Alex needed help to figure out what it was.

* * *

Drifter smiled grimly as the reflection in the mirror changed back to that of his own smooth face. Part of him loved this little bit of rebellion against his Master. Drifter didn't think he could stay away from time travel even if he wanted to. It was in his blood. He understood the danger of what he did. Mark watched him like a hawk, waiting to catch him in another one of his "episodes". He couldn't allow that to happen and yet he couldn't stop himself from checking in on the man whose body he would soon be taking over.

He sighed and rolled out of bed. While he would rebel in this small way, he would also follow Master's orders to the letter. Drifter sat down at his computer and typed in the URL that he had memorized. He had been doing that more lately. Anything he could commit to memory, he did. The mission depended on him being able to memorize something more complicated than a website address.

Drifter grabbed his notepad from the hidden compartment in his desk. He hated to have physical evidence of his mission but the only way to know for certain that he had memorized the research article was to write it out. He switched to a blank sheet and wrote what he remembered from the article. He got most of the way through the introduction before needing to look at the paper again. He read the three paragraphs he couldn't remember and tried again from the beginning, the only sound in the silent room was that of his pencil scratching on the paper.

Chapter 12

ALEX AWOKE to the blaring of the alarm, her mind fuzzy from lack of sleep. Her dreams had been plagued by nightmares and whirling thoughts. Her nightmares were a strange combination of time travel and Bruce cutting her mom into little pieces. She had gotten to bed later than usual since she waited up for her mom to get home. Part of her wanted to sit with her mom and ask her about her date.

Alex gasped and grabbed her phone off the nightstand. The icon indicating she had a text waiting flashed on the top of the phone. She checked her texts and breathed a sigh of relief when she saw one from Sean indicating they had arrived and would see her at 11:30 the following morning.

She dragged herself into her bathroom and turned on the water, brushing her teeth. Her mom was in the kitchen rushing through breakfast. It wasn't like her mom to oversleep.

Alex fought the urge to pick a fight. Today was a big day and she didn't want to start out on a sour note. She opened her mouth and was surprised to find herself about to spill her guts about everything, the time travel, the Traveler, Sean and Gavin.

What the hell's wrong with you?

She shook her head, blaming her almost-lapse-in-judgment on her exhaustion. Rather than pick a fight or tell her mom her big secret, she filled the time with chit-chat about the upcoming theater show. Her mom nodded and gave her daughter single-word answers, barely looking at Alex when she left for the store.

Alex watched her mom leave, eyes stinging with tears. Her mom had never given her the brush-off quite like that before. Alex knew when her mom was angry and this morning she wasn't angry. More like indifferent.

She brushed at her eyes and finished breakfast even though her stomach was threatening to eject everything she had just eaten. She grabbed her bag and waited for Jenn.

Jenn showed up almost half-an-hour early, which was fine with Alex. She didn't want to sit in the house.

"What time did they get in last night?" Jenn asked.

"More like this morning, about two. We're supposed to meet them at 11:30 out at the Village Inn on Horizon Drive."

"Sounds good. Are you nervous?"

"I don't know what I feel. I'm sort of numb." Alex filled in her best friend about her mom's strange behavior that morning.

"Maybe she had a super awesome date and was replaying it in her mind. Sounds like she was distracted, not mad."

"Yeah, I guess." Alex couldn't explain it but she thought there was something more to it than that.

The morning crawled at a snail's pace. Alex fidgeted so much she was certain her teachers would ask her to leave class, perhaps visit the nurse to see if she had something contagious. Jenn hissed at her to sit still during their pop quiz in Spanish class. Her constant motion was responsible for her desk creaking like a rusty hinge. The other students glared at her. Alex blushed and willed her muscles to behave. She took a deep breath, trying to remember how to put together a simple sentence in Spanish, but her brain was shrouded in fog. The words eluded her.

The teacher came by to pick up the quizzes and Alex turned hers upside down, hoping the teacher wouldn't notice that she hadn't even answered all the questions.

When the bell rang, Alex glanced at Jenn and they shared a nervous grin. They jumped up and grabbed their books, shoving them into their bags. Alex followed Jenn to the door.

"Alex, can I see you for a minute?"

Alex gulped and turned to face her teacher. She glanced at her watch.

"It won't be long."

"Go ahead, I'll meet you at the car," Alex told Jenn.

"I'd like to chat with you about your quiz. I don't think I've ever seen you not answer every question before. And you seem anxious and out of sorts. Everything okay?"

Alex took a deep breath. She was used to her teachers noticing when she didn't perform to certain standards. *Sometimes being smart sucks.* She had never been ashamed of her brain power but the minute she lapsed, even a little, her teachers swooped down, ready to pry into her personal life, certain she was about to have a nervous breakdown.

"Everything's fine. Just dealing with some stuff at home," Alex said.

Mrs. Rodriguez narrowed her eyes. "Whatever this thing, it isn't going to distract you for a long period of time, is it?"

Alex shook her head. "No." She glanced at her watch and switched her weight from her left foot to her right. "Can I go now? I sorta have somewhere to be."

"Of course. If there's anything you need to talk about, we have excellent counselors here."

"I know. And if I need to, I'll look them up," Alex said as she walked out of the classroom.

She trotted out to the parking lot, trying to remember where Jenn had parked that morning. She heard a horn honking from somewhere near the middle. She spotted Jenn's Pontiac pulling out of the space. Alex ran toward the car and shrieked as the speeding car came to a halt mere inches from hitting her knees.

"What are you trying to do, kill me?" Alex shouted as she flung open the passenger door.

"I thought I'd save some time and meet you in the middle," Jenn hollered over the music blaring from the stereo.

"We only have a few minutes so hit it." Alex couldn't believe she was giving her best friend permission to drive even crazier than she usually did.

"I'm on it."

Alex gasped as her body was pushed back against the seat from the force of acceleration. Her heart beat wildly, in time to the rock music. Normally her friend's driving terrified her but today, all she felt was exhilaration.

Jenn swerved into the parking lot of Village Inn, hitting the curb with the front tires, forcing Alex's body into the seat belt.

"Told you I was on it," Jenn said with a grin.

Rather than answer, Alex grabbed her bag from the back seat and exited the car on wobbly legs. She didn't know if it was from the ride or the prospect of meeting Sean and Gavin in person.

In her time.

Jenn was ahead of her and opened the door to the restaurant. Alex burst into laughter, more from nerves than because anything was particular amusing.

"What's so funny?"

"You going first. Do you even know what they look like?"

Jenn sputtered. "Well, no, but..."

"It's fine. I'm just giving you a hard time."

Alex told the hostess that they were meeting some people and the woman told them to take a look around. Jenn stayed strained to see the customers despite not having a clue about what they looked like. Alex pursed her lips to hold back another hysterical giggle. She wracked her brain to remember the picture of the two of them she had seen on their website.

Suddenly a pair of older gentlemen stood from the corner table and stared her way. Alex couldn't breathe. It was so strange seeing Sean as someone so much older. She remembered him as an awkward gangly kid when she visited him in the past. The man standing next to the booth was old, maybe in his forties with dark hair just barely showing some grey at the temples. Gavin, on the other hand, was super old, like maybe older than sixty.

"Is that them? That's gotta be them, right?" Jenn gripped her arm so hard Alex feared she would lose circulation in her hand.

Alex walked toward the men on wooden legs so stuff she feared she would pitch right over on her face. Sean was smoothing his clothing and bouncing on the balls of his feet as though he wanted to run away.

"Alex?" Gavin said as he held out his hand.

Alex nodded, throat clenched tight against the sob that was trying to escape. She wanted to fall into his arms like she should have been able to do with her father, if he was still around. His face was warm and inviting and oozed sympathy, all of the things she so desperately needed and didn't quite know it until this very moment.

She took a deep breath and held out her hand. "Yeah, it's me."

"And who is this?" he looked behind Alex.

"This is my best friend, Jenn. I told you about her."

"Ah, yes, I do recall. Please, sit." Gavin motioned the girls to sit in the booth. Alex and Jenn scootched around, letting the men sit on the outside.

"What can I bring you two?"

Alex glanced at the waitress and didn't like what she saw in the woman's eyes. They were hard and accusing, as though wondering what two teenage girls were doing with much older men.

"Can we have a shake, Grandpa?" Alex gave Gavin a pointed look.

"Oh, pleasepleaseplease!" Jenn really laid it on thick, holding her hands under her chin.

"Your mother will kill me, but what the heck. Chocolate shakes all around!" Gavin included the whole table with his gesture.

The waitress visibly relaxed and smiled for the first time since arriving at their table. "I'll be back to get your order after I get those shakes started."

"Quick thinking, Alex. It never even crossed my mind that folks would think something strange was up," Sean said.

"The last thing we need is for people to pay too much attention to us. Now they think we're just a family out for some lunch," Alex said.

"We just have to hope no one recognizes them," Jenn said.

"What do you mean?"

"They are famous authors, Alex. Grand Junction may not be California but there are people here who read fantasy novels."

Alex turned white and glanced around the restaurant, certain a gaggle of fans was about to descend on their table.

"Not to worry. We've been here for half an hour and no one has given us a second look. Most people don't expect to see someone famous at a local diner. So even if they thought they recognized us, they'd brush it off as coincidence," Gavin said.

The waitress returned, halting all talk at the table. The four hurriedly glanced at their menus and ordered lunch. Alex glanced at her watch, hoping they could get their food and finish eating before she and Jenn had to be back at school.

"What time do you have to be back?" Gavin asked, reading Alex's nervous gestures.

"A little over an hour. And we have a quiz so we can't be late."

"We will make sure to be done by then. Let's get down to business then, shall we?" Sean said.

Alex was grateful for Sean's bluntness, and yet she wasn't ready to spill her guts. It was so surreal, sitting in a Village Inn with a Master and his time traveling pupil, seeing them in her own time. Her head felt like it was floating off her shoulders.

"Alex needs your help. Big time," Jenn said, ignoring Alex's glare.

"I figured as much by the cryptic message you sent. Very clever, by the way. You have a good head on your shoulders. Kind of important for someone with your special abilities," Gavin said. "Spill it, Alex. What's going on?"

Alex took a deep breath and glanced to the nearby booths, making sure no one was paying attention to them. She told Sean and Gavin about the last trip through the mirror, only spending a few seconds in the body of the Mongol girl before ending up back in the void and yanked back to her body, the nurse appearing in the mirror, and yet without the urge to touch the mirror. By the time she finished, the waitress was back with their lunch.

When she left, Gavin spoke softly, "I think I know what happened to you with the Mongol girl. If something happens to disturb a Traveler, being awakened before they can finish their merging, the Protector is also yanked back to their own body. They will only return to the past when the Traveler returns. The fact that you haven't yet and that you are seeing someone new means that this guy you are dealing with has other plans."

"So why haven't I had the urge to touch the mirror? That's never happened before."

"I would imagine it's because he isn't going back in time yet. There seems to be a connection between you two that doesn't exist between anyone else, at least not that I've ever heard of or even read in the Master's tome. Maybe you only travel back in time once he does. But this connection is giving you a hint as to his plans. If you can figure out when he's going back to, you can take steps to protect yourself."

"All I know is that she's a nurse. I got a look at her uniform but haven't had a chance to look anything up on the Internet yet."

"This man worries me. We are clearly dealing with someone with a nefarious plan."

"What *is* his plan? He's been all over the place. There's nothing connecting all of the people I've saved."

Gavin took a huge bite out of his burger. "I've been thinking about that. The excursions you have taken thus far almost seem like practice. Or..." He glanced at Sean.

"Or what?" Alex said, stomach clenching at the shared look.

"He's been traveling back in time to random points with the sole purpose of killing you."

Chapter 13

ALEX SWALLOWED HARD. "You really think his only mission in life is to kill me?"

Gavin shook his head as he wiped his mouth with a napkin. "I don't believe it's his *only* purpose, no. But after defeating him twice, he must have known he was dealing with someone special. If he is to carry out his mission, whatever that may be, he needs to be free and clear to do so. And that means taking you out of the picture."

"Great." Alex sat back in the booth, appetite gone.

"You've already proven you're more than a match for him," Sean said.

"For how long? How do I know that the next time he won't succeed in killing me?"

Gavin looked at her with eyes that oozed sympathy. "You don't. All you can do is keep fighting."

"I have an idea."

Alex looked at Jenn who had been furiously writing in her time travel journal. She sat with the journal hugged tightly to her chest, face pale and drawn.

"What about trying to do what you did with Sean when you traveled back to see him as a teenager? Only do it with this evil Traveler instead."

Alex opened and closed her mouth, her thoughts scattering so fast that she couldn't hang on to one of them long enough to form a sentence. She looked to Gavin who sat with his brow furrowed, staring at Sean.

"It may be the only way," Gavin said.

Alex shook her head and waved her hands in front of her. "No way in Hell am I doing this."

"Alex—"

She turned to Jenn. "Seriously? You really think I have it in me to inhabit the body of some girl and what, kill him? I can't do it."

"Would you rather spend the rest of your life being hunted by this guy?" Jenn asked quietly.

"Of course not. There has to be some other way. Why can't you guys do it?" She looked at Sean and Gavin hopefully.

"I can't do what you do, Alex."

She stared at the faces around her, wanting a giant hole to open up and swallow her whole. *I can't do this!* Her throat sealed and tears threatened to fall. Rather than lose it in front of everyone, Alex excused herself, hoping a trip to the restroom would give her time to get it together.

Alex locked herself in a stall and sat down, breath hitching in a chest that felt much too tight. She wondered if this was what people with asthma dealt with on a daily basis.

Get a grip, Alex!

Her usual mantra had the desired effect. Her heart rate slowed and she felt strength rather than fear flowing through her veins. She wiped her eyes and left the stall. As she stared at her reflection in the mirror, she replayed each visit back in time, the faces of the women her spirit had inhabited flashing through her mind, each of their faces as real as her own. They all had such strength and character. Alex closed her eyes and prayed that their spirits would help her now.

She didn't know what to do. Part of her knew the others were probably right and yet the thought of actually killing someone seemed repugnant to her. Alex thought she might be capable of it if she was fighting for her life but to simply walk up to someone and kill them made her want to puke up all her lunch.

And yet she didn't want to spend the rest of her life traveling at someone else's whim, never knowing if that would be the trip that would end her life. What kind of a life would that be? How could she ever have a husband, a career, even children, if she was under the cloud of this secret?

Alex walked back to the table and slid in next to Jenn. She tried to smile but could barely manage to make her lips twitch.

Gavin patted her hand. "Nothing has to be decided today. Sean and I will be in touch. Besides, you need to be back off to school."

Panic closed Alex's throat and her muscles wouldn't obey her brain's command to stand. She glanced back and forth between Sean and Gavin, unwilling to leave their comforting presence. Scotland was too far away. She needed them here.

"Do you have to go back home?" she asked quietly.

Gavin smiled sadly. "I'm afraid we do. Our agent has us booked solid for the next year and we have to finish a book in the next few months. But you know where to find us. We can email or Skype if we have to. In this modern age, technology can bring us together in seconds."

Alex felt a little better but she hesitated saying her good-byes. Only Jenn's frantic gesturing to the door forced her hand. She hugged both men, feeling a bit awkward but still playing up the relative bit for the waitress.

"If you see this woman again, let us know. We can help you do some research, try to figure out what time period she lives in. And give Jenn's idea some thought. If you do decide to go after this guy, we'll be right there with you." Sean blinked a few times then stammered. "Well, we won't be able to be with you when you go back in time of course, but we can be with you while you're here..." He shrugged and gave Alex a lopsided grin.

Alex watched as they drove away, eyes burning with tears. For once, Jenn didn't start chattering and she even left the radio off. Alex wasn't sure that the silence was any better than the usual noise.

The afternoon passed just as slowly as the morning. Alex wanted to seek refuge somewhere and think about Jenn's idea, to formulate some sort of plan in case she decided to take a man's life. She stared at her desk surrounded by a sea of washed out voices. When her biology professor wrote the five questions on the board, she stared without blinking, feeling as though she wasn't even really sitting in the classroom doing something as ordinary as taking a quiz.

The words written on the chalkboard didn't make sense. They ran together and reformed into a shape that was vaguely human, perhaps even a man. The white chalk man ducked and dodged a variety of white chalk weapons: a sword, gun, a bottle of poison.

Her breath came in gasps and her stomach roiled. The chalk man bled red, mixing with the white chalk and black board. He raised his hands to fend off the invisible attacker. Alex screamed at him to run, knowing that the invisible attacker was *her* and that she was actually considering the idea of going back in time to kill someone just to save herself.

Alex stood, grabbed her bag and ran from the room, ignoring the startled gasps from the students and the shouting of the teacher. She ran into the nearest bathroom and locked herself in a stall. Her knees buckled and she sat heavily, reaching for the metal bar to steady herself.

Her phone buzzed in her back pocket. Jenn sent ten text messages so quickly Alex couldn't keep track of them. She sent one back saying that she was fine and would meet her at the car.

"What the heck happened back there?" Jenn asked when Alex climbed in the car.

"Don't know. Freaked out, I guess."

"That's an understatement. Half the class thinks you're on drugs."

Alex groaned. "Great."

"Just play off like you had to puke or something. No big."

"That's not a bad idea. Not like I can tell anyone what's really happening."

"You have me, and you have Sean and Gavin now. That's gotta count for something, right?"

"Damn right. Now I just have to figure out how to live long enough to figure out if I have it in me to kill someone in cold blood."

"I know it's not the best solution but it sort of seems like the only one, ya know?"

"Yeah, I know."

"Hey, isn't your mom supposed to be taking you driving today?" Jenn asked as she pulled into the empty driveway.

Alex frowned. "I thought we were supposed to. Maybe she isn't home yet."

"I'll see you tomorrow. Happy driving!" Jenn shouted as she backed out of the driveway.

Alex unlocked the door, checking her phone to see if her mom had left a message about being late for their practice driving. She tossed her bag on the couch, headed into the kitchen for a snack, and noticed the note on the table.

Out for a walk with Bruce. Back after dinner.

Alex crumpled the note and threw it in the trash, body shaking with rage. How dare her mom blow her off for some dumb guy? They had planned her driving practice around theater and work. She couldn't get her license without having at least fifty hours practice behind the wheel with her mom. She wasn't allowed to practice with anyone else.

Alex considered texting her mom but figured it would be a waste of time. *I'll confront her when she gets back.* She grabbed her bag off the couch and headed to her room, giving the door a good slam even though there was no one around to hear it but her. She had a little homework to do but couldn't concentrate. Alex read and re-read the assignment, her mind unable to focus long enough to come up with the answers to the questions. The only thing she seemed capable of thinking about was trying Jenn's idea to find the evil Traveler and get him out of her life once and for all.

Chapter 14

THE MORE ALEX THOUGHT about it, the queasier she became. Even remembering the time she had been inside the body of Agy and the evil Traveler had killed the old black woman didn't strengthen her resolve. Alex was terrified of actually seeing the Traveler face-to-face, like some Wild West show-down. And there was a distinct possibility that it might actually involve guns.

I don't even know how to shoot a gun!

Alex imagined their confrontation being a bloody hand-to-hand affair, with the pair of them trying to get a chokehold on one another or perhaps doing the eye gouge. He would be bigger and stronger and there was no way she could win in a fight. Unless she could get her hands on a gun, figure out how to shoot it, and aim from far away. Maybe an airplane.

I probably couldn't make the mirror change anyway.

As her anxiety grew to unbearable levels, Alex jumped off the bed and grabbed her hand mirror out of her bathroom. She stared at her reflection in the large wall mirror, putting off what she knew deep down she needed to do. Her phone vibrated, causing her to squeal out loud.

-Eating out. You're on your own

Alex stared at the text from her mom and resisted the urge to throw her phone against the wall. She couldn't believe her mom was doing this to her again. Blowing her off for a guy.

She called Jenn and spent the next hour crying and slamming her mom for leaving her alone again to go out with Bruce. Alex ignored Jenn's attempts to smooth things over and ranted about the unfairness of it all, how she couldn't wait to turn eighteen so she could move out on her own.

"It just sucks! I mean, what mother leaves her daughter home alone to hang out with some guy? And not even a cool guy. He's totally lame," Alex said.

"She's single now, Alex. She just wants to have some fun. It's not like they're getting married next week."

"At the rate they're going, they just might."

"Hey, mom's calling me to dinner. Chat on Facebook later?"

"Sure."

Alex hung up and wandered into the kitchen to find something to eat. There were some left-overs, but that didn't sound appealing. She randomly opened and closed cupboards and finally settled on a can of soup. She microwaved it and brought the hot bowl into the living room hoping that the television would distract her for a few hours.

As she watched TV, she rehearsed the speech she would give to her mom when she returned from her date. Alex refused to sit by and be treated like this. The more she thought about what she was going to say, the angrier she became until her hands were shaking too badly to hold the bowl of soup without sloshing it on herself.

Several hours passed and rather than calming down, Alex became more and more agitated as she pictured her mom out having the time of her life. She turned off the TV and stormed into her room, pacing back and forth, hoping she would hear the Blazer pulling into the driveway. Alex felt like she was going to explode if she had to bottle up these feelings much longer.

Her hand mirror lay on the bed, calling to her. Alex walked slowly to the bed and picked up the mirror, handling it like she would a venomous snake. She was terrified to look at the reflective surface. What if the evil Traveler was staring back at her?

I don't have to travel back in time just yet. Maybe just see if I can make the mirror change when I think about him.

Just knowing that she had control of whether she went back in time helped her decide to at least try to make the reflection change to someone close to the evil Traveler. She wished it wasn't so late. She wanted Jenn here but Alex knew Jenn's mom would never let her come over at this time of night.

Alex grabbed her computer, hoping she had a message from Sean and Gavin. She checked her Facebook and Twitter, knowing she was putting off the task. If she went that far, she had to admit that she might be willing to go further and actually travel back in time, and if she was willing to admit *that*, then she had to admit to herself that she may be capable of murdering someone.

Is it still considered murder if I kill a bad guy?

Alex was fairly certain that it would be. Even though Alex herself wouldn't be caught for the crime, the woman whose body she inhabited would and Alex wasn't sure she could live with that. Not even if it meant saving the world from someone trying to alter the past.

What if I just hurt him? Scare him?

That idea sounded a lot more appealing. She had no idea how she could scare someone as ruthless as this Traveler but she would rather try that than attempt to take his life. Alex pondered what would happen to history if he wasn't around any longer. Would it be as devastating as altering the path of someone with more influence? Then again, Alex didn't know who this guy was so she couldn't say how much influence he had. Maybe he was a ruler of a country, or maybe his son would stop world hunger.

There was another possibility that Alex didn't want to contemplate. That by going back in time and alerting the evil Traveler that she could hone in on him and find him would start a war that she wasn't sure she could win. *If I can find him that way, maybe he can find me!* Alex didn't know if she wanted to tip her hand.

She stared at the back of the mirror, her mind whirling so quickly she feared she would get sick, much like she did when on the Tilt-a-Whirl at the local fun park. Tears streamed down her face as she felt the overwhelming urge to call her mom and tell her everything that had happened since that fateful day in the bathroom at Burger King. While she was grateful for Jenn, Sean, and Gavin, she wanted her mom to tell her everything was going to be fine.

Her father's face flashed across her mind. Alex tried to shove it to the side like she usually did but it persisted. This face was from younger years when she had been happy and unaware of the hammer that would fall and change her life. She wanted to go back to that time. Maybe if her dad hadn't left them, they wouldn't have been forced to come live with her aunt, and she never would have seen that girl from Ireland and she would be living the life of a normal teenager.

Maybe she could stop her dad from running off with that blond floozy. If she was a better daughter, he would tell Blondie to take a hike, spend more time at home, and show interest in what she was doing. Alex knew her thinking was terribly flawed and that she wasn't to blame for her dad leaving. He had made that choice and nothing she or her mom could have done would have changed his mind.

Alex wished her dad was in the room so she could shout and scream and curse and tell him exactly how he had ruined her life. If he had been around, her mom wouldn't be out dating some loser. They would be a family, like they were supposed to be. It wasn't fair that she didn't have a father to turn to when things got rough.

She buried her face in her pillow and cried until the tears finally dried up. She made her way to her bathroom, wiping her face. Her eyes were hot and heavy, like they got when she spent too much time underwater at the pool. Alex blew her nose and stared at her face in the mirror. What should be a teenager's best friend was something that spurned mixed feelings in her. Every time she gazed at her reflection to comb her hair or put on make-up, her heart would race as she waited with bated breath for her reflection to change to that of a stranger. Gavin's voice echoed in her head, telling her that killing the Traveler was the only way to ever live a normal life.

How does he know that?

What's to stop another one from taking his place? Gavin assumed that her duty was to stop this one man since he was the only one she ever encountered in the past. *What if Gavin was wrong?* That thought scared Alex. She could go back in time, kill the evil Traveler, and still not be free of this curse; she would never be able to call it a gift.

She went back to her bed. With shaking hands, Alex turned the mirror, light from the ceiling fan overhead reflected in the shiny surface, nearly blinding her. The face in the mirror could almost be that of a stranger. Her hazel eyes were puffy and bloodshot, like those of someone who was much older than seventeen.

With a silent prayer, Alex took deep breaths to slow her heart rate. She focused on the times she had met the evil Traveler and the feelings she experienced when he was near: revulsion, terror, wrongness emanating like the stench off a corpse. Just remembering her previous encounters shattered her concentration as her mind fled from the emotions.

Get a grip, Alex!

She closed her eyes and flexed her muscles to hold the mirror steady. Rather than let the emotions cause her to break her focus, she faced them head-on, refusing to back down.

The image shifted for a brief moment and Alex caught a glimpse of a woman with dark skin before it flickered back to her own familiar face. Alex placed the mirror on the bed next to her and stared at the wall. She couldn't say how much time passed. She had heard the expression of someone's mind going blank and for the first time, she knew exactly what they meant. There was literally nothing that she could remember thinking for that period of time.

Alex heard the slam of a car door. She jumped off the bed, heart racing as she remembered her previous desire to hash it out with her mom about blowing off their driving lesson. Her mom was talking and laughing. *Is he here this late at night?* When she didn't hear any other voice, she figured her mom was talking on the phone.

She waited until her mom had moved down the hallway and into her own room before she opened the door. She considered foregoing the impending fight she knew was about to occur until the next morning, but anger fueled her steps toward her mother's bedroom.

Her mom was in her own bathroom. Alex could hear water running through the closed door. She sat on the edge of the bed, trying to remember the speech she had rehearsed hours earlier but the words were tangled with the image of the African-American woman she had seen in the mirror.

Alex couldn't even meet her mother's eyes when she exited the bathroom.

"I thought you'd be in bed."

"The car woke me up." The lie came easily to Alex's lips.

"Well, I'm tired and we both have to work tomorrow so I'd suggest we get to bed."

Alex jumped off the bed, too angry to sit. "How could you? How could you run off with him and blow off my driving lesson?"

"Bruce wanted to come with me for your driving lesson. But your behavior is unacceptable. He's a perfectly nice man and I'm a grown woman who can spend time with whomever I choose. I like spending time with him. How would you like it if I acted like you in front of your friends?" Her mom stood with her hands on her hips.

"It's not the same thing."

"It *is* the same. Until you learn to behave like an adult, I'll spend time with Bruce without you. If that means you don't get as much driving time, then so be it. The world doesn't revolve around you."

"I never said it did! But when you and I have plans and you break them to hang out with that dork—"

"That's enough out of you. I will not stand for this attitude, Alexis. I deserve to be happy." Patricia took the throw pillows off the bed and tossed them against the wall.

Alex wanted to rant and scream at her mom but it was obvious she had pushed her mom too far. She stormed back to her room and slammed the door knowing it could bring down her mom's wrath but not caring if it did. She couldn't believe her mom was justifying breaking their plans.

She acts like I don't want her to be happy.

Her laptop beckoned her from the desk. Alex grabbed it and brought it over to the bed. She needed to tell Jenn what had happened with her mom and with the reflection changing in the mirror. Jenn's name didn't show up on the chat menu but Alex sent her a message anyway. She knew she was going to be awake for a while and was willing to take the chance that Jenn would receive the notification on her phone and get on her computer. Alex wished she could have internet capability on her phone but her mom refused to pay the extra money and still forbade it even when Alex offered to pay for it herself.

Thinking about that incident only added fuel to the anger bubbling inside her. Her fingers shook as she typed the message to Jenn. She hit send and checked her email and Facebook newsfeed to kill the time.

In moments, Jenn was online and asking her about the woman in the mirror. Alex filled her in on the details she could remember about the woman she had seen.

-Are you going to try again?

-I don't know. I'm scared to try.

-Maybe I can come over, bring you back after a certain time or something?

-That's a good idea. Maybe tomorrow after work?

-Text me when you're done and I'll come get you.

-Good idea. Mom will probably be with Bruce the Dork anyway.

-I think you should give him a chance, Alex. If he makes your mom happy and he's nice, then what's the harm?

-I don't want to give him a chance. Mom and I don't need anyone.

-Sounds like maybe your mom does.

Wanting to end the conversation, Alex said good night and slammed her laptop closed wincing a little hoping the noise wouldn't bring her mom in to ground her. She couldn't believe her best friend in the whole world wasn't on her side when it came to her mom dating someone. Alex just didn't think it was appropriate. The more she thought about her mom choosing Bruce over her, the angrier she became until she was literally seeing red, another of those expressions she didn't really understand until now. If Bruce walked into her room right now, she thought she had it in her to punch him in the face.

Some dim part of her mind reminded her that she wasn't the type to go around hitting people no matter how angry they made her. The voice sounded suspiciously like Jenn's. She stuck out her tongue at the voice in her head and walked to the bathroom in a huff, barely able to brush her teeth because her hands were shaking so badly.

As she tossed her throw pillows on the floor under her desk, she caught site of her hand mirror on the bed. Alex was glad she had decided to try to find the evil Traveler again while Jenn was there. She liked the idea of having someone to wake her up.

As she lay there trying to calm her nerves and emotions, Alex thought about the two women, the nurse with the tired blue eyes, and the African-American woman she had barely glimpsed, hoping she had it in her to save the one and use the body of the other to take someone's life.

Chapter 15

"HOW DO I wake you up again?"

Alex rolled her eyes at Jenn. "Take the mirror out of my hand."

"That's it? Seems too easy."

"That's what Gavin said when I emailed him last night. All someone has to do is break the contact of my eyes with the mirror. Seems like the easiest thing would be to take the hand mirror out of my hands."

"What if I can't?" Jenn looked a little panicked.

"What do you mean?"

"What if you hold it too tight?"

Alex laughed. "You are such a drama queen. It will be fine, seriously."

Alex settled back against the pillows on the bed and held the mirror with shaking hands. Jenn sat next to her with her notebook in her lap. Alex took a deep breath and closed her eyes to help her focus on the evil Traveler. Just as before, she trained her mind on the feelings he invoked in her, all things bad and wrong.

The image shifted to that of the African American woman. Alex held her breath as she watched the woman's dark brown eyes widen in shock and fear. She ignored the part of her mind gibbering to throw the mirror against the wall and stop this dangerous experiment. She reached out a finger and touched the mirror.

* * *

Alex gasped and braced herself against the counter. She found it strange how easy it was to acclimate to the new body when she chose to do the traveling rather than being forced to do it. As she gazed at her reflection in the mirror Alex noticed how muscular she was, even larger than Arachadamia, the Spartan princess she had visited. She had close-cropped black hair and the largest eyes Alex had ever seen. As she turned and flexed in the mirror Alex was reminded of the movie *Aliens* and thought this girl bore a striking resemblance to Vasquez, her favorite character in the movie.

A quick look around revealed that she was in a large bathroom with several stalls and showers. *Am I in a gym?* Her arms pebbled with goose pimples when she noticed how modern the bathroom looked. Her heart beat so fast and hard that she feared she would pass out.

Something's wrong.

She left the bathroom, hoping to get answers as to why she didn't appear to have traveled back in time — at least not very far — and stepped into a large room with rows of bunks. *Seems more like summer camp.* Alex thought the woman a little old to be in summer camp. *Counselor, maybe?*

Why don't you access her memories you twit?

Alex snorted laughter as Sean's voice rang through her mind. As she relaxed, Alex ran through the woman's memories. Her name was Annabel Jennifer Jensen, her friends called her AJ, and she was a Lance Corporal in the Marines. She was an intelligence analyst and was supposed to report to Colonel Jackson at 0830. There was a calendar on the wall and Alex walked closer as though in a trance.

She's living in my time!

While the year and month were the same, AJ's memories indicated that Alex had indeed traveled back in time, just not very far. As close as Alex could tell, she had traveled back in time about half a day.

Alex walked to the bunk that belonged to the woman and opened the wall locker that held her fatigues and got dressed quickly, spurned by the urgency she felt from AJ at not wanting to be late for her meeting with Colonel Jackson. Alex knew she couldn't let the woman get in trouble. It would probably mean being kicked out of the military for treason or something. She would have to play out the next hour until Jenn woke her up then she would try again.

She walked quickly to her destination. It was all she could do not to break into a trot. Her right hand came to her forehead in an automatic salute whenever she saw someone with a higher rank insignia badge on their arm. Alex bit the inside of her cheek to keep from giggling at the strange mantra that was playing through AJ's mind: Shiny badge on the arm, salute! Shiny badge on the arm, salute! One of her superior officers had taught her that and she couldn't help but hear his voice in her head.

You mean you are hearing his voice in AJ's *head.*

She didn't think she'd ever get used to the idea of having her own thoughts jumbled together with those of a stranger. Then again, the girls didn't feel like strangers while her spirit was in their bodies. They felt closer than sisters. Accessing their memories was a bit like trying to remember that person's name you only met once and only for a brief moment. The knowledge was there but it sometimes took a while to retrieve it. If she was relaxed and not consciously trying to sift through the girls' memories, they came easily and quickly. Yet another aspect of her "gift" that she didn't understand and probably never would.

A pair of men walked toward her. One of them looked familiar, even from this distance. And there was something else. Her skin prickled and her hair stood on end. Alex fought the urge to vomit and run in the opposite direction. She needed to see the men and figure out which one was the evil Traveler. As they drew closer, she caught her breath and stopped dead in her tracks. She knew one of the men.

Before she could stop herself, she blurted out, "Uncle Mark?"

*   *   *

"What did you say?" Mark asked the startled woman standing in front of him.

She looked around as though waking from a dream. "I don't remember. Sir, what am I doing here? The last thing I remember was getting out of the shower."

"Did you imbibe any alcoholic beverages or take any recreational drugs this morning, Lance Corporal...?" Mark left the question hanging.

"Jensen, sir, AJ. And no, sir, I did not." She saluted.

"Did you hit your head?"

"No, sir."

"I suggest you report to the doc immediately."

"I'm to meet with Colonel Jackson at 0830."

"I'll inform the Colonel that you are indisposed. Dismissed."

Mark watched the young woman walk away, skin tingling and heart heavy with dread. The only one that called him Uncle Mark was Alex. And this tough-as-nails Marine definitely wasn't his niece.

"What do you think that was all about?" Mark turned to speak to the man beside him.

Lane Stygian was pale as a ghost and stared at the young woman making her way to the medic as though he wanted to devour her on the spot. His lips were pulled back from his teeth in a feral grin. Mark took an involuntary step away from the man, fear twisting his guts. The last time he had seen Lane this angry was on a mission where the man had gleefully shot someone at point blank range, not even flinching as the enemy's blood drenched his face.

"Hey, wait, where are you going?" Mark called fruitlessly at the retreating man's back.

He debated whether to follow or visit Colonel Jackson. He didn't want the Lance Corporal to get in trouble for being late for her duties. *Jackson first, then I'll see what Stygian's up to.*

As he walked to Colonel Jackson's office, Mark pondered the strange event that just took place. If he had to come up with an explanation on the spot, he would swear that for a split second, AJ Jensen had somehow transformed into his niece.

But that's impossible. Isn't it?

Chapter 16

ALEX AWOKE with a start and stared into the worried face of her best friend.

"Are you okay? I waited exactly an hour before I took the mirror away from you." Jenn held up the hand mirror so Alex could see.

Still trying to get her mind around what she had just seen, she sat up slowly.

"Did you find him?" Jenn asked.

"Oh, Jenn, it's worse than that." Alex put her hands to her eyes and cried.

"What happened, Alex? Did you run into the guy? Did he hurt you?"

Alex ignored her friend's incessant tugging on her arm. Things were spinning out of control and Alex needed time to think, to sort it all out. Only one thought kept raging through her mind: get in touch with Sean and Gavin.

She reached for her laptop, vision blurry from crying. Jenn's worried voice was a buzzing in the background. Alex opened her browser and got into her Gmail account. It took her several tries to compose the email as her hands were shaking so badly and every blink brought an onslaught of fresh tears to her eyes.

"Alex, I swear to God, if you don't tell me what the hell is going on, I'll—"

"Jenn, I need to you please shut up. Seriously. I can't right now. I...I just can't." Alex didn't look up from her computer screen as she hit send.

Jenn got up from the bed and threw the time travel journal into her backpack. Alex wanted to shout at her best friend to please stay, that she just needed some time to sort things out, that it wasn't personal but the words stuck in her throat. Jenn opened the door and glanced back and Alex looked away, chest hitching with barely controlled hysteria.

"My God, Alex, something *really* bad happened, didn't it? I don't even know what it is and I'm scared out of my mind." Jenn came back and sat down next to Alex.

Alex leaned on her friend's shoulder and sobbed, unable to hold back the emotion raging through her. She thought if she didn't get a handle on things she would simply cry herself out of existence. *Is that even possible?*

"Enough is enough, Alex, okay? Seriously. Time to bring in the adults here. It's great you found Sean and Gavin but you need to tell your mom about what's been happening."

"I can't do that and you know it."

"You're in over your head. When are you going to finally decide this is too much for you to handle? When this guy finally manages to kill you?"

"Sean and Gavin can help—"

"They're on the other side of the freaking ocean!"

Alex cringed at the anger and fear in her friend's voice. She knew Jenn was right but the thought of telling her mom the secret she had kept for the past three years was just too much to handle on top of what she had just seen. Her phone buzzed and she pushed away from Jenn to grab her computer, hoping the notification was from her email account.

Her shoulders sagged with relief when she saw the email from her Scottish friends. She opened it and motioned Jenn to come closer so she could read what the email said. Alex wasn't sure she had it in her to actually verbalize seeing her uncle walking next to the man who was trying to kill her and change history.

Dearest Alex,

My heart is heavy with dread at this new development. When the suggestion was brought up about you using your gift to seek out the Traveler, I never imagined that he would actually be living in the here and now. The fact that he has ties with your uncle makes me even more concerned for your safety. Did you do anything that would give the Traveler any hint of who you are? I eagerly await your reply and will speak with Sean about possible options. The first order of business is to ensure your safety. Do not attempt to travel to find him again until you hear back from me.

Alex wanted to crawl into a hole and hide for the rest of her life. Screw driving, screw graduation. She just wanted to live long enough to see her eighteenth birthday.

"This can't be happening. I'm more convinced than ever that it's time to tell your mom. And you may want to consider telling your aunt and uncle. I mean, this guy could easily slit your uncle's throat in the middle of the night or something."

"Uncle Mark is a highly trained officer. I'm sure he can take care of himself." Alex bit her lip, remembering her childish outburst at seeing her uncle. *I called him Uncle Mark!*

"I guess if he doesn't know that Mark is your uncle...Alex, what's wrong? What did I say?"

"Oh, Jenn, I messed up so bad. It was just so shocking to see my uncle walking right in front of me, ya know? And then knowing that the evil Traveler was right there with him."

"Slow down and tell me everything that happened." Jenn hurriedly grabbed her time travel notebook from her bag.

Alex started from the beginning and told Jenn everything she could remember, from her first realization that the girl she was inhabiting was actually living in the present and not the past to seeing her uncle and blurting out "Uncle Mark" just before she awoke back in her own body.

Jenn's face turned pale and she gulped audibly. "Oh man, oh man."

"Is that all you can say?"

"What do you want me to say? It's going to be hard for that other girl to blow that one off. What are we going to do?"

"I don't know. That's why I emailed Sean and Gavin. And they don't seem to have any answers either. Maybe I should try to travel again, just to see what damage I caused."

"Oh, no way, Alex. Nope. You read that email. They said not to do any such thing until they figure things out."

"But what if my uncle figures it out? I'm the only one who calls him Uncle Mark. And that poor girl. She'll never be able to explain why she called him that. Why am I the great Protector anyway? I can't even keep my mouth shut in a situation that clearly calls for it." Alex sighed and covered her face with a pillow.

"I don't know what to tell you." Jenn looked as miserable as Alex felt.

"It would be nice if you could say that this was no big, that I just didn't screw everything up royally. Something along those lines would be helpful, thanks." Alex knew she shouldn't be taking it out on Jenn but there was no one else around to unleash on at the moment.

"There's no way to know for sure."

"Unless the guy comes knocking on the door. 'Hey, I couldn't help but figure out who you are. Thanks for the 'Uncle Mark' hint and all.' He's going to come here and kill me and continue with his plan, whatever that may be."

"Something to do with a nurse, that's all we know," Jenn said as she scanned the notebook.

"Yeah, let me just use that little bit of zero information to solve the case and save the world."

"It's all we have to go on unless you see the woman again and can figure out what time period she lives in." Jenn bit her lip. "Sean and Gavin said not to use the mirror to find the evil Traveler but they never said anything about not using it to find out who the nurse is."

"I'm so frazzled, I don't think I could make it change even if I wanted to. Maybe tomorrow would be better."

"The longer you wait, the worse it will be. If your uncle or that guy figures out what's going on, you will be in danger really soon."

"Really not helping, Jenn."

"What do you want me to do? Sit by and tell you what you want to hear? Well excuse me for wanting to keep you alive a little longer."

Alex was shocked at the thick emotion in Jenn's voice. They had never really discussed deep subjects like dying. It made Alex a little uncomfortable discussing the possibility of her death. She didn't want to die. Like *really* didn't want to die. *At least the nightmare would be over.*

Get a grip, Alex!

The voice had the desired effect. She would never give up. She didn't ask for this duty but she would do it to the best of her ability. The thought of her mom or her friends' lives being altered or maybe snuffed out prematurely made her angry. And if there was one thing she had learned about herself in all of this was that she could be a pretty formidable force when she was good and pissed off.

"Sorry for all the drama from me, it's just that this is a little rough, ya know? Of all the things I expected, seeing my uncle wasn't one of them. And knowing I may have put his life in danger just makes me sick to my stomach. And knowing the Traveler could be on his way here now makes me want to run away to Scotland or something."

Jenn sat up straight and grabbed Alex's arm. "Alex, that's it! You need to leave, go somewhere he'll never think to look for you. And what better place than with a fellow Traveler and his Master?"

Alex snorted. "Oh sure, just pack up and leave school, work, my mom. I can just stow away on a plane and live out the rest of my days in the highlands."

"I'm serious, Alex." Jenn crossed her arms.

"I'm sure you are but leaving is out of the question. I can't just pack up and leave in the middle of my junior year. What do you think mom would say to that?"

"She may agree to it and maybe even pay for it if you tell her the truth. She'd have to believe you if you traveled and came back with a wound you didn't have before you left, wouldn't she?"

"Or she might think I'm possessed by the devil and perform an exorcism."

Alex giggled and couldn't stop. She put her hands over her mouth and snorted laughter until tears fell down her cheeks. *That's just what I need.*

"You have lost your mind," Jenn said with a shake of her head.

"You know what they say: laughter is the best medicine."

That sent her off into another fit of giggles that lasted so long she feared ever being able to breathe again.

"Yeah, well, whoever said *that* lame phrase obviously never dealt with someone in complete hysterics."

Alex got her giggle fit under control and laid back against the headboard of her bed, body suddenly exhausted from the terror of her trip to find the evil Traveler, not to mention the crying and now the laughter. She felt like she'd been run over by a truck. Or this is how she imagined someone would feel.

"Got it under control?" Jenn asked.

"I think so."

"I guess you better reply back to Gavin and tell him about your little slip up. They need to know everything if he's going to be able to help you."

Alex grabbed her computer and hurriedly typed a reply, blushing as she typed out the details of how she blurted out the words "Uncle Mark" and how the evil Traveler has been standing right there when she said it. She imagined Gavin pinching the bridge of his nose and shaking his head in disappointment. *I bet Sean never screwed up this bad.* Guilt made her hesitate to hit the send button but she knew she had to confess everything she'd done if any of them had a chance of helping her out of the enormous blunder she found herself in.

She hit send and put her hands over her eyes as though that would somehow block out the reply she was sure would come swiftly. She didn't know Gavin or Sean that well, but she didn't want to disappoint either one of them.

Her hands shook and she felt her face flush as her computer chimed that she had a new message waiting for her. Alex took a deep breath and clicked on the link, hoping the reaming would be kept to a minimum.

"So what did Gavin say?" Jenn asked, bouncing on the bed beside Alex.

"He's more scared than mad," Alex said, sighing in relief. "He says I may *have* to switch places with the girl again to find out how badly I screwed up."

"I don't like the sound of that, Alex."

"What else do you suggest? Hang around until the guy comes to kill me?"

"You have to leave. And that means telling your mom the truth."

"I don't know if I can do that. She'll never believe me."

"We'll have to find some way to prove it to her, Alex. You have to leave and the only way to do that is to 'fess up to your mom." Jenn bolted up on her knees and grabbed Alex's arm in a death grip. "Alex, if the evil Traveler tracks you here that means your mom will be in danger too."

Alex put her head in her hands and cried softly. It was one thing knowing that her own life was in danger but it was another knowing that her mom's life was at risk because of her outburst at the Marine base.

The girls chatted and rehashed their options until Alex was so exhausted she feared her eyes closing mid-sentence. And yet they were no nearer a solution than they were hours ago

Her mom's voice echoed down the hallway.

"Alex! Phone!"

"Just take a message, okay?" Alex knew she couldn't leave her room in her current state without having to answer questions she wasn't ready to face.

"It's your uncle calling long distance!"

Chapter 17

ALEX COULDN'T BREATHE. Her chest and throat locked tight, unable to draw in much-needed oxygen.

A knock on her door unfroze her muscles.

"Did you hear what I said? I said your uncle—" Her mom's voice cut short when she walked into Alex's room. "What is going on in here? Have you been crying?"

"It's nothing, Ms. D. Just Drake being rude online," Jenn said.

"I see. Well can you pull yourself away from your computer long enough to see what your uncle wants? If he's calling it must be important." Patricia held the phone, one hand covering the receiver.

Alex hated the tone in her mom's voice, the one that said she thought her daughter was being immature and self-absorbed.

"Thanks for bringing me the phone." She hated that her voice was so shaky.

"Are you sure you're alright, Lexi?"

The concern that replaced the annoyance almost sent Alex into another bout of crying. She told her mom she was fine and put the phone up to her ear, hoping her mom would get the hint and leave the room. Alex stomach turned when she thought about the reason for the phone call. She glanced at Jenn and swallowed hard at the look of terror on her friend's face.

"Hello?" Alex cleared her throat as the word she meant to say sounded garbled and barely audible. "Hello?" Her voice was stronger this time.

"Alex?" Her uncle's voice sounded strained.

"What's up?" Alex tried to sound nonchalant but just forcing the words out was harder than she thought.

"Oh, not much. Just had something weird happen this morning on base."

Alex glanced up at Jenn. She wanted to hang up the phone and throw it against the wall, anything to stop the conversation occurring between herself and her uncle. Her lower lip and jaw quivered and her eyes filled with tears. She swallowed hard to push down the lump in her throat.

"What does that have to do with me?" She tried not to sound accusatory but she feared it came out that way anyway.

"One of my junior officers called me 'Uncle Mark' and yet claims she doesn't remember doing it. You're the only one who calls me that. Is this some sort of prank or joke you're playing with Lance Corporal Jensen?"

Oh, God, what do I say?

The silence stretched on for what seemed like ever. Alex was surprised to find that her mind had gone completely and totally blank. There was not one coherent thought flitting through her mind at that moment. She felt as though she were sitting outside her body and was merely an observer of the conversation. Jenn sat to her left with the time travel notebook held tightly against her chest.

"You still there, Alex?"

"I gotta go." Alex hurriedly hung up the phone and tossed it down to the foot of her bed. She jumped up and paced her room, raking her hands through her dirty blonde hair.

"Alex, what's wrong with you? I can't believe you just hung up on him!"

She waved her hands to ward off any more questions. A decision had to be made and it had to be made immediately. Alex grabbed her computer and sent off another email to Gavin explaining about the phone call and asking for his advice. She paced again, unable to sit still to wait his reply. Her breath came in gasps and as she walked she felt lightheaded. Her vision darkened at the periphery and she felt as though she was moving through a tunnel. She stopped and swayed on her feet.

"Oh my God, Alex!"

Alex felt Jenn grab her before she hit the floor but the other girl wasn't strong enough to keep her on her feet. The pair slumped to the ground in a heap of tangled arms and legs. Her stomach lurched and she turned her face to the carpet so she didn't puke all over Jenn.

"Gross, Alex. You stay here. I'll grab a towel or something."

Alex heard Jenn rummaging around in her bathroom. She lay her cheek against the rough carpet, trying to reclaim control of her body. Her heart still hammered in her chest but she didn't feel like she was going to faint anymore.

Hard to faint when you're already on the floor.

"You owe me big time for this."

She glanced over and saw Jenn wiping up her vomit with a bathroom towel. Alex wondered absently if Jenn planned on throwing the towel away or if she would throw it in the hamper with the rest of Alex's dirty clothes.

Her computer dinged, bringing her out of her stupor. Alex tried to stand but as soon as she got half-way up, she felt woozy and faint again. She stayed on her knees and scooted to the edge of the bed where her laptop still sat. She turned the screen to face her and clicked on the reply from Gavin.

Dearest Alex,

I am horribly afraid at this latest news. It's clear that your outburst did not go unnoticed. If your uncle was able to put things together, then my guess is the evil Traveler has too. It's only a matter of time before he comes for you.

I wish I had the answers for you. If you think you can trust your uncle, perhaps it is time to bring him into your confidence. He can keep an eye on the Traveler and tell you if he leaves the base. At least military personnel can't just leave whenever they choose. That makes it a little easier to avoid him. I could advise you to leave home but I know that isn't a decision to be made lightly. Perhaps if you did tell your uncle the truth he could help you figure out what to do next.

I have forwarded on these correspondences to Sean. Maybe he will have some idea that eludes me. Please keep me informed as to your decision of whether or not to confide in your uncle and what comes of it.

You will be in my thoughts and prayers,

Gavin

"Alex, he's totally right! He will take a lot less convincing than your mom. Not to mention the fact that he's a Marine."

"You really think so?" Alex felt the terror and anxiety lessening at the thought of telling her uncle her secret.

"Think about it. He's with the Traveler and can keep an eye on him. And he's got awesome weapons in case the guy tries anything."

"That's true." Alex chewed her lip, battling between wanting to keep her secret and needing someone else's help.

"Absolutely. Look, Alex, the time has come to get some adult help here. And who better than a bad-ass Marine?"

She wanted to argue but there was no flaw in the logic. *If Gavin thinks it's a good idea, who am I to argue?* "So how should I break the news? Call him? Send him an email?"

"Can you even call someone on base?"

Alex shrugged. "I don't know. He called me, didn't he?"

"Yeah, but that's different. I'm not so sure it's as easy to call someone on a base as it is for them to dial out. Maybe you could ask your mom? Pretend like you guys got cut off or something?" Jenn suggested.

"I don't know. She may want to know what he was calling about and I don't have a good story worked out yet. I still feel weak and sick and I don't know..." Alex lay back against her pile of pillows.

"Maybe you need something in your stomach. It's been awhile since breakfast."

"I need to tell Mark before I even think about food. I won't be able to relax until I finally do it."

"Maybe just send him an email and tell him to call you as soon as he can."

Alex glanced at the hand mirror sitting on her bed. "Or I could do something even more convincing."

* * *

Alex gasped and grabbed the edge of the sink. She was in a bathroom, a different one this time. Just a single toilet and sink. She glanced at the now-familiar face of Lance Corporal AJ Jensen in the mirror. The woman was wearing a hospital gown and her eyes looked haunted and scared. Alex lifted her arm and winced at the slight pinching pain. She looked down and saw a piece of white gauze stretched around the crook of her arm.

There was a full urine sample cup sitting on the edge of the sink. Alex read the girl's thoughts and knew she was supposed to bring it out to the lady at the desk just outside the door. Alex took a deep breath and exited the bathroom.

"Just set that down on that shelf and have a seat there." The woman tilted her head to the left, indicating a row of pale blue chairs against a pristine white wall.

She placed the urine cup carefully on the metal shelf next to a half dozen other samples and sat in one of the chairs. Her skin pebbled in goose pimples as her flesh touched the cold plastic seat.

After only a few minutes, a nurse called her into a small room.

"The doctor didn't find anything unusual during his exam but he is going to run a few more tests just to rule out anything serious. For now, he's ordering you back to barracks. You are to resume your regular duties the day after tomorrow. He's already informed your superior officers."

Alex nodded at the young woman who looked barely old enough to be out of high school let alone old enough to be a nurse in the military. The woman closed the medical chart and left the room. Alex glanced around and found her clothing in a neatly folded pile on a chair against the wall. She dressed, wondering what her next plan of action should be. Jenn was under strict orders to wake Alex only if her mom came into the room. They had locked her door to give them some time in case her mom tried to walk in unannounced.

If the doctor ordered her to barracks, she had no choice but to do directly there. If he caught her out and about, AJ would be in big trouble. Alex didn't want the poor girl suffering any more than she already had. Guilt made her face flush when she realized that AJ could be discharged if her superiors thought she had mental issues.

Uncle Mark will fix everything.

Alex walked to the barracks, hoping the answer would come to her as she made her way across the base. Part of her hoped her uncle would be walking along just like he had that morning, but Alex didn't hold out too much hope. And she damn sure didn't want to run into the evil Traveler.

Her senses were on high alert and she was a little distracted looking for Mark and the Traveler but she saluted when she was supposed to and didn't think her manner was in any way suspicious. Alex wondered if the barracks had a phone book. If she couldn't wander around the base the next best thing would be to try to get a hold of her uncle some other way.

The barracks were blessedly empty. That didn't happen often and Alex knew she had better take advantage of it. She retrieved AJ's laptop from the woman's footlocker and got into the Outlook program. By using AJ's memories, Alex knew the best way to get her uncle's number was to use the directory associated with Outlook. She had wanted to simply email her uncle rather than call but the military would have access to any emails. Alex couldn't take that risk so a phone call was the only option.

She found her uncle's private number and dialed before she lost her nerve. Her heart raced so fast she feared she would faint. When ring after ring met her ears she feared he wouldn't answer. And part of her feared he would.

A computerized voice announced that the person she was trying to reach was not available.

Oh, God! What do I do now?

Her mind raced as she tried to decide whether to hang up or leave a message. Jenn could be waking her up at any moment and she needed to tell her uncle the truth. But she didn't know what to say. Should she leave a message as AJ or as herself? Which would he be most likely to believe or respond to? Would he come alone or with a squad of military police to arrest AJ for being crazy?

Get a grip, Alex!

The beep shattered through her rambling thoughts. She took a deep breath and spoke into the receiver, "This is Lance Corporal Jensen and I think we need to talk about what happened earlier. I remember what happened and it's urgent that you come to my barracks as soon as you get this. Come alone."

Alex slammed the phone down and put her head in her hands. There was nothing else she could do. *At least I have less chance of running into the evil Traveler if I'm stuck here.*

She jumped up and paced the length of the barracks and hoped her luck would hold out and the place would remain empty. Every time she approached a window, she peered out and looked for her uncle. When he didn't appear, she threw up her hands in disgust and paced again. Alex feared that if he didn't get here soon she would have AJ's fingernails chewed down to nubs.

The sound of rapidly approaching footsteps stopped Alex in her tracks. She held her breath as she waited for the door to open. And yet she hoped that whoever it was would keep on walking.

She had kept her secret for so long that the thought of telling someone terrified her. Jenn found out by accident so Alex didn't have a choice but to tell her.

He can help you.

The footsteps stopped outside the door and the door handle turned ever so slowly. Alex backed away, gripped by sudden fear. Her legs hit the bed behind her and she fell backward gracelessly. As the door opened, she stood and tried to look casual in case it was someone coming back to the barracks.

Alex wanted to weep when she saw her uncle's familiar face. They had never been super close but just seeing him standing there in his fatigues made her feel safer.

"I want answers and I want them now, Lance Corporal."

She blinked a few times. His brusque statement left her bewildered. She had hoped there would be some awkward stammering, perhaps even an uncomfortable silence but this right-out-of-the-gate demand had her flustered.

"I'm not sure you're going to believe me—"

"Don't worry about what I won't or won't believe. Just spit it out." He stood with his arms crossed over his chest and his facial expression was nothing but angry.

"I'm not who you think I am," Alex said.

"What's that supposed to mean?" he asked.

Tears welled in her eyes. "It's me, Uncle Mark. It's Alex."

Chapter 18

"COME AGAIN?"

Alex wiped her eyes and swallowed the lump in her throat. "It really is me. It's Alex."

"I don't know what kind of stunt you're pulling, but I don't like it."

Alex took an involuntary step backward as her uncle advanced on her. He was all military at that moment, graceful and deadly. She side-stepped the bed as she moved away from him but he kept coming and had her pinned against the wall in seconds.

"Please, Uncle Mark, you have to believe me. You're married to Karen who owns two clothing stores in Grand Junction, mom and I came to live with you guys when dad left us."

Alex spoke so quickly the words tumbled over themselves. As she spoke Mark's eyes grew larger and he backed further away until Alex was the one chasing him down. She told him things AJ couldn't possibly know.

She stood as her uncle sat on the edge of one of the bunks looking rather shell-shocked. He ran his hands through his hair and mumbled to himself.

"So do you believe me?" Alex asked.

"I need time—"

"I don't have time. That's why I came back. I need your help."

"If I'm going to help, you need to start at the beginning. I need to have all the facts before I can even begin to deal with this."

Alex grabbed a chair, sat in front of her uncle, and told him everything that had happened since she had seen Aine in the mirror in the Burger King off I-70. As she spoke, she kept a watch on the door in case someone wandered into the barracks. She ended with the reason behind the last trip that she had blundered so badly.

"I was trying to locate the evil Traveler and that's how I ended up in AJ. Which is strange since I always thought the traveling thing could only occur to the past," Alex said, staring off into space. She shook her head and continued. "Anyway, I knew that AJ lived in somewhat recent times as soon as I saw the modern facilities in the bathroom. I figured I had traveled back a few years at most. When I spotted you and that guy, I lost all sense of control and blurted out your name without thinking."

Mark gave a small smile. "Imagine what I was thinking."

"So here's the thing. That guy you were with? I think he's the evil Traveler I've been fighting all these years."

"I wish I could say that I didn't believe you or that you must be mistaken, but I actually think you're right."

Of all the things her uncle could have said, Alex never expected that. "What do you mean?"

"I think I interrupted one of his missions back in time. He played it off like it was some sort of medical condition but I knew better. He was ice cold. The only medical condition I know of that has that symptom is death."

Alex nodded. "That's what happens to me. Poor Jenn nearly lost her mind when she found me in one of my episodes."

"I'm glad you've had someone to open up to. I still think you need to tell you mom. I don't like the idea of you being home and dealing with this without an adult."

Alex shook her head. "I'm not ready. The only reason I came to you was because Sean and Gavin suggested it."

"And they are time travelers like you?" Mark asked.

"Sean is. Gavin is his Master. This guy I've been dealing with has killed most of the others. Which is why Gavin thinks I don't have one."

Her uncle jumped to his feet so suddenly Alex gave a squeak of fear. "So does Gavin think this evil Traveler has a Master?"

A chill raced down Alex's spine at the look in her uncle's eyes. "I suppose so."

"Because I think I know who it is."

"What? Are you serious?"

"And if it's who I think it is, we're in big trouble."

* * *

Alex rubbed her eyes. She had shared years of information with her uncle in a very short period of time and the bombshell he had dropped on her about the identity of the evil Traveler and his Master had her more scared than ever.

"I can't believe this is happening. How am I supposed to fight a top military official? I bet he has connections I never even dreamed of."

"There's more. Your little outburst didn't go unnoticed. Lane will put two and two together, if he hasn't already. I can keep an eye on him here but if he can do what you do and travel into someone close to you in the present time, he could harm you and I couldn't do a thing about it."

"Just don't let the guy around any mirrors then, okay?"

"I'll watch Stygian like a hawk, but I can't draw suspicion to myself or do something that will get me discharged."

"I don't want you to get in trouble, Uncle Mark. But I admit confiding in you makes me feel a hell of a lot better and ... What are you laughing at?" Alex raised her eyebrows.

"I've worked with Lance Corporal Jensen before and she is so different from you. It's so weird seeing her sitting here and yet all of your mannerisms manifesting themselves. Even the way you talk is different."

"Well, I'm glad you're having fun with all of this. I have a madman after me and all you can do is laugh."

"I'm sorry, kiddo. Look, we'll figure something out, okay? You focus on finding out who that nurse is and I'll keep an eye on Lane Stygian. I'll keep you apprised of everything he does and if I see him with a piece of mirror, I'll take it away like you said. Maybe he'll give up."

Alex sighed. "I don't think that will be enough to stop him. I've beat him more times than I can count and he still keeps coming. This Max Poder you told me about has him doing something big, so big that he won't let anyone stop him. Not me and not you."

"Don't worry about me. You have enough to worry about."

"I can't help it. I've put you in danger just by telling you the truth. If you interfere with Lane, he'll try to take you out."

"In case you hadn't noticed, I'm a Marine. Rumor has it we're pretty bad ass. I can handle Lane."

"Yeah, but can you handle your superior officer? Couldn't he send you on a mission to Russia or something just to get you out of the way?"

"That's a very real possibility. But we'll deal with that when we get to it. Right now, focus on the nurse and what time she's from. It may give us a clue as to what Max's plan is."

Mark glanced at his watch and stood. "I have to run. Duty calls."

Alex stood and raised her arms to give him a hug but remembered she was in the body of an older woman and someone that her uncle knew. He scratched his head, aware of the awkwardness and they both ended up laughing and shaking hands instead.

"Keep in touch. And stay safe." Mark walked out of the barracks and closed the door softly behind him.

Alex sat on AJ's bed and sagged with relief. Her uncle was in her corner. For the first time in a long time, she felt like she would be able to beat this guy. She made her way into the bathroom and stared at AJ's reflection in the mirror. She focused on her own face and in seconds the reflection in the mirror shimmered. She reached out to touch the mirror.

I hope Uncle Mark will help cover for poor AJ.

Chapter 19

ALEX SAT UP in bed and turned at a squeal of fright just to her left.

"It's just me, Jenn."

"I'm aware of that. But when you've been lying still for a while and you all of a sudden sit up, it's a little scary," Jenn said sarcastically.

"I didn't do it on purpose." Alex sat up and rubbed her hands across her face. Even though traveling like this was easier on her, it still took a few minutes to acclimate to being back in her own body again. She turned at an impatient tapping sound.

Jenn drummed a rhythm on the time travel notebook with her pen. "Spill it, Alex. And don't forget to tell me everything."

Alex filled Jenn in on the conversation she had had with her uncle, trying to remember the details. She would rather gloss over everything and just get right to the point but Jenn would bug her until she recalled the color of the paint on the walls of the barracks, the positioning of everything, the sounds she heard.

"Lane Stygian? That's the guy's name? It sounds creepy." Jenn shuddered.

"Yeah, and we think his Master is a General named Max Poder."

"I can't believe that the evil Traveler is at the same base as your uncle. At least he can keep an eye on the guy for us. Give us a head's up if he leaves."

"Mark said Lane isn't due for leave for a while. But that doesn't mean that the General can't have Lane go away on some fake mission so he can do whatever it is he is going to do." Alex waved her hands vaguely in the air.

She grabbed her laptop and sent an email to Gavin. For the first time in a long time, she felt hopeful about the future. She had other people in her corner, *adult* people who wielded far more power than she had. And with Mark keeping an eye on Lane Stygian, she figured she would focus her attention on trying to find out more about the nurse she had seen. She was tied to Max and Lane's plans, Alex was certain of it.

Alex glanced at the alarm clock sitting on her end table and groaned. "I gotta get ready for work. Wanna drive me and we can figure out our next move?"

"Sure. It's not like I have anything else to do."

Alex jumped in the shower and threw on some clothes, hardly giving any thought to what it was she was wearing. Her mind was so distracted. She threw her hair up in a quick bun and put on a little make-up.

"Alex, you ready to head into work?" Patricia rapped on Alex's door.

"Jenn's taking me."

"Okay. Better hurry or you'll be late."

Alex rolled her eyes. She'd never been late to work a day so far and her mom was treating her like a child. *Like usual.*

On the way to the store, Jenn grilled Alex one last time to make sure she didn't leave anything out. Alex assured Jenn that she had told her everything.

"I need the details if I'm ever going to write the books about this stuff. I'm tellin' ya, they will be big. Maybe even have movies made out of them. Which reminds me, I need to get online and figure out what actors I want to play our parts."

Alex laughed. "I think you're dreaming, girl."

"You'll change your tune when I'm walking on the red carpet. I need to get online and pick out my dress and shoes!"

The two girls chatted about dresses they had seen their favorite stars wearing, what kind of shoes they would wear, what accessories they would have on. They even went so far as to dream about what male actors would accompany them down the red carpet. With each passing moment, their imaginations got more and more carried away until they were walking arm-in-arm with top A-list actors.

Jenn braked hard in front of the store. "Need a lift after?"

Alex shook her head. "Mom and I are supposed to go driving after work but who knows. She'll probably blow me off again for Bruce."

"Well, if you need a ride, give me a holler." Jenn gave a quick wave before she drove away.

Alex walked into the store and stopped short. Catelyn Montgomery was browsing through the store with her mom. Alex hadn't seen her arch nemesis all school year and it had been a truly blissful year because of it. She had been sent away to a private school when her parents had come home from vacation early and caught her and Beau in a rather embarrassing situation.

Catelyn looked up and met Alex's eyes. Alex wanted to look away but her hazel eyes were locked onto the girl's blue ones. Catelyn's face grew redder by the second until finally she broke contact and stalked past Alex, brushing her so hard she nearly knocked Alex over. Catelyn's mom looked up at the sound of the door opening and followed after her daughter, shouting and gesturing.

"What was that about?" Karen asked as she came from the stockroom at the back of the store.

"Just a little mother-daughter spat. Nothing to worry about," Alex said.

"I got some new stock in the back. Want to take a look?" Karen asked.

"Sure. Need me to inventory it?"

"Not yet. I don't have room for it anyway. But there's some new stuff in the men's store that needs sorting through if you wouldn't mind doing that."

"Sure."

Alex walked back into the stockroom to see the new stuff that had arrived yesterday. She loved looking at the new clothing all wrapped in plastic, so pristine and perfect. Although she received some items for birthdays and Christmas, she couldn't afford to shop here herself. Alex walked down the length of the back room until she came to the back entry into Downtown Boy. When her aunt had purchased the neighboring building, she had the construction crew knock out the wall between the stockrooms so she, Patricia, and Alex could move between stores without having to go outside first.

She looked at the rows of boxes and sighed. The men's store had really taken off and moved quite a lot more inventory than did the women's store, which meant a lot more boxes to open and clothing to inventory. Alex turned on the small radio and got to work.

At first it seemed as though she wasn't making a dent in the rows of boxes but as the hours wore on, the pile of broken down boxes grew ever taller and the racks more full. When the last box had been unpacked and counted, Alex wheeled the first of several full racks over near the doorway into the store. When the squeaking of the wheels stopped, she heard voices coming from the store.

Oh, great, it's him.

Alex rolled her eyes as she caught the sound of Bruce's voice, laughing at something her mom was saying. She tiptoed closer to the doorway to eavesdrop, face burning when she imagined what her mom would do if she caught her. And part of her wasn't sure she wanted to hear what they were talking about.

"...not sure what to do," Alex heard her mom say when she got within earshot.

"She needs time," Bruce said.

"How much time? How long do I continue to choose between the two of you?"

"I never meant for you to have to choose between me and your daughter. Maybe it's best if I stay out of the picture for a while."

Alex felt a little guilty at the sadness in Bruce's voice at the thought of not spending time with her mom and yet she couldn't help but grin. She and her mom were better off without a man in their lives. Her mom would see it in time.

"That's not going to happen. I'm not going to let my head-strong teenager decide who I spend time with."

"Not to make things worse, but when you are supposed to be spending time with me, you're not really there because you're thinking about Alex."

"Oh, Bruce, I'm sorry about that." Her mom sighed loudly. "I just wish she would come around so we could spend time together."

"Just so you know I'm okay with doing dinner and such even if her behavior is less than exemplary."

Alex sputtered. She couldn't believe the man had the nerve to bad-mouth her in front of her own mom.

"I'm not okay with her behavior and I won't subject you to it. She is going to learn one way or the other that I have a right to live my own life."

Alex gripped the doorway so hard her hand hurt. Before she knew quite what she was doing, she barged into the store and stormed over to where her mom and Bruce were standing. Her mom turned with a smile but it faded just as quickly.

"How *dare* you talk about me like this behind my back?"

Her mom's face turned red but refused to look away. "I'm sorry you had to hear that, Alex, but perhaps that will teach you not to eavesdrop on conversations that don't concern you."

"Doesn't concern me?" Alex shook her head. "You were talking about *me*! I'd say it concerns me."

"I won't allow you to talk to me like this, young lady, and certainly not in front of Bruce."

"Why not? He was in on it too. Who the hell is he to talk about my behavior?"

Alex nearly screamed in rage when her mom actually broke into laughter. "Maybe you should head in back and watch the store security tape. Maybe you'll understand."

"I can't believe you're choosing him over me." Alex shook so badly she thought her knees would give way.

"It's not as hard as you think when you act like this. I have a right to spend time with whomever I choose and I also have a right to expect my nearly adult daughter to treat my friends or boyfriend with respect."

"Boy...boyfriend?" Bruce asked.

Alex and Patricia looked at him for the first time since Alex began her tirade. He opened and closed his mouth a few times before turning and walking out of the store. But not before Alex saw the sappy smile plastered on his face.

"We'll discuss this later, Alexis. You best get back to the other store." Patricia turned her back on Alex.

"I'm not discussing it any more. You want to see him, fine. But leave me out of it."

"What is it you have against Bruce? He's perfectly nice!"

Alex turned to face her mom with tears running freely down her cheeks. "He's nice now, sure. But what happens down the road, Mom? What happens when he starts drinking and sleeping around and ruins everything? Will you pack up and move us somewhere else and ruin my life again? You probably would and not even care, wouldn't you?"

Alex's voice broke at the end and a sob broke through her tightened throat. Each word she had spoken, her mom's face had gone a shade paler. By the time Alex was done her mom was sheet-white and looked like she was about to faint.

"Alex, it wouldn't be like that..."

"You don't know that. Guys are lying, cheating bastards and we don't need one in our lives screwing things up." Alex walked out of the store and back into the storeroom, ignoring her mom's cries for her to stop.

Rather than return to the women's store, Alex wasted time in the back so she could get it together before being around other people. She walked into the small bathroom to splash some water on her face. When she saw her reflection she burst into tears at seeing her father's hazel eyes staring back at her. Anger and bitterness welled from deep inside, threatening to choke the life out of her. She gripped the sides of the sink to keep from hitting something. Sobs ripped from her constricted chest, making her sound like an injured animal.

"Alex, are you back here?"

Her aunt's voice echoed through the storeroom. Alex tried to answer but she literally couldn't draw a breath. She absently wondered if it was possible to suffocate because of crying. *Death by crying!*

The knob to the bathroom door turned as her aunt frantically tried to get into the bathroom. Alex reached out blindly and unlocked the door.

"Alex, my God, what is it? What happened?" Karen gathered Alex into her arms.

Alex couldn't say how long she cried on her aunt's shoulder. If anyone asked, she wouldn't be able to tell them what she had said. But words came pouring out from some dark place where they had been hiding for years, just waiting to come out. Her aunt never said a word, just held her, rocked her, and smoothed her hair.

When the sobbing subsided somewhat, Alex pulled away from her aunt and almost started crying again when she saw the mess she had made on her aunt's blouse. Karen simply stood and got a box of Kleenex from the bathroom and brought it to Alex.

"If you need to get back, I'll be okay now, I think," Alex said.

"I have Chloe watching the front so I'm here as long as you need me," Karen rubbed the back of her head and neck.

"I'm sorry about losing it while at work. It won't happen again."

Karen hugged Alex with one arm. "It's okay. We can't always choose when our emotions need to come out. At least you did it back here and not in front of customers," her aunt teased. "And I think you've been keeping too much inside for too long."

Alex tried to remember what she had said while sobbing against her aunt's shoulder. *I hope I didn't say anything about the time travel stuff!* "Yeah, I guess I have."

"Honey, you have to know that just because your father left doesn't mean that every man will be like that. Look at your uncle Mark and me. He's not a thing like Gary. And neither is Bruce."

"But how do you *know*? Dad wasn't always like he was at the end."

Karen hesitated before replying. "Is that what your mom told you?"

"No. But I don't remember him being drunk like that or being mean when I was little."

"Honey, your dad was always like that. Your mom was able to hide it from you easier when you were little is all. But Gary was always a womanizer and a drunk."

Alex cringed at the venom in her aunt's voice. She remembered another time when she had eavesdropped on a conversation where she heard something she wished she could take back. It wasn't easy learning your dad had hit on your aunt.

"Why did she stay with him?"

"Gary swept your mom off her feet. And while he was a slime ball, he could also be charming and attentive. Your mom and Gary got married so young. And when you have a child, it complicates things."

"So you think Bruce is good enough for mom?"

"I have only talked to him once but I've been in this town for a long time and people talk, especially rich ladies with nothing else better to do than spend money. And not one has anything bad to say about Bruce. In fact, more than a few are jealous of your mom. Seems Bruce is considered quite the catch and no one else has been able to get him to do more than say a few nice words."

"Really? Out of all the ladies he could have he picked mom, huh?" Alex sniffed.

"Your mom is pretty amazing, Alex. And she really does deserve someone in her life to make her smile again. Besides you and me and C.C."

Alex knew her aunt was right and the knowing made her want to lock herself in the bathroom and cry for another few hours or so until she purged the guilt eating at her insides.

"Honey, I know why you fought so hard to keep Bruce away. What Gary did to you and your mom was inexcusable and tore your life apart. But you guys made it and have a good life here. Everything happens for a reason, Alex, I truly believe that. But life *can't* happen if you build walls so high that no one can get in. We can try to protect ourselves from getting hurt but those walls will also keep out people and things that bring us joy."

"I just don't want my life turned upside down. I can't go through that again." Alex shook her head, feeling the crushing weight of bad memories.

Karen kissed her on the top of her head. "I know, honey. But this time will be different. Bruce really is a good guy. He didn't leave his wife. She passed away. People have nothing but good things to say about him. Give him a chance. I'm not saying you have to call him 'Dad' right away but it might be nice to spend some time with him and your mom."

Alex caught the tone of rebuke in her aunt's voice and her face reddened. It took her a minute to raise her head. It felt stuffed with cotton or more like nasty mucus. Alex thought it was impossible that the human body could produce that much mucus and not totally dehydrate.

"Let's get you cleaned up. It's quitting time soon." Her aunt helped her to her feet.

Alex once again entered the bathroom and groaned aloud when she saw her face in the mirror. She barely looked like herself with her eyes red and puffy. The rest of her face was a blotchy mixture of normal skin tone and raw red.

As she blew her nose she wondered what she was going to say to her mom. Even though she felt horrible about the confrontation earlier, part of her was still angry that the two of them had been talking about her. And she still wasn't totally convinced that her mom spending so much time with Bruce was a good idea. But she would rather be forced to have dinner once in a while with the guy than have this strained relationship with her mom.

She walked slowly back to the men's store, wishing she could put this task off. She hated apologizing even when she was in the wrong. Especially when she was in the wrong. And in the wrong big time. *At least Bruce isn't there.*

Her mom was closing out the cash register. She turned and stopped when she saw Alex in the doorway. Alex's wanted to die at the look of hurt in her mom's eyes. They were red-rimmed so it was obvious she had been crying. She put the drawer down on the edge of the counter.

Alex's eyes filled with tears again – *how can I possibly have any left?* – and she walked to her mom and hugged her tight.

"I'm so sorry, Momma. I didn't mean what I said earlier. I'm afraid, so afraid." That was all Alex managed to get out before another bout of crying stole her ability to speak.

"Afraid of what, Lexi? That I'm going to run away with him?"

"No," Alex pulled away so she could look at her mom. "I'm afraid that he'll run away from *us.*"

Her mom laughed a little and held her close. "Oh, honey, I know how you feel. Believe me. Bruce has been after me to go on a date with him for the last year."

"Wait, you've put him off for a year and he is still around?"

"Apparently he's patient as hell. I kept him at arm's length but he persisted and I finally gave in. I figured a date or two couldn't hurt. And then before I knew it, I realized that I enjoyed his company. A lot."

Alex smiled a little at her mom's blushing. "He must really like you to wait for that long."

"I guess he does," Patricia stammered.

"I'm not saying I'm all of a sudden fine with this but I suppose it wouldn't hurt to give the guy a chance," Alex mumbled.

"That's all I ever wanted, Lexi. Why don't we get out of here. If I remember correctly, you and I have a driving date, don't we?"

"If you still want to."

"Absolutely," Patricia said.

*   *   *

Later that night Alex sent a text to Jenn about what happened that afternoon, leaving out most of the things she had said to her mom and Bruce. There was no need to tell her everything.

-Just don't do any traveling without me there. You need someone to watch your back now that Lane might know who you are

-I won't

-When do you think you want to try to connect with the nurse again?

-So busy the next few weeks with the play and work. Not sure. Will let you know

-K. See you Monday morning

Alex got ready for bed, in better spirits than she had been in a long time. It felt so good to have adults on her side with the time travel stuff and the emotional tsunami that had overtaken her earlier left her exhausted, but purging all of that negativity was the first step in healing.

She closed her eyes and sleep took her almost immediately.

Chapter 20

"**I'M TELLING YOU,** he has to go."

Drifter tried to stand at ease in Max Poder's office but anger tightened his muscles making it impossible to relax.

"One doesn't simply get rid of a high ranking Marine officer, no matter how difficult he's being," Max said.

"It's more than him following me around. I'm telling you, I think his niece is the Traveler who has been thwarting me at every turn."

"Highly unlikely. Whoever heard of a Traveler passing into a body in the present time? You must have heard wrong."

"I didn't hear wrong. Lance Corporal Jensen clearly said 'Uncle Mark' before reeling in confusion, claiming she had no memory of how she got outside. And the girl didn't have to travel into someone in the present time. Traveling back in time doesn't have to mean years or decades. A few minutes or hours in the past is *still* traveling back in time." Drifter tried to keep his voice steady.

"Perhaps she had some sort of medical condition—"

"Like *my* medical condition?" Drifter threw as much sarcasm into his tone as he could without stepping over the line. Like it or not he was still in the presence of a higher ranking officer.

"What occurred yesterday is of no concern. You still have a job to do. Find a way to keep Mark off your tail so you can do it. Is that clear?"

"Yes, Sir." Drifter turned on his heel and stalked out of his Master's office. His fury must have shown on his face because people made it a point to avoid him as he made his way to his barracks.

He couldn't believe Poder refused see what was right in front of him. Lane didn't know much about Mark but he knew that he only had one niece which meant only one person who would ever call him Uncle

Mark. He wanted to jump on a plane, head for Grand Junction, and kill the girl but he couldn't disobey an order from a superior officer.

Or from his Master.

If the girl dares to return to Lance Corporal Jensen, I'll leave base, permission or no.

Drifter spotted the very woman he had been thinking about walking toward him. She saluted in perfect form, though she looked a little confused. He glared at her and smiled a little at the look of utter and complete shock on the woman's face. He turned and watched her walk away, visions of how he would kill her flashing in his head. He could kill with nothing more than his bare hands.

But killing the girl would raise eyebrows and questions would certainly be asked. Mark would suspect him and would stop at nothing to see him convicted. Besides, killing AJ Jensen before the Traveler was inside her body did him no good at all. The meddling girl would only hone in on someone else.

Drifter walked into the barracks and grabbed his laptop out of his footlocker. He had a long way to go before he memorized the journal article Master had told him about. The formulas were complicated and science wasn't exactly his strong suit. His mind was distracted and he couldn't recall more than a few sentences at a time. He slammed the top of the computer and paced the room, hoping it would clear his head. All he could think of was looking into Lance Corporal Jensen's dark brown eyes as he choked the life out of her.

As was his usual practice when his anger threatened to boil over, he went to the shooting range to take out his anger on a paper target. It wasn't as good as shooting at a real person, but beggars couldn't be choosers.

*   *   *

Mark watched Drifter leave the barracks and head for the shooting range. He had witnessed the man's reaction to Lance Corporal Jensen and had been ready to step in if Lane looked like he was going to do more than intimidate the poor woman.

If Alex is right, Jensen doesn't even know why he's glaring at her.

He shook his head at recalling the conversation he had with his niece. It was a tough story to swallow. If he hadn't heard his fellow officer call him something only his niece ever called him and if Alex hadn't told him things Jensen couldn't possibly know, he would never buy it. Mark considered himself of sound mind and body and every instinct was screaming at him that his niece was right and that she was in grave danger. He had served with Lane Stygian for many years and knew what the man was capable of.

Do you really?

If what Alex said was true, Stygian was more than a cold-blooded killer. He was hell-bent on changing the past for some purpose Mark couldn't begin to fathom and that would have far more disastrous consequences than a murder or two.

And his seventeen-year-old niece was the only one who could stop him.

Mark was glad she had confided in him. The thought of Alex facing not only a man who could travel through time but a highly trained killer as well made his skin crawl. He vowed to do whatever it took to keep Alex safe. If that meant trailing Stygian every second, then that's what he would do. Maybe if he made Lane's life difficult, he would give up on his mission.

Unlikely.

Mark snorted and headed to the headquarters building for a debrief. As he walked across the hot pavement, he hoped it didn't mean a mission away from base. If he had to leave, there would be no one to watch Lane Stygian. And it wasn't as though he had someone else he could tell this story to. What frightened him more was the fact that he was seriously considering going AWOL if the debrief meant he was on an away mission.

He opened the door and tried to relax as he took a seat at the large round table. It was a full house which made him relax further. In the past when he had been sent on an away mission, there had been only six others present. A full room generally meant that he wouldn't be going anywhere.

"Worried you may be going off base?"

Mark jumped at the sound of Lane Stygian's voice coming from right behind him. "Why would that worry me?" Mark said, surprised at how calm his voice sounded.

"Oh, I don't know. If you were gone, you couldn't follow me around." Lane met his stare with a small smile that never reached his flat gaze.

"Follow you? What are you talking about?" Mark fought the urge to wipe his sweaty palms on his pants.

"Don't play dumb with me. I've known you too long for that."

"Why are you worried about me following you? Afraid I might catch you doing something you shouldn't be?" Mark said, hoping to put Stygian on the defensive.

Lane laughed, drawling curious stares from those seated around the conference table. "Whatever you *think* you know believe me, you're way off the mark."

"And what do you think it is that I *think* I know?"

Lane shook his head. "I'm as highly trained as you. It's going to take a lot more than that to get me to talk."

Mark set his jaw and curled his hands into fists under the table. "I really don't care what you're up to."

"You need to work on your skills at lying," Lane said with a whisper.

Further talk was cut off by the entrance of a senior officer carrying a clipboard under her arm. She called for attention and directed the man standing to her left to pass out several packets of information.

Mark tried to focus during the meeting but as soon as he knew he wasn't going off-base any time soon, his thoughts drifted and he tried to think of a way to keep an eye on Lane without being so obvious about it. If they weren't on a military base, he could probably set up some sort of surveillance equipment. But there was no way he could do that here without someone asking why. It wasn't as though he could tell anyone that his niece could time travel and that Lane Stygian was also a time traveler and that Alex had to somehow stop him.

I'd get a medical discharge for sure.

He could feel Lane's eyes on him but he refused to turn around.

I'll do whatever it takes to stop him and help Alex.

Chapter 21

SHE WALKED THROUGH a magical wood unlike anything she had ever seen in her life. The trees were so tall they blocked the sky and yet the sun warmed her skin as though she stood out in the middle of an open meadow. It gave the woods a peaceful warm feeling rather than being closed in and dark. Soothing melodies drifted on the breeze and mist curled around her legs.

A man called her name. She turned, trying to locate the source of the voice that made her knees tremble and her heart race. The voice drew closer and Alex wished desperately to find out who called to her. There was something familiar about the voice but she couldn't place where she had heard it before. Her heart ached as the voice moved further away.

Alex called out but her voice was lost in the fog. She ran after the man, hoping he would hear her and return.

The blaring of the alarm woke Alex from the dream. She groaned and buried her face in her pillow, wishing she could return to the magical woods and find out who the mystery man was.

Her mom was already in the kitchen drinking coffee at the table. Things still felt a little strained between them but Alex was glad the icy wall had been mostly broken down.

"What did your Uncle Mark want the other night when he called?"

Alex forced her feet to keep walking. Her mind went completely blank as she tried to think of an answer that would satisfy her mom. "He was just seeing how the driving was going. Said he would take me out on the interstate if you were too scared to do it."

"Really? That seems a weird thing to call about that late at night."

"I kinda thought so too but maybe he just figured we'd still be up." Alex was growing nervous and wanted to get the conversation off her uncle.

"I suppose it was nice of him to offer. Did he say when he'd be home?"

"He said in a few months. Speaking of driving, are we still on for this afternoon?"

"I should be done at the store by the time you're out of school so how about if I come get you?"

"Sounds good."

"Oh, I'm running late! See you this afternoon." She planted a kiss on the top of Alex's head on the way out of the kitchen.

Alex finished her breakfast and got her books packed into her bag. While she waited for Jenn to come pick her up, she searched for pictures of nurses in the past to see if she could spot the same uniform she had seen the nurse in the mirror wearing. Alex hoped she would find it so she wouldn't have to try to make the mirror change. What if the evil Traveler was alerted to what she was up to? If he didn't already know her identity, he would certainly double his efforts to find out. Not only would Alex be in danger but so would her mom.

Her search didn't prove fruitful. Alex sighed. She had no choice now. She would have to make the mirror change and try to find out more information about the woman and the time period she lived in.

If I can do that, I'll have a better idea how to stop the Traveler.

* * *

"We're already halfway through the semester and most of you have done a great job. You'll be able to pass and keep playing next year. However, some of you are in real trouble." Alex stared hard at Beau and his little group of friends. As usual, they had their phones out and were not paying her the slightest bit of attention.

She resisted the urge to throw an eraser at them. She grinned at the image of their phones falling to the floor and shattering into a million pieces.

"What are you smiling at? You think it's funny that we won't be able to play ball our senior year?"

Alex shook her head but couldn't quite wipe the smile off her face. "I think that if you really wanted to play ball, you'd buckle down and get to work." She kept her eyes glued to his face so that he wouldn't notice Mr. Edwards approaching from behind.

"We'll just blame you for not tutoring us and the coaches will let us play. This is all a waste of time." Beau smirked as he lounged back in his chair.

Mr. Edwards knocked Beau's feet off the desk and stood right in front of him. "I don't think that little story will work. You see, I've been keeping a good watch on all of you." His gesture took in the whole group. "I've spoken to your coaches. If I were you I'd focus more on studying and less time screwing around on Facebook or Twitter or whatever crap you guys are doing."

Alex stood there stunned at Mr. Edwards' outburst. She knew he was aware of this one particular group's laziness but she never thought he'd go to the coaches. Beau glared at Mr. Edwards' back as he walked back to his group of students.

"We'll just see about that." Beau stood so quickly his chair fell backwards.

He stalked out of the room, dialing his phone as he shoved the door open. Two other boys and one girl followed. The other three students stared at the door and Alex before deciding to remain behind.

As she stared at Beau's retreating back, the true nature of his personality finally hit her like a smack between the eyes. And suddenly, he wasn't as good looking as she had always thought. In fact, the sight of him repulsed her.

Alex spent the remaining hour in a daze. If someone asked what subject she helped the students with, she couldn't have said with certainty. Maybe some history, definitely some English. By the end of the hour, the ones who usually played with their phones were taking notes and comparing their note cards to those that had managed to bring their grades up in a few short months.

The bell rang and Alex headed outside to meet her mom. She didn't see the Blazer so she pulled out her phone and chatted with Jenn via text messages. She told Jenn what had happened in the latest tutoring session.

-I have a feeling the rest of the year is going to be miserable now.

-Don't sweat it, Alex. Maybe Beau and his little cronies won't even come back.

-Hope not. Anyway, mom just drove up. Gotta go!

Alex shoved her phone in her bag and trotted to the car. Her heart skipped a beat when she saw Bruce sitting in the passenger seat. She slowed to a walk, wondering what her mom was thinking inviting Bruce to come along on her practice drive.

Her mom got out of the car, followed closely by Bruce. Patricia walked around the front of the car while Bruce moved to the back seat. Just before her mom climbed into the passenger seat of the Blazer, Bruce planted a quick kiss on the back of her neck. Alex's throat closed at the look of happiness that flashed across her mom's face. She hadn't seen her mom smile like that in a long time.

She forced herself to smile as Bruce waved to her from the back seat.

"Ready to hit the highway?" Patricia asked as Alex climbed in to the driver's seat.

"Ummm...sure, I guess so." Alex tried to swallow past the dry lump that had suddenly taken up residence in her throat.

"Everything okay?"

"Just had a rough day in tutoring." She glanced in the rear view mirror and her gut tightened with a flash of guilt at how uncomfortable Bruce looked just sitting back there all by himself tugging at the pleats of his trousers.

"Are you sure that's all that's bothering you?"

Alex turned her head to look at her mom. "Well, I wasn't expecting company on our drive." She cleared her throat and began picking at the skin around her nails. "What if I do something really dumb?" She finished in a whisper.

"Oh, honey, you're a great driver. Much better than I expected, actually. Everything will be fine," Patricia said.

Alex blushed. The only reason she was any good was because her friends let her drive their cars. *If mom finds out, she'll never let me get my license.*

"Just pretend it's just the two of us." Patricia patted Alex's hand.

Alex took a deep breath and put the Blazer in drive, pulling out slowly onto 5th street. She deftly maneuvered the vehicle through traffic as she made her way to Horizon Drive, the closest place to get onto the interstate. Despite her mom's confidence in her abilities, Alex was a bundle of nerves as she accelerated onto the on-ramp. She'd been on the interstate plenty of times with Jenn but it was different with her mom.

Get a grip, Alex!

She glanced into her rearview mirror and turned her head, checking her blind spot for cars. Seeing none in her path, she merged into the right lane of I-70, heading west.

"You're lucky to live in such a small place. I grew up in Chicago and had to drive on a maze of highways that held thousands of vehicles at all times of the day. I got into my first wreck on an interstate highway," Bruce said, his voice dropping to a whisper by the end.

Alex gasped. "Was it a bad one?" She glanced at Bruce in the rear view mirror.

It felt like a hand closed over her heart at the look on his face. "I lost my best friend that day. It wasn't my fault. Some kid was out joyriding in his mom's car and over-corrected when he swerved onto the shoulder. I didn't even see him coming. Just felt the impact and heard the sound of screeching. Then I woke up in the hospital."

"Oh my God, Bruce, you never told me that. I'm so sorry." Patricia turned and put her hand on his knee.

Bruce patted her hand absently, his eyes far away. "After that I didn't drive until I was in my mid-twenties. I was terrified to get behind the wheel of a vehicle. It took many years of therapy to help me get over my fear."

Alex shook her head, blinking hard against the tears that threatened to fall. She didn't know why Bruce had shared that story with her. *Could he know I've been going out without mom?*

"Does it make you nervous to have me driving?" Alex asked timidly.

Bruce smiled. "Not at all, young lady. Your mother is right. You're really a very good driver." He cleared his throat before continuing. "But just remember the rules of the road and to always watch what other drivers are doing. Things can go wrong in a split second and at high speeds, there isn't much room for error."

They traveled the rest of the way in silence. Alex took the 24 Road exit and wound her way through the roundabouts as she headed south toward the mall.

"Where to now?" she asked.

"Go down the business loop and head for Orchard Mesa. You pick whichever route you want," Patricia said.

Alex turned on the radio to a station both she and her mom could agree on as she drove through town. She never kept her head still as she passed side streets and went through lights. Bruce's story hit a nerve. Alex didn't want to be behind the wheel and have something happen to a passenger.

"How about letting me take you lovely ladies out to dinner?"

Patricia glanced at Alex. "What do you say, Lexi?"

"Sure, I guess so."

"Head out to Palisade, Alex. I'm going to treat you guys to dinner at Inari's."

"Inari's? That's pretty fancy, isn't it?" Patricia said.

Bruce laughed. "It's not *that* fancy. You'll love the food, I promise."

Alex mumbled and kept her eyes on the road. She had promised to be nice to Bruce but she wasn't quite ready to spend an evening at some fancy restaurant with him. She fought the urge to pout and ignore the guy, hoping he would go away and leave her and her mom alone. Deep down she knew that she had to learn to trust again and allow her mom the ability to meet someone nice. But it was so difficult considering opening her heart even just a little, and even harder watching her mom fall head over heels knowing that it could end in a shattering blow that would be worse than the one her father handed out. Heartache was always worse the second time around.

"Turn left here, Alex," Bruce said.

She parallel parked between two large SUVs. It only took a couple of tries, backing in and out until she had the Blazer far enough off the road so it wouldn't get side-swiped. Bruce held the door for them. Alex gave him another point for being a gentleman. She had never seen her father open the door for her mom.

The waitress led them to table in a semi-secluded section of the restaurant that was surrounded by heads of African antelope.

"Wow, these are so cool!" Alex said.

"That one is a gemsbok, that one is a kudu, and he is an eland," the waitress said as she pointed to each of the heads in turn.

"They're enormous! I can't believe what it must be like seeing them out in the savannah in Africa," Alex said.

"I've always wanted to go on an African safari," Bruce said.

"Me, too." Alex smiled.

"You guys are both nuts. I'd rather stay here than get eaten by a cheetah or bitten by a poisonous snake," Patricia said as she picked up a menu.

"It's not like you just wander about the savannah on your own, Mom," Alex said rolling her eyes. "You'd be safe and sound inside a vehicle."

"I'd be the one in the vehicle that gets attacked by a mob of angry rhinos or something," Patricia said.

Bruce laughed. "I suppose this isn't a good time to tell you I bought tickets for a walking African safari." He winked at Alex and she giggled behind her menu.

"Oh two tickets? Good, you can take Alex along." Patricia said after sticking her tongue out at them.

By the end of the dinner, Alex wondered if her abdominal muscles would be sore the next morning. She had no idea Bruce was that funny. He knew a lot about history, which moved him up a rather large notch on her score sheet. They all shared dessert and followed Alex back out to the Blazer. Part of her wanted to let her mom drive so she could veg out in the back seat and digest the amazing meal. But she also needed the practice and she knew her mom would never sign off on the driving hours unless Alex had *actually* driven.

When she reached the business loop she realized she didn't know where to drop Bruce off.

"So where are we headed now?"

"Bruce's car is at our house, Alex, so just head on home," Patricia said.

Alex let her mom and Bruce chat and simply listened, enjoying the sound of her mother's laughter while still feeling scared of the outcome of the relationship. She didn't want to see her mother get hurt again. *And I don't want to deal with someone leaving us again either.*

"You're going a little fast there, Lexi."

"Sorry, Mom." Alex took a deep breath and focused on her driving rather than worrying about what the future might hold with Bruce in their lives. She vowed to think positively about him and the role he would now play. Alex knew it wouldn't be easy but she owed it to her mom to at least put the fear and bitchiness aside and give the guy a chance.

Chapter 22

THE MORNING of her birthday dawned cool and crisp, a typical October day. This was Alex's favorite time of year and not just because of her birthday. She loved everything about fall: the changing colors, the cool weather, Thanksgiving, and Christmas right around the corner. But as was the case for the last couple of years, a dark shadow robbed her of her enjoyment of autumn. This year it was made even darker knowing her uncle was in harm's way because of her. Whenever the phone rang, her heart would skip a beat, certain it was her aunt calling to say Mark had been killed. Or perhaps shipped off to some foreign land where he couldn't keep an eye on the evil Traveler.

As part of her morning routine, Alex checked her email and smiled when she saw one from Gavin.

> *Dearest Alex,*
>
> *Sean and I still can't find anything pertaining to this particular Traveler that you seem linked to nor why you can sense him. I wish I had better news for you. It's like trying to find information on a Yeti or Sasquatch. So much of what we read or hear is so ludicrous as to defy reality and yet here you are. A legend in time travel circles. We need to add your story to the tomes so that others in the future will know that you are indeed real and that you had a pivotal role to play in preserving time. Please be safe and let us know if your situation changes.*
>
> *All my best,*
> *Gavin*

Thanks to Jenn and her meticulous notes, she could email Gavin every detail about all of her trips through time. She forwarded the email to Jenn and added a note about sending a copy of her notebook to Gavin so he could add it to the Masters' tomes.

Her mom had left for work early so Alex ate breakfast alone: a bowl of Cheerios swimming in milk. She spotted a note from her mom on the kitchen table: *I asked Bruce to join us for your birthday dinner. Hope that's okay. See you when you get home! Love, Mom*

Alex actually found she was looking forward to the evening out with her mom and Bruce. As promised, she had opened her heart just a tiny crack and allowed herself to get to know Bruce a little better. She had been mildly surprised at how much she enjoyed his company. He asked her about the theater, came to the latest show, chatted about history, even asked her about boys.

But it was her mom's happiness that kept her going despite the reservations she still had. She seemed to glow when she was with Bruce, perfectly at ease, smiling and laughing. Alex thought she had never looked more beautiful.

At lunch that day, her friends surprised her with a small cake and gifts. They presented her with the cake in the middle of the cafeteria, which left her blushing.

"Oh, Alex, don't look now but there are so many cute boys staring right at you," Paul said in a falsetto.

Amy punched him in the arm. "You shouldn't be so mean." She glanced around the lunch room. "But he's right, Alex. Lots of eyes on you at the moment."

"She's used to it. Girl's a natural in front of a crowd," Simon teased.

"That's different," Alex said, trying to be as inconspicuous as possible as she began opening her gifts.

"What's different? Actually, when you are on stage you're in front of a lot more people than this." Simon swept his arm dramatically to indicate the students sitting in the cafeteria.

"Beau certainly can't keep his eyes off you. But he doesn't look too happy," Paul said.

Alex refused to rise to the bait. "Mr. Edwards got on his case in tutoring weeks ago and he's just pissed at me."

"Why would he be pissed at you?" Paul asked.

"Because I wouldn't let him slide in the tutoring and he's going to be benched for the rest of the semester."

"Ouch. But I'm glad you stuck to your guns."

"It's not fair. Just because he plays ball he thinks he's better than everyone else." Simon turned and glared at Beau's table.

"I know, right? All the jocks are the same. They walk around like they rule the school. Too bad they don't realize that they can't play the game forever. If the guy can't pass high school, how's he ever going to make it in college?" Paul said.

"Not all of them. Most of the ones in the tutoring session have pulled their grades up. At least they're trying," Alex said.

"I can't believe you're sticking up for them," Paul said.

"I'm not sticking up for them. Just giving credit where credit is due. The ones in my session have worked really hard to bring their grades up."

"Well, it doesn't change the fact that the huge pain-in-the-ass that is Beau Johnson isn't very happy with you," Simon said.

Alex glanced up and gulped audibly when Beau's blue eyes seared into her chest. Rather than the fluttering in her stomach coming from how hot she thought he was, this time it was from pure discomfort and wanting to avoid seeing him in tutoring ever again. To distract herself, she opened her presents. Jenn gave her a gift card to Kohl's with a note that promised a girls shopping trip. Amy bought her several history books. Paul and Simon got her movie tickets and several boxes of movie candy.

After lunch, she shared her cake with her friends and thought that she was a pretty lucky girl to have these wonderful people in her life. During moments like these, she considered coming clean about her big secret. Of all her friends, only Jenn knew the truth of her time traveling. It would be so great to share the burden with the people she was closest to. *Maybe they can help.*

Get a grip, Alex! You'll only get them killed.

She put her fork down next to her half-uneaten cake, a dark cloud moving over her good mood. It was difficult to enjoy the little things when her life was in mortal danger and knowing that the evil Traveler could hurt her uncle at any moment.

"Something bothering you?" Amy asked.

Alex gave her a half-hearted smile. "Just ate too much."

Amy frowned. "You do this all the time. Just when the group is having a good time you go all quiet and broody."

"I don't do it *all* the time," Alex mumbled as she poked her cake with a fork.

"Yeah, you pretty much do. You're not depressed or anything, are you? My cousin suffers from depression and she has to be on meds."

"I'm not depressed. Just got a lot on my mind, that's all. I mean, mom has a new boyfriend and I'm still not sure what to think about that, I'm anxious to get my license, the tutoring has been rough lately, and between work, school, and theater, I just don't feel like I have enough hours in the day."

Amy blinked slowly. "Alright, I was just asking. Guess I can see why you'd be a little stressed and quiet."

"That's exactly it. Stressed." Alex hoped she was convincing enough to end the conversation.

"I think she needs herself a guy to loosen her up."

Alex turned a withering glare on Simon who was wiggling his overly large ears at her. "I don't need a man thank you very much. I don't have time for one."

"Oh pooh, there's always room for one of those."

"This conversation is over, Simon."

The bell sounded. Alex picked up her tray, giving Simon a dirty look as she passed. She rolled her eyes and laughed when he waggled his eyebrows.

The afternoon passed quickly. After her last class, Alex ran outside to meet her mom and Bruce. She wished she knew where they were going to dinner but Bruce wanted it to be a surprise. She heard someone shouting her name. Alex looked around in confusion. An arm waved frantically at her from a sleek black sports car. As she got closer she recognized her mom, beaming from the passenger seat. Bruce exited the car and tossed his keys over the hood to Alex. She juggled them and almost dropped her phone in the process.

"Are you sure? I mean, this is a *really* nice car," Alex said, hardly daring to believe that she would be driving this awesome machine.

"I've driven with you before. I trust you."

Alex grinned as she tossed her backpack to her mom and slid into the driver's seat. She didn't think she would ever forget the feel of the real leather seats or the look of the fancy instrument panel. She shoved the key in the ignition and gunned the engine, feeling a sense of power she'd never felt while driving the Blazer.

"Take us out of space dock, Captain," Bruce said from the back seat.

Alex laughed and pulled away from the curb. She fought the urge to floor it so she could feel the vehicle lunge forward but she didn't want to overstep the privilege. She kept the car right at the speed limit.

"Head to Main, Alex. We're going to Le Rouge," Bruce said.

She nodded and headed down 7th Street. She wanted to roll the window down and blast the music but she settled for a face-splitting grin. The fact that they were headed to a fancy French restaurant could have something to do with it.

Alex parked in a large lot behind the restaurant. She sighed in disappointment when she turned the engine off. She kind of wished Le Rouge was about a hundred miles away so she could continue driving.

"This way, ladies," Bruce said.

Alex walked behind her mom and Bruce. He was wearing a pair of dark denim jeans, a white button down shirt and a suit jacket. Her mom was wearing one of the new outfits her aunt had recently stocked for Uptown Girl. The slacks and cream-colored blouse was very flattering. Alex felt out of place in her outfit.

"Ummm, am I dressed okay for this place?" Alex asked with more than a hint of trepidation in her voice.

"You look great, honey," Patricia said over her shoulder.

Alex fidgeted with her clothes as she followed Bruce and her mom to the restaurant. Bruce held the door for them making Alex feel like a real lady. The greeter checked her ledger when Bruce gave her his name and she promptly led them to a semi-secluded table near the back. Bruce held their chairs as they sat. Alex smiled and blushed as she sat down.

"Isn't this place great?" Patricia whispered.

"It's beautiful. I feel a little out of place," Alex said.

"You look fine. Working at your aunt's store definitely has its perks, doesn't it?"

"Absolutely."

The waitress arrived to take their drink order. Bruce suggested wine for himself and her mom and Alex ordered a water and iced tea. She sat and listened to her mom and Bruce chat, a warm flush filling her when she saw how happy her mom was.

Maybe this guy isn't bad news after all.

The rest of dinner passed in a blur. The menu items were unlike anything Alex had ever seen. It was nearly impossible to choose something. Bruce was able to suggest several things. Alex picked one at random and handed the waitress her menu.

"While we wait for our entrees, why don't we give Alex her gifts?" Bruce suggested.

"You didn't have to bring them here. I could have opened them at home." Alex didn't want a replay of her birthday at the school cafeteria.

"Apparently Bruce can't wait that long," Patricia said with a grin.

Bruce shrugged as he pulled a small back box out of his jacket pocket. "It's just a little something. I saw it and knew you would love it."

Alex took the sleek box with shaking hands. She never expected her mom's boyfriend to get her something for birthday.

"Open it. I'm dying to see what it is," Patricia said.

"You don't know what it is?" Alex asked.

"Bruce wouldn't tell me."

"I wanted it to be a surprise. The fewer people who know a secret, the easier it is to keep," Bruce said.

He's not wrong about that.

Alex opened the box and her breath left her chest in a whoosh. She reached out and grabbed the silvery necklace, unable to believe what her eyes were seeing. Attached to the necklace was an intricate book made of silver. It even had spidery black writing on the open pages. She had never seen anything to beautiful and perfect, like it was made just for her.

She looked at Bruce and shook her head, unable to speak. Her throat was so tight she feared she would pass out right there on the table.

"What is it, Lexi? Hold it up so I can see."

Alex placed the necklace back into the box and shoved it across the table to her mom. She bolted upright so quickly she barely missed running into a waitress. She ignored her mother calling after her and ran to the bathroom with tears spilling over her cheeks.

She locked herself in a stall and put her face in her hands, trying to get a handle of the emotions surging through her. It wasn't possible one person could be expected to deal with this many feelings at once.

Get a grip, Alex!

That sharp voice in her mind helped to calm her down a little. After taking a deep, shuddering breath, she wiped her face and exited the stall so she could wash her face before heading back to the table.

She stared at her face in the mirror for a moment to let the emotions wash over her one at a time. When she had first seen the book necklace, she had been ecstatic. No one had ever given her anything that beautiful and grown up before. And it meant that Bruce cared enough about her to get her something completely appropriate, something he knew she would love.

Her hands curled into fists. Her father had never given her anything this nice. The only gift he bought her that her mom had nothing to do with was a baseball and glove. Alex remembered opening the box and staring at the sports equipment with stunned disbelief. Her father had been so excited to go out and throw the ball with her. After missing every toss and taking a hit to her face that left her with a fat lip, the ball and glove ended up in the back of her closest. He knew she wasn't into sports but he somehow thought that the perfect gift for her was a baseball and glove.

I wish dad would have been more like Bruce.

Guilt chased away the anger, leaving her hunched over the sink trying to stop the tears. Bruce wasn't her dad and would never be her dad. She didn't *want* him to be her dad. But she wanted him to be...*something*. It was all such a jumble that Alex couldn't put a name to what she wanted.

She glanced up at the mirror and gasped. Her reflection was that of the nurse. The woman was in uniform and staring at the mirror in her time with wide blue eyes. There was a man in uniform standing behind the scared nurse but Alex couldn't see enough detail. *Move just a little to the left!* Alex motioned with her hands, hoping the woman would move in that direction.

Just then, the man stepped into view and Alex got a good look at his clothing.

That looks like a Nazi uniform!

Chapter 23

"**ALEX, WHAT IN** the world has gotten into you?"

Alex gave a yelp of surprise and turned to face her mother. She had been so intent on the man she had seen in the mirror that she hadn't even heard her mom come into the restroom.

"What are you doing in here?" Alex said the first thing that popped into her mind.

"What do you mean? You left the table in another temper tantrum. I thought you were over this, Alex."

Alex shook her head trying to focus on what her mom was saying. She had almost forgotten about leaving the table after opening Bruce's birthday gift.

"It's not what you think. I don't even know if I can explain it."

"Well, you better try, young lady, because you hurt that man's feelings and embarrassed the hell out of me." Patricia was breathing heavy and Alex could tell she was near tears.

"I was just overwhelmed by the gift. It was so beautiful and perfect and I don't have anything even nearly that nice. And all of a sudden I felt angry that dad never got me anything that nice and then I felt guilty for being angry at dad but I'd rather have Bruce's necklace than that dumb old baseball..." Alex trailed off as she burst into tears.

"Oh, Alex. I don't even know what to say."

Alex fell into her mother's arms. "Just when I think I'm over what dad did something comes along and brings it all back."

"It did the same to me for a while too, Lexi. But you know something? I can't change what your dad did and neither can you. We can either let what he did keep us from being happy again or we can move forward. I chose to move forward. I admit there are times when the anger still gets to me but it fades quickly."

"Does it make me a bad daughter that I like Bruce? That I wish dad had been more like him?"

"Of course not, Alex. Your dad wasn't very nice to either of us. But we came out alright. And there is someone nice that wants to be a part of both of our lives. I know it's hard, honey, but you can't enjoy true happiness without experiencing sorrow as well."

"I know, it's just so unfair."

"It is unfair, you're right. You deserved to have a good father and I deserved to have a loving husband. But life just didn't play out that way. We can't go back in time and change the past so all we can do is live for the future."

Alex snorted laughter before she could stop herself.

"What's so funny?"

"Nothing. Just weird emotional stuff running through my head. Let's go back to the table before Bruce thinks we ditched him."

Alex's heart sank as she followed her mom back to the table. The water works almost started flowing again when she spotted Bruce all alone at the table looking miserable. As soon as he spotted them returning he stood awkwardly and shoved his hands in his pockets. His eyes were glued to the table. Rather than take her seat right away, Alex forced her feet to walk around to Bruce's side of the table. She gave him a quick hug and backed away before it could get any more awkward.

"Well, perhaps we should sit and enjoy the rest of our evening," Patricia said as she took her seat.

"Great idea. The evening is young so we should definitely enjoy it," Bruce said a little too loudly and with just a tad too much enthusiasm.

"I'm sorry I freaked out. It's just..." Alex couldn't speak around the lump in her throat.

"We don't have to discuss it here and now," Patricia said.

"It's okay, Mom, I want to try to explain," Alex said. She took a deep breath and turned to face Bruce. "The problem wasn't with you and it wasn't with your gift. It's all the jumbled up feelings about my dad."

Bruce blinked and opened his mouth a few times, looking at her mom for some guidance.

"Just be honest. I think that if we are going to be spending time together, we need to be open with one another. Both of us have painful pasts that will rear their heads from time to time. Hiding from it or pretending the events never happened won't help," Patricia said.

Bruce nodded. "Your mom's right, as usual," he said with a smile. "I know your dad did a very hurtful thing and I am in no way trying to take his place. After my wife died, I never thought I would date again. Meeting your mom changed all that." He reached over and took her hand.

"It's really great that you and mom found each other. Really. I guess I just need to try to forgive my dad for what he did and let go of the anger," Alex said.

"Take all the time you need, Alex. There's no rule book for how long this stuff is supposed to take. We all handle pain differently. There's no need to rush things. I'm not going anywhere. I will try to be more mindful of how my actions come across," Bruce said.

"And I'll try to keep my temper in check and think about things rationally," Alex said with a small grin.

"So what do you say?" Patricia asked as she held up the black velvet box. "Want to put it on?"

Alex nodded and took the shiny silver book necklace from her mom and clasped it around her neck.

"Oh, it's so pretty, Lexi."

Alex glanced at the wrapped box still sitting on the table in front of her mom. "Can I open that one too?"

"Of course you can." Patricia handed Alex the large box wrapped in Doctor Who wrapping paper.

Alex was careful to unwrap the box with minimal tearing. She planned on saving the paper and hanging it up in her room. She gave a little squeal of delight when she saw what was inside: a new touch-screen phone, a book on the 14th century, and a gift card from Kohl's.

"It's hard to believe you're seventeen," Patricia said.

"Seems like it took forever to get here," Alex said.

"Ah, to be young again," Bruce said, smiling at her mom.

Alex hurriedly put her gifts on the floor when the waitress returned with the meal. She was sure it was delicious but it tasted bland to her. As soon as she started eating, her mind returned to the nurse and the German officer she had seen in the bathroom mirror. Her heart skipped a beat when the implications of what that might mean hit her. *The evil Traveler couldn't possibly be trying to alter the outcome of WWII.*

"Alex, are you okay? You look like you might faint," Patricia said, her voice full of concern.

"No, I'm okay. Just need to use the restroom." Alex grabbed her purse and headed back to the restroom.

As soon as she closed the stall door she grabbed her phone and sent a text to Jenn with her suspicions about the Traveler and his plans.

-Email Gavin. As soon as I get home, I'm going to visit my uncle again and warn him.

-Are you sure U want to do this without someone there?

-I'll be okay. Text U later.

Alex hurried back to the table and smiled, hoping it was convincing. She tried to focus on the conversation, urging her mom and Bruce to eat faster so she could get back home. Her shoulders felt heavy with the terrible weight of the burden she carried. For the hundredth time she wished she could tell her mom the truth.

At least I have Uncle Mark.

That thought gave her strength. Her uncle was a Marine. Surely he would be able to help her stop the evil Traveler, Lane Stygian, and his Master, Max Poder. She tapped her feet under the table as she watched her mom and Bruce slowly lift forks to their mouths.

Stop talking and just eat!

After what seemed an eternity, they finished the last bite and laid their napkins on their empty plates.

"Now for dessert!" Bruce said rubbing his hands together.

Alex groaned inwardly. She couldn't refuse dessert without raising suspicions. She had never been known to say no to something sweet after dinner and she couldn't very well say no to a birthday dessert.

After an interminable wait that made Alex fear she would die of suppressed tension, the dinner was finally at an end. She led the way this time, walking so fast her mother yelled at her several times to slow down.

She stood next to the car and waited for her mom and Bruce to arrive. She ignored the look her mom gave her and hopped into the back seat as soon as Bruce unlocked the door. As they drove, she silently urged him to drive faster. Alex wanted to scream at him that the fate of the world and the human race counted on him getting her home as quickly as possible. Instead of screaming, she sat in the back and willed the car to move faster.

When they reached the house, Alex jumped out of the car, shouted a hurried "thank you" to Bruce and ran to the house, snatching her keys out of her purse. She ran to her room, grabbed her laptop off the desk, and headed for the bathroom.

Before the computer even had a chance to boot up, her mom was banging at the locked bathroom door.

"Alex! What are you doing in there?"

"Sorry I ran into the house so quick. My tummy was feeling a little icky after the main course."

"Oh, I see," her mom said as though she didn't understand at all.

"You know how I feel about doing that sort of thing in public, Mom," Alex said, trying to get her mother to leave.

"Yeah, I guess I do. Well, I'm going to bed. There's some Pepto in my bathroom if you need it."

Alex mumbled goodnight and hoped she hadn't made her mom angry again. Seemed she did that an awful lot lately. But she couldn't worry about that now. She had a job to do. Alex opened her email and there was a message from Gavin.

What you saw through the mirror scares me, Alex. If Stygian is going back to WWII Germany, he can be trying to help Hitler win the war. I don't know why else he would be going back to that time period. But is this his Master's ultimate plan or is this just another random trip back like the others? I don't know and that scares me as well. I fear you may have to contact your uncle and have him push to get some answers. The fate of the world could be riding on this.

Alex closed the laptop with a frustrated sigh. She had hoped Gavin had something more to tell her. How was her uncle supposed to push for answers without putting himself in harm's way? Unless that's exactly what Gavin meant for him to do. His last line had read "the fate of the world could be riding on this." Maybe he thought her uncle putting his own life at risk was worth it if he could expose Stygian and Poder, prevent them from whatever it is they planned to do.

After getting ready for bed, Alex grabbed her hand mirror from a drawer in the bathroom and settled into bed. She held the mirror in one hand and focused on AJ. In moments, her reflection changed to that of the African American woman. *This gets easier every time.*

Alex took a deep breath and reached out to touch the mirror.

*   *   *

Drifter sighed as the reflection in the mirror returned to that of his own familiar face, that of the German doctor fading. He put his hands behind his head and wondered when Master would give him the word to travel back to WWII Germany.

The man is too cautious.

He had no doubts that he could beat the girl who had caused him so much grief. She was working without a Master. Drifter had even suggested to Max Poder to allow him to take care of the meddlesome girl in the present time.

Thinking about the strange turn of events that put the gifted Traveler almost within his grasp, made him cackle with glee. If the silly girl hadn't slipped and called Mark "uncle" he never would have found out who she was. Even though he didn't know Mark all that well, he knew the man only had one niece living in Grand Junction, Colorado.

Master insisted that the girl be left alone for the time being. Killing was such nasty business. And unless he killed Mark at the same time, the man could make Drifter's life troublesome. And there was no guarantee that the girl hadn't told others about her ability.

"There are too many unanswered questions regarding this girl. We'll continue as though we don't know who she is. I need time to figure out what to do to minimize the danger to my plans," Max had said at their last meeting.

If the girl dares to interfere with me again, I'll kill her despite Master's protests.

Chapter 24

ALEX OPENED HER EYES and sat up slowly. Even though traveling this way was easier to acclimate to, it still left her feeling disoriented and dizzy. She was in the bathroom, the same as last time. Alex peered from around the partially closed door and glanced around quickly, hoping she was alone.

She stepped into a long hallway. After accessing AJ's memories, she knew she only had about half an hour left until the end of her shift. Alex made her way to AJ's cubicle and sat down, hoping she could just hang out and do nothing until she was free to leave. The last thing she wanted to do was flub some big secret, military intelligence stuff. AJ would end up in the brig or tried for treason or something.

Being surrounded by three and a half walls meant that Alex could sit in privacy and avoid talking to anyone. It was strange. When she had gone back in time previously, she had been nervous at first but had ended up enjoying her sojourns, interacting with the people, seeing the sights, watching history unfold right before her eyes. Fighting for her life with the evil Traveler was something she could do without of course, but up to that point had been rather fun.

But somehow this was different. She didn't feel any urge to hang out and learn the inner functioning of a military base. Perhaps it was because she was in the present time, give or take a few minutes or hours, so there wasn't anything historical to learn. It could be knowing the evil Traveler was here, plotting with his Master to do God knows what. Whatever the reason, Alex wanted to talk with her uncle about her suspicions and go back to her own body.

As soon as her shift was over, Alex logged out of the computer and headed for her quarters. Her heart was beating about a mile a minute. The last thing she wanted to do was run into Stygian.

At least I know what he looks like.

What scared Alex more than coming face-to-face with Stygian was coming face-to-face with this Max Poder guy. She didn't know anything about him. He could be behind her right this very minute and she wouldn't know it. Alex glanced over her shoulder nervously and let out a laugh that sounded almost like a sob when she saw that there was no one behind her.

As soon as she got back to the barracks, she dialed her uncle's number, praying he was there. There was no way she could leave him a message. Her mind raced. What if he was off on a mission somewhere and not even on base? What if Max Poder had succeeded in doing something to her uncle? Or perhaps Stygian had him held captive somewhere.

Get a grip, Alex!

She gripped the phone tighter as it rang and rang. Just when she was about to hang up, a fuzzy, yet familiar voice answered.

"Who's this calling?"

"It's me. I need to see you right away," Alex said.

"I'm on my way."

Alex hung up the phone, amazed at how quickly her uncle had gone from sleepy and disoriented to wide awake and alert. She supposed it had to do with his military training. Soldiers couldn't afford to be caught unaware.

She paced the room while she waited for her uncle to arrive. When the door opened she turned, ready to spill her guts. Her heart sank when one of her barrack mates came in.

"Wanna hit the gym with me?" The petite girl began peeling her clothes off and rummaging around in her foot locker.

"Not tonight. Think I might be coming down with something." Alex coughed a little for effect.

"What? You never get sick."

"There was a guy in the cubicle next to mine that coughed all damn week. I bet that's where I got it."

Two more Marines walked into the barracks. Alex hoped they would run off to the gym along with the girl she had just been talking to.

"Hey, you guys want to hit the gym with me?" the first girl asked.

"Nah, I'm beat. Ran drills today so I already got my work out," one girl said as she sat on the edge of her bunk.

"I'm out too. Been dying to read this new book my husband sent me," the second girl said.

Alex bit her lip and tried to think of a way to get all the girls to leave before her uncle arrived. She needed to have privacy for the conversation they were about to have. Alex didn't know if it was against protocol for her uncle to come to the barracks but the last thing she wanted was to call unwanted attention to herself. That could mean problems for AJ and Alex had gotten the girl in enough trouble already.

"Suit yourselves. I'm heading to the gym before dinner. Bye!" The first girl waved as she jogged out the door.

"Mmmm...dinner. Not a bad idea. Want to join me for a bite, ladies?" the second girl asked.

"I'm game. What about you AJ?" the third girl asked.

"I'll meet you guys over there. I need to send an email to my mom first," Alex said.

She avoided the urge to shoo them out the door. Alex paced and chewed her nails while waiting for her uncle all the while hoping more girls wouldn't come back to the barracks. When a sharp knock sounded at the door she gave a little squeak and laughed nervously.

Get a grip, Alex!

Alex ran to the door and flung it open, startling her uncle.

"I need you to come with me, Lance Corporal," her uncle, Mark, said.

"I'm alone so we can talk here if you—"

"Not here. Follow me."

Alex followed her uncle, fear causing her heart to race out of control. She didn't know how he would react to being told to find out about what Max Poder and Lane Stygian planned. Alex knew it was common for soldiers to put themselves in the line of fire but this was asking him to go above and beyond the call of duty.

Mark led her to a series of buildings shrouded in the shadows of the larger ones around them. He kept his head up and his eyes straight ahead, hands behind his back. Alex tried to walk as confidently as he was but all she could manage was hunched shoulders and shuffled footsteps.

He opened the door to a small building and indicated that she should enter before him. Alex squeaked in fear when the door slammed closed behind her. There were no windows in this building and she squinted against the blankness around her.

"We don't have much time. I assume you're here with news?"

Alex turned to his voice. "I wish. Actually it's news I'm hoping to get from you. Well, Gavin and Sean are hoping."

"I've followed Stygian when duty allows but I haven't seen him try anything. And I can't follow Max without arousing his suspicions. To tell you the truth I'm waiting for Poder to send me on some fool mission to get me out of the way," Mark said.

"Gavin is worried about that too. But he thinks we're running out of time and wants you to... well, push harder for answers," Alex finished, hoping he wouldn't grow angry.

"I'm doing the best I can. I won't be any good to you if I get sent away. And if I push too hard that's exactly what Poder will do. He has the power and he knows it. And Stygian knows it." Mark punched the wall to his left so hard it made Alex jump.

She watched her uncle pace the tiny room, wishing he would turn and give her the answers she so desperately sought. For too long she had borne the burden of saving the world alone. True, she had Jenn, but she didn't have her uncle's power. Gavin and Sean were an ocean away and didn't seem to have answers.

Please help me figure this out!

Mark turned to her and sighed, shoulders slumping. "I'll try harder to figure out what they're up to. It's not going to be easy. I can't jeopardize my career. Besides, I wouldn't be much good to you if I end up in the brig. Or worse."

"Worse?"

"Do you have any idea how easy it would be for Max Poder to have me killed? It's so easy it scares me and I don't scare easily."

Alex put her hands to her face, the truth of what her uncle was doing for her hitting home. "Then you can't push further. I'll figure something out."

"I can't let you tackle this alone. You're just a kid."

Alex raised her eyebrows. "A *kid* who's managed to do pretty dang good on my own."

"Okay, okay, point taken. But you still need help. And I'll give it. I just have to figure out what to do."

Alex nodded. "I'll take all the help I can get." She tried to keep the disappointment out of her voice. She hoped he would come up with a grand scheme that would rid her of Max Poder and Lane Stygian for good. It would be nice to be a normal teenager for once.

*   *   *

Drifter smiled in the darkness as he spotted Mark and Lance Corporal Jensen exit the storage building. His eyes followed them through the camera lens as they made their way back to Jensen's barracks. Mark exited alone a short time later, unable to hear the sound of the camera as it captured his every move. Drifter walked slowly toward the barracks, a coldness seeping into his veins.

He had been watching the barracks and knew that Lance Corporal AJ Jensen was alone inside. Drifter boldly walked through the door, eyes darting to the right and left. AJ was on her bunk, sitting up slowly as though she had just awakened from a nap.

I'm too late!

Drifter wanted to catch the Traveler while she was still in this body, to give her a message.

"What am I doing here? The last thing I remember I was at work," AJ said as she looked at him with terrified eyed. "What's wrong with me?"

He tilted his head to the left and watched her silently. The girl sat mesmerized, like a deer in the headlights of an oncoming car. She must have seen something of his intent in his eyes because she slowly scooted to the side of the bed and tried to stand.

Quick as lightning, Drifter grabbed her by the throat and shoved her back down on the bed. Strong as she was, she was no match for him. He pinned her arms to the bed with his knees. His alibi would be blown if he was covered in defensive wounds.

His skin tingled as her pulse quickened under his grip. Soon, it would slow then come to a sweet stop. Her dark brown eyes pleaded for mercy, as she no longer had a voice. He lost himself in those eyes, the pistol all but forgotten in this moment of ecstasy. Her eyelids fluttered, obscuring his view of her terror. Drifter closed his eyes as her pulse lost its strength and slowed. He often wondered what people thought in these last moments of their existence. Did they wonder at the damnable unfairness of it all, curious as to what had brought them face-to-face with a killer. Or perhaps anger that they would be nothing more than worm food, that all their hopes and dreams were dashed with the clenching of a fist around a delicate throat, fear at what comes next, pondering that age old question of the existence of heaven or hell.

Drifter kept his hand in place long after her heart stopped beating. The last thing he needed was some medic bringing the girl back from the brink. He positioned her on the bed facing the wall and covered her with a blanket. To anyone coming into the room, she was merely sleeping.

He took a piece of paper from his pocket and shoved it in her open mouth. Drifter walked calmly to the door, and paused for one last look around. There was no indication that he had even been here. He smiled at his handy work and closed the door softly behind him.

Chapter 25

MARK WOKE UP instantly at a knocking at the door. It was a trait his wife, Karen, had always found incredible. She insisted it wasn't natural, being able to be alert the second your eyes opened but he shrugged it off as something he had trained himself to do over the years he'd spent as a Marine.

It wasn't just knocking. More like insistent pounding.

"Captain Mark Reynolds. Open up, Sir."

Mark walked to the door, icy fingers of dread threading their way up his spine. He couldn't say why, but he was certain that whoever was on the other side of that door wasn't here for a friendly chat.

"What's this about?"

"Open the door, Sir."

Mark opened the door and swallowed the lump that formed in this throat as the sight of the two MPs standing on his stoop. Their presence definitely didn't bode well.

"We are under orders to place you in restraints if necessary. I hope it won't be," the man said with no hint of a smile.

"Can I at least put some clothes on?"

A curt nod was all the response he got. Mark left the door open and walked quickly to his bedroom, mind whirling. *MPs mean I'm being placed under arrest.* He wasn't an expert in military law, but he knew enough to make his skin grow cold.

As he dressed he tried to think of anything he might have done to warrant being arrested. The only unusual thing about the day was the chat with his niece while she was in the body of Lance Corporal AJ Jensen.

Could this have something to do with Alex's ability to time travel?

He wracked his brain but couldn't come up with a connection. At least, none that would mean his arrest. His hands shook a little as he buttoned his shirt. He had always planned on being career military. A court martial would end those dreams.

Mark took a few deep breaths to slow his heart rate as he walked back his front door, a trick he often did while out on missions. He needed to remain calm and in control of his faculties if he was going to come out of this unscathed.

Neither MP said a word as they escorted him out of his house and into the night, their footsteps echoing as they hit the concrete. His skin tingled in fear when he saw they were escorting him to the brig.

The MPs led him to an interview room and left without speaking a word. Mark kept his hands flat on the table in front of him, back straight, face impassive. He knew he hadn't done anything wrong. The minute someone from the Criminal Investigation Division came to begin the questioning, he would demand a lawyer, and buy some time.

He didn't have long to wait before the door opened and the CID walked into the room. The man was dressed in a smart looking navy blue suit and matching tie. The man didn't look happy at being awakened in the middle of the night. The CID set some papers down on the table.

"Captain Reynolds, you have been placed under arrest for the murder of Lance Corporal Jensen. You have the right to remain silent. Any statement you say may be used against you in trail by court-martial..."

Mark's thoughts whirled and his mouth went dry while the CID read him his rights. Although he felt sadness at losing a good soldier like Lance Corporal Jensen, his main concern was for Alex. He had no doubt who was responsible for AJ's death and his niece's life was in grave danger.

"I'd like a lawyer," Mark said as the CID pushed the paperwork across the table.

The CID kept silent while Mark filled out the forms. As he checked boxes and filled in his personal information, Mark wondered what he was going to tell his wife. The charges were serious and Mark wondered what evidence there was of his guilt. It had to be pretty convincing for him to have been arrested and brought to the brig. Mark hoped his lawyer would come to visit him soon so he could ask exactly why they thought he had murdered Lance Corporal Jensen.

Maybe I should use my phone call to contact Alex.

He couldn't ask his wife how Alex was. She would be suspicious and Mark didn't want to be the one who gave away Alex's secret. Part of him wondered if he should tell Karen what was happening. With him in the brig, there wasn't anyone else to watch Alex's back. She would be in danger from Stygian and Max Poder. He had to get word to her somehow.

The CID took the forms and left the room without saying a word. While he waited, Mark tried to think of a way to contact Alex without letting anyone else know about it. He couldn't use his one phone call for anyone other than his wife. He wouldn't be allowed any other contact with the outside world unless the case was brought to trial.

What if I used Alex as my alibi?

His hands twitched in excitement. If he told his lawyer that he had been on the phone with Alex during the time of the murder, that would get him off the hook and he would know whether or not Stygian had managed to hurt Alex while killing Lance Corporal Jensen. There was no way to contact Alex to get their stories straight. There was a lot of risk involved in bringing her into it. What if Alex said that she hadn't been in contact with her uncle? What if the military asked what the conversation had been about? What if they asked to see phone records?

The more he thought about it, the more he realized that he would have to bring Alex in only as a last resort. For now, he would wait and talk with his lawyer, see what the evidence the CID had against him before he jumped the gun about using his niece as an alibi.

* * *

"If I didn't need you to complete my plans, I would kill you where you stand!"

Drifter stood with his hands behind his back. He crossed a line with the murder of Lance Corporal Jensen, knew it the moment his hands had wrapped around her slender throat, but had been unable to help himself.

"Nothing to say for yourself?" Poder stood nose-to-nose with Drifter.

"We need Reynolds out of the way. I made that happen," Drifter said.

"I could have sent the man away. It won't take long for the investigators to figure out that Reynolds didn't kill that girl. Once they look at the surveillance tape—"

"Oh, you mean the tape that doesn't exist?"

Poder backed up but didn't break eye contact. "Go on."

"The recording devices in several barracks haven't been working for weeks."

"That may be true but the cameras are manned twenty-four-seven. Plan on killing every person in front of the cameras too?"

"There was only one person on duty tonight and fortunately for us, he was sleeping during the incident." Drifter smirked.

"Your doing?"

"It was easy enough to slip a little something in a cup of coffee. Even if it can be traced back to me, it gives us the time we need to finish the mission."

"I will decide when we will complete the mission."

"I'm ready. I memorized the papers you required. There's no better time than now."

Poder moved back and sat on the edge of his desk. He watched Drifter for a moment. "If you are ready, then go. If you are successful, the murder won't matter. Who knows if Mark Reynolds will even exist?"

"Should I take care of the girl before I go back?" Drifter asked.

Poder shook his head. "No. It will be too difficult to make an excuse for you to leave at this time. With Captain Reynolds in the brig, you are needed here."

"She can make things difficult for us."

"I think I may have a plan for that. And if she shows up in the past, deal with her. It doesn't seem like it should be too difficult for a man of your talents."

Drifter clenched his jaw. He had faith in his abilities but this girl was something unlike he had ever encountered when going back in time. She had stopped his every plan thus far and there was no reason to think she wouldn't prevent his meddling in World War II Germany. His hands tightened into fists. He wanted to find the niece and wrap his hands around her throat, much like he had done to Lance Corporal Jensen.

* * *

The door opened and Mark stiffened. Max Poder stood in the doorway, in full uniform, a slight smirk on his face.

"What did poor Lance Corporal Jensen do to you? From what I hear, she must have really made you angry."

Mark willed his face to show no emotion and his hands to remain still on the table. "I'm not speaking to anyone without a lawyer present."

Poder waved his hand. "That's quite all right. I'm sure he'll be along any moment. I hoped he would wait until morning but the seriousness of the charges warrants swifter action. You've been a very bad boy."

Mark refused to rise to the bait.

Any further conversation was interrupted by Mark's lawyer coming into the interview room.

"My client is not to be questioned without me present," the man said as he walked up to the table.

"I'm his commanding officer. Just telling him to keep quiet until we can sort all this out." Poder turned to face Mark. "And don't worry about your *family*. I'll phone them personally and let them know your situation." Poder left the room.

Mark's skin crawled at the inflection on the word 'family'. He knew exactly who Poder was referring to. It took all of his will power to focus on his lawyer.

"My name is Matt Schmidt. The charges against you are serious, Captain Reynolds."

"I didn't kill the girl."

"The evidence seems to suggest otherwise."

"And what is the evidence against me if I might ask?"

"There are photos of you leaving Lance Corporal Jensen's barracks around the time of the murder and a note on a piece of paper shoved into the victim's mouth that implicates you."

Mark blinked slowly. "Photos? Who took them and what were they doing outside the barracks? Doesn't that mean they were also around at the time of the murder?"

"The man who took the photos has an alibi for directly before and after the murder. Apparently he found evidence that you meant the Lance Corporal harm and took it upon himself to follow you to find proof."

"You can't seriously believe that load of crap! Let me guess, the man who took the photos is Lane Stygian and his commanding officer is his alibi."

The lawyer's wide eyes and open mouth told Mark that he was correct.

"All this can be solved in about ten seconds. Check the security tapes for the barracks."

"Already been done. The recording devices in that particular building haven't been working for weeks."

Mark sat back and rubbed his face. He wouldn't put it past Stygian and Poder to damage the recording devices. Suddenly, he wasn't so sure about the ease of proving his innocence.

"What about the guy on watch duty?"

"Fell asleep and facing demotion because of it."

"So what else do we have? Surely they will find someone else's fingerprints on the scene. And simple handwriting analysis will prove I didn't write the note."

"That is true but that takes time. Until the evidence can be analyzed, you will be stuck in the brig for a while. I tried to get you released to your own home under guard but because of the seriousness of the charges, I was denied."

"Thanks for trying." Mark sighed in frustration. He hoped he could prove his innocence before the night was through but it looked as though he would be here awhile.

"Would you like to make a phone call now or wait until morning?"

"I'll wait. No sense waking Karen in the middle of the night."

"I'll return at 0800. And don't worry. The evidence against you is flimsy at best. If you are telling the truth, you won't be here more than a few weeks." Mr. Schmidt stood and left the room.

The same MPs who had escorted Mark to the brig entered the interview room a few minutes after the lawyer left. They led Mark to a cell and closed the door. The sound of the metal clanging together sent a shiver down Mark's spine. He was in serious trouble and the only one who could get him out of it was his lawyer.

He paced his cell, wondering how he could get a message to Alex without arousing Karen's suspicions. He grew more worried as he walked until the only thing he wanted to do was rattle the bars and demand to be released. Mark didn't know what Poder had planned for Alex but the man's tone left Mark's skin ice cold with worry.

Chapter 26

"SO DO YOU THINK your uncle will be able to get information out of Stygian and Poder?"

Alex turned to face her best friend and sighed. "I don't know. Part of me hopes he does and yet part of me doesn't want him to. He could be in real trouble if he gets caught. And yet, if he doesn't come up with any information, I'm sort of screwed." Alex flopped down on her bed.

"Hey, don't do that while I'm trying to write in the book!" Jenn said as she erased furiously. "Did you email Gavin yet?"

"No. I am dreading it, actually."

"Why?"

"I'm supposed to be some mystical time traveler or something and yet I can't figure this out. I don't want him to be disappointed in me."

"Don't be so hard on yourself, Alex. You've done better than anyone else could have. This Stygian sounds very dangerous. I mean, he's already tried to kill you, more than once. And if your uncle isn't careful, he might figure out who you are and come after you in the here-and-now."

Alex shivered. "Don't even bring that up. It's all I can think about. And it's not easy to focus on midterms when the nightmares keep me up half the night."

"Maybe you should get some pepper spray," Jenn said.

"And how do I explain that to my mom?"

"Why does she need to know? Just get it and hide it under your bed."

Alex nodded. "Might not be a bad idea. But I'm sure Uncle Mark will warn me if Stygian leaves the base."

"That's true."

"Are you almost done with your notes? We really need to get our homework done," Alex said.

"You're going to thank me for this someday." Jenn finished with a flourish and placed the time travel notebook back in her backpack.

Alex lost herself in homework for the next few hours. It was soothing to have her mind occupied by something other than time travel and her possible death at the hands of an evil Marine who just happened to be in her uncle's unit.

The sound of the front door opening signaled the end of the homework session. Jenn grabbed her backpack and Alex walked her to the door.

"Busy day today, girls?" Patricia asked.

"Yeah. The teachers really pile on the homework during midterms," Jenn said.

"What is your family doing for Christmas this year?"

"We're heading to Oregon this year. My aunt and uncle want to have Christmas in their new house."

"That sounds like fun. I'm sure Alex will be miserable without you."

Alex forced a smile to her face. "I think I can manage a few weeks on my own."

The truth was, she didn't want Jenn to leave for the holidays. If Stygian managed to find out who Alex really was, she would be forced to deal with him alone.

Jenn gave Alex a small smile as she walked down the driveway as though she could read Alex's mind and knew her best friend was scared.

Alex made her way to the kitchen and helped her mom with dinner. Alex couldn't help but notice that her mom was unusually chatty and acted nervous.

"Everything okay mom?" Alex asked after her mom laughed a little too loudly at a lame joke.

"Fine. Why do you ask?"

"You're acting weird. Is it Bruce?" Alex almost hated to ask the question.

"No, he's fine, we're fine." Her mom chopped salad a little too vigorously.

"But there's obviously something bothering you. Did I do something wrong?" Alex wracked her brain trying to think of anything she could have said or done to make her mom mad.

"Oh, Alex, it's not you. Something's happened, Lexi. Something bad."

148 SHAY WEST

The breath left her in a whoosh. She wanted to leave the kitchen so she wouldn't have to hear the news. Her instincts told her it had something to do with her uncle.

"It's your uncle, honey. He's in trouble. The Marines think he killed some girl."

Alex turned from her mom and put her hand over her mouth, hoping to hold back the vomit making its way from her stomach but it was no use. She bolted from the kitchen and into the bathroom in the hallway.

As she knelt in front of the toilet, her mind refused to deal with the news of her uncle's arrest. *It's all my fault!* Tears ran down her cheeks as she dry heaved into the toilet.

Her mother's frantic knocking broke through the haze.

"I'm okay. Just give me a minute!" Alex shouted.

"If I'd known you would be this upset, I never would have told you," her mom said.

"I'll be okay. Maybe it was something I ate."

Alex flushed the toilet and stood on shaking legs. She rinsed her mouth out and hung her head, unable to stop the sobs from tearing their way past her tight throat. Alex knew the dead girl would be Lance Corporal Jensen. Guilt made her stomach clench again but Alex fought the dry heaves with every ounce of will power she possessed.

She left the bathroom and went down the hall to her room. She frantically grabbed her laptop and opened her email account. Her fingers trembled so badly she had to backtrack and correct the spelling on almost every word she typed. She hit send, praying that Gavin would still be awake.

Alex grabbed her phone and took it to her bathroom. She dialed Jenn's number and shifted her weight from her left to her right foot as she tried to control her rapid breathing.

"Didn't get enough of me when I was there earlier?"

"Jenn, something awful's happened," Alex whispered.

Alex told Jenn about Mark being arrested for murder and her suspicions about who the dead girl was. Alex couldn't get through the conversation without the tears flowing and her throat closing, choking off the words.

"Oh, jeez, Alex, you gotta tell your mom about this. Things have gotten way out of hand. This guy could be coming after you." Jenn's voice was tight with barely suppressed panic.

"I can't tell her. I sent an email to Gavin—"

"What good will that do? He's a whole continent away!"

"Just because my uncle has been arrested doesn't mean that Stygian knows who I am. Maybe Mark pushed Stygian and Poder too hard and they wanted him out of the way," Alex said, trying to convince herself as much as Jenn.

"The only way you'll know is if the guy shows up on your doorstep."

"He would probably use a sniper rifle and shoot me from like five miles away."

"Don't joke around, Alex. You have a highly trained, dangerous individual who probably knows who you are. You are the only thing standing between him and his plan, whatever that is."

"Well, we know it involves World War II."

Jenn snorted. "That doesn't help anything."

"Look, if I see anyone strange hanging around, I'll tell my mom. Okay?"

"I guess." Jenn didn't sound convinced.

Her computer beeped, indicating an incoming email message.

"Jenn, I gotta go. I have an email and it's probably from Gavin."

"You better text me as soon as you read it. And every five minutes until this whole damn thing is over with."

Alex hung up, walked out of her bathroom, and gasped when she nearly ran into her mother who had her hand raised ready to knock on the bathroom door.

"Who are you talking to? And why were you talking to them in the bathroom?" her mom asked.

"I was talking to Jenn and I was in the bathroom because I was afraid I was going to be sick again."

Her mom nodded. "Are you going to school tomorrow?"

"That's what I was talking with Jenn about. She said she would take me home if I get sick again at school."

"Are you sure you feel up to going tomorrow?"

"It's too close to midterms. I think I'll be okay."

"He didn't do it, you know that right?"

"Of course he didn't! I'm sure the Marines will find out who the real killer is," Alex said.

"Your aunt is beside herself, naturally, but is refusing to take any time off."

"I can watch the store after school and on weekends if you think it will help."

Patricia smiled and hugged Alex. "It actually might. I'll talk to her about it tomorrow." She walked out of the room but peeked back in. "Dinner is still on the stove. Want me to bring you a plate?"

Alex shook her head. "I don't want to put anything in my stomach. I'll probably just head to bed."

"Okay. See you in the morning."

"Night, Mom."

Alex sat on her bed, wishing she had never traveled into AJ Jensen. Her decision had cost the girl her life. Not to mention that her aunt's life was now in upheaval, worrying about her husband.

Get a grip, Alex!

She grabbed her laptop and opened her email.

Dearest Alex,

I am so sorry to hear of this latest development and I fear my demand to push for answers may have been the cause of this. Your life is in grave danger. Sean and I will be leaving for the States in a few days. We will contact you as soon as we reach Grand Junction.

Take care of yourself. We will see you soon.

Alex breathed a sigh of relief, fresh tears falling down her cheeks. She wished the waterworks would stop, already. Her eyes were going to be puffy and red tomorrow if she couldn't stop crying. Alex sent Jenn a quick text and told her Gavin and Sean were coming to help. Alex could practically hear the squeal Jenn made when she texted back in all capital letters how glad she was.

Feeling a little better, Alex brushed her teeth and climbed into bed. She wished she could talk to her uncle and tell him how sorry she was that she had gotten him into this mess. Alex wondered if it would be possible to travel in time into someone that would have access to her uncle so she could get the whole story but quickly decided against it. She had already caused enough damage. The last thing she needed was to have another death weighing on her conscience.

Chapter 27

ALEX COULD HARDLY pay attention in class. She had barely slept the night before, being awakened every hour or so by vivid nightmares or sounds from outside that made her bolt upright in bed, convinced Stygian was going to come bursting into her room to kill her.

Her friends knew something was wrong but Alex didn't say anything about her uncle. She didn't want them to think he had actually killed someone and her reasons for knowing that he was innocent couldn't be explained without giving away her secret. Her friends simply chalked it up to midterm nerves and left her alone.

Only Jenn stayed by her side, afraid to leave Alex alone for a minute. Alex thought it was sweet at first, but when Jenn insisted on accompanying her to the bathroom, Alex had to try to put a stop to it.

"Stygian wouldn't be dumb enough to come after me in school. Too many people," Alex said.

"He killed someone in a Marine barracks. If he can pull that off, he can find a way to kill you in front of all these people and get away with it." Jenn's eyes widened and she grabbed Alex's hand.

"He can obviously do what you do. I mean, he can travel back in time whenever he wants so he can obviously inhabit anyone he wants," she whispered, glancing around at the people passing in the hall as though any one of them could be the evil Traveler.

"I know that. Believe me, I know. At least I can feel when he's near. If I didn't have that ability, I'd have been dead a long time ago."

Jenn visibly relaxed. "I'd forgotten about that part."

"Gavin and Sean will be here in a few days. Hopefully they can help keep an eye on things. I don't just worry about myself. I worry about mom, and Karen, and you."

"I'm sure everything will be fine. Your uncle will be out of trouble soon. Hey, what are you looking at?"

Jenn voice was a low buzz in her ears. Alex wasn't listening to a word her friend was saying. Someone was walking down the hallway, someone she'd never seen before. Her heart beat wildly, her breath quickened, and her skin pebbled in goose pimples.

The young man walking down the hall was the most beautiful thing she had ever seen. His dark brown hair was long but not so long as to make him look messy and his eyes were the color of melted chocolate. His hands were shoved in the pockets of his blue jeans and he glanced shyly to the left and right.

But that wasn't what took her breath away. It was the feeling that she knew this boy, had known him her whole life.

Their eyes met and Alex couldn't catch her breath. The boy's eyes widened and his pace quickened as he drew closer to Alex. He stopped a pace away from Alex and simply gazed at her face. His hand lifted as though he wanted to touch her but stopped just shy of making contact.

"Can we help you?"

Jenn's question broke through the moment.

"Umm, yeah. Hi. Sorry to interrupt, but I could swear I know you from somewhere," the boy said.

Alex wanted to tell this boy that she knew where the feeling had come from. She had felt it each time she had traveled back in time. One boy in each time period, someone she knew better than she knew herself. Someone who made her heart melt and her knees weak.

And she had the exact same feeling when she looked at the young man standing in front of her.

"I'm Jenn and this is Alex."

The young man glanced at Jenn and smiled. "I'm Chandon. My family just moved here."

Even his name is hot!

"Is this your first day?" Jenn asked.

"Yeah. Mom said I could wait until after Christmas break but I wanted to get started early."

"Gee, Alex, a nerd like you who actually likes school," Jenn said.

Alex shoved Jenn. "If you want me—" she blushed and stammered. "I mean, if you need anything, just ask." Alex looked away, hoping a giant hole would appear and swallow her whole.

"Don't mind her, she always like this," Jenn said as she tried to catch Chandon's eye.

Students pushed their way past the trio standing in the middle of the hallway. Alex knew the bell would ring any moment, signaling the start of afternoon classes. She wanted to ask Chandon to ditch so they could spend the rest of the day together. And by the way he smiled at her, Alex thought he felt the same way.

"We gotta run. See ya around," Jenn said as she tugged on Alex's arm.

Alex shouted good-bye over her shoulder as her best friend dragged her away.

"What was that about? I've never seen you like that with a boy," Jenn said.

"Remember me telling you about the boys I met back in time? The ones I felt like I knew? I felt the same thing with Chandon just now," Alex said.

"So maybe he's your soul mate in the current time! Oh, how romantic," Jenn sighed.

"The last thing I need right now is to be distracted by some guy."

"Maybe a distraction like this is just what you need. I mean, you haven't dated anyone since you and Drake broke up."

"I just haven't had the time. Between school, work, and fighting a time traveling maniac, I don't have time for anything else."

"You had time when you dated Drake."

"I barely said two words to Chandon. He'll probably ask out one of the cheerleaders."

"Are you kidding me? Didn't you see the way he stared at you? I was surprised he didn't have drool running down his face."

"Now that's a sexy thought," Alex said as she rolled her eyes.

"I bet he asks you out by the end of the week," Jenn said with a sideways grin.

"I could end up dead at the hands of Stygian by the end of the weak," Alex whispered miserably.

Jenn gave her hand a quick squeeze. "I'm sure everything will be fine."

Alex's phone buzzed in her back pocket. She took it out and answered without looking, assuming it was her mom.

"Hello?"

"Listen, and listen very carefully. I know all about you and your little gift. By now, you must have heard about your poor uncle. If you interfere in my plans again, I'll kill him. Do you understand?"

Alex couldn't move, couldn't speak.

"Alex, what is it?"

Jenn's voice sounded like it was coming from a thousand miles away. Alex's skin tingled and her vision narrowed.

I believe I might faint.

"I'm waiting for an answer."

Alex opened her mouth but nothing came out. She couldn't breathe.

"DO YOU UNDERSTAND?"

Alex cried out and nearly dropped the phone. "Yes, yes, I'll do whatever you want, please, don't hurt him!"

Alex heard soft laughter before the phone went dead.

"Alex, *what* is going on?" Jenn grabbed her arm.

"I need to sit..." Alex's knees gave way and she crumpled to the floor, her back against a row of lockers.

Jenn grabbed the phone from her hand. She didn't protest. "It says the number is restricted."

"It was him. He said he'll kill Uncle Mark if I try to stop him. What do I do? Jenn, he's going to *kill* my Uncle Mark!" Alex's chest tightened in terror.

"Oh, God, Alex! You have to tell Sean and Gavin right away. Come on, let's get out of here," Jenn helped Alex to her feet.

"We have classes—"

"Screw classes! This is a little more important."

"What do I do, Jenn?" Alex's voice broke and tears fell from her eyes.

"I don't know. I wish I had an answer for you."

"I can't just let this guy change the past. But I can't let him kill my uncle either, can I?" Alex swiped the tears off her cheeks. Her shoulders slumped with the weight of the decision she would have to make.

"Maybe it's time to tell your mom. This is too big now."

"Sean and Gavin are on their way. They'll know what to do."

"Do you want to wait that long? What if the evil Traveler goes back before they get here?"

"I'll have to take that risk. I made the mistake of bringing my uncle into this and look what happened. He's in jail and could be killed if I don't do that the guy wants."

"Okay. We'll wait it out and tell Sean and Gavin when they get here." Jenn's eyes filled with tears as she hugged Alex. "I hope your uncle is proven innocent soon. And soon. We can use all the help we can get."

*   *   *

Mark paced his tiny cell, waiting for his lawyer, Matt Schmidt, to arrive. He'd been stuck in this cell for days, only being allowed out for meals and an hour of exercise each day. When he was out among the other prisoners, he did his best to ignore the looks of hostility. Most of them were in for petty crimes; murder was another thing altogether.

Hurried footsteps came toward his cell.

"Stand with your back facing the door, hands behind your back," the voice outside the door ordered.

Mark complied. The door clanked open and hands slipped cuffs around his wrists. Mark hated the feel of the metal cuffs around his wrists. He had never broken a law in his whole life and his service in the Marines had been exemplary. The cuffs chaffed, and not just his skin. He hated the thought of anyone believing he was actually capable of strangling a woman. The silver metal on his wrists marked him as guilty and he hated that he had to wear them.

The MP led him to an interview room, let him inside, and closed the door. Mark took a seat, trying to get comfortable with his arms behind his back.

Matt arrived shortly, dressed in the same suit as previous visits. The man looked confident as he placed his briefcase on the table in front of Mark.

"The good news is, the analysts have moved this case to the top of their list. The bad news is, it's still going to take a few weeks for them to get through all the evidence. But if you are innocent, the analysts should be able to prove it soon," Matt said.

Mark sighed. He had hoped the analysts had already proven he didn't write the note that had been stuffed into Lance Corporal Jensen's throat or found evidence that someone else had been in the room with her at the time of her death.

"I understand. At least it's a few weeks rather than a few months," Mark said.

"Just hang tight. We have your handwriting sample, your prints, DNA sample, everything we need to prove your innocence."

"Thanks. Anything else you need to tell me?"

Matt shook his head. "Right now we're just waiting. Wish I could give you more information than that."

Mark nodded. "I can handle a few weeks in here. Especially since I know I didn't do it."

Matt closed his briefcase, started to stand, but sat back down. "I have to ask. What exactly were you doing at the barracks that night?"

Mark knew this question was going to come up sooner or later but he still wasn't prepared to answer. "Just visiting with a fellow officer."

"That's it? Just visiting? At night? Alone? Is there any truth to the accusation of an affair?" Matt held up his hands when Mark leaned forward in anger. "I have to ask. If this comes to trial, you will be forced to answer these types of questions on the stand."

"I have never cheated on Karen. Like I said, just visiting with a fellow officer."

Matt shook his head. "Have it your way. I'll let you know when the evidence has been analyzed." He put his papers back in his briefcase and left the interview room.

The MPs arrived to take Mark back to his cell. He had put on a brave face while speaking to his lawyer but now that he was alone, fear reared its ugly head. He dropped to the floor and started doing push-ups. As he lost himself in the rhythm of his muscles, his fear turned to anger. Max Poder and Lane Stygian had turned his life upside down, killed an innocent woman, and put his niece's life in danger. Mark meant to see them pay for what they had done.

* * *

"I'm going to travel tonight."

Max Poder glanced at Drifter. "You know how important this mission is. Everything you've done up to this point has been to prepare you for this. You cannot fail."

"I know what's at stake. The girl will not stop me this time. We could be guaranteed of that if you would let me leave the base and kill her."

"I have made my decision. It would look suspicious to let you leave now. Besides, I don't think she'll be a problem." Poder said with a smirk.

"What do you mean?"

"I made a phone call. Told the girl I'd kill her uncle if she meddled in my plans."

"Do you think she'll keep out of it?"

"I think I scared her enough. If not, you'll have to make sure to kill her yourself."

Drifter walked slowly to the shelf holding Master's most prized photos. He moved the front photos out of the way and glanced at the ones in the back, noting the German uniforms, the hard lines of their faces, the fierce eyes. A family one could be proud of.

"Rumor has it that Reynold's case has been moved to the front of the queue," Drifter said.

"I know."

Drifter waited for more. "Doesn't that worry you?"

"Of course it worries me!" Max Poder snapped. "We wouldn't be in this mess if you hadn't lost control of your urges."

"I won't fail in my duty. In a short time, Mark Reynolds and his whole family will cease to exist."

Chapter 28

"JENN, THEY'RE HERE!" Alex jumped up from the lunch table.

"Wait, who's here?" Simon asked.

Alex glanced at Jenn, cursing herself for forgetting where she was in the excitement of receiving the text message that Gavin and Sean had arrived in Grand Junction.

"Umm, just my cousin and uncle, visiting from out of town."

"Why does she know and the rest of us don't?" Amy asked.

"She was at the house when mom said they were coming," Alex said, hoping that would ease the hurt in her friend's voice.

"Oh. So are you off to meet them or something?"

"I'm just taking Alex home," Jenn said.

Alex gave her friend a grateful look. "Mom is stuck at the store all day so I'm kinda stuck with them till she gets home."

"Oh. Just seems like you two have been thick as thieves lately. Like you have a secret or something," Amy said.

Paul piped up. "Don't think we haven't noticed you two whispering. Not to mention Jenn's scribbling constantly in that purple notebook of hers."

"So what gives, guys?" Simon asked.

"Nothing, seriously. You guys have been watching too many shows about conspiracy theories or something," Alex said as she slung her backpack over her shoulder.

She grabbed Jenn and led her out of the lunch room.

"Alex, they know something's up. Why don't you just tell them?"

"I can't, Jenn. They'd never believe me and if they knew my secret, they would be in danger. I feel bad enough that *you* know about it."

"Do you think they know what I've been writing about in the notebook? I thought I was being careful but guess we aren't as sneaky as we thought."

"I don't think they've seen inside it. I just wish this whole thing was over," Alex said.

"I wish there was more I could do to help."

"Just you knowing the truth is enough. I couldn't have come this far without you."

Alex stopped and turned at a gasp from behind them. Her heart skipped a beat when she spotted Chandon standing there. *How much did he hear?* Jenn hurriedly shoved the time travel notebook into her backpack trying her best not to look guilty.

"I'm sorry. I didn't mean to eavesdrop," Chandon said.

"How much did you hear?" Alex tasted bile in the back of her throat.

"Not much. Just that you have some sort of secret. And that it has something to do with that notebook you put in your bag."

"It's nothing, really," Alex said.

"You're in trouble, I can tell," Chandon said.

"It's nothing I can't handle."

"Nothing *we* can't handle," Jenn said.

"Look, if you're in trouble—"

Alex held up her hand as she backed toward the door. "Everything's okay. Please, just stay out of it."

Chandon took a couple of steps toward her, eyes pleading. "You can trust me."

Alex merely shook her head and shoved Jenn out the door.

"What are we going to do?" Jenn whispered fiercely.

"The new guy in school is the least of my worries right now," Alex said as she glanced back, making sure Chandon wasn't following them.

The girls made their way to Jenn's car. As they drove to the hotel where Sean and Gavin were staying, Alex wished she had more news about her uncle. The last she heard he was still in the brig and the investigators on the base were analyzing the evidence. Alex knew who had really done the killing. She couldn't believe Max Poder was powerful enough to pull off framing a man for murder. The evidence would prove her uncle's innocence and he would be out, hopefully within a few weeks.

"Does it seem weird to you that someone in the military would even dare to murder a person and then try to frame someone else? Seems like it would be impossible to pull off," Alex said.

"If Poder is a super high ranking official, then he may have ways. Still, you're right about it seeming impossible," Jenn said.

"He had enough power to frame someone for murder and get away with it. I must be crazy thinking I can stand up against this guy. Maybe I should just let him do whatever he wants and hope another Traveler takes care of things," Alex said.

"Maybe Gavin will have some ideas," Jenn said as she pulled into the parking lot of the hotel.

Alex practically ran into the hotel, eager to see the faces of two people who had the power and knowledge to help her in her fight against Lane Stygian and his Master, Max Poder.

But she had to be careful. People would begin asking questions if they saw her hanging out with two strange men with Scottish accents. She wished there was some way to come up with an excuse that her mom would believe so she didn't have to hide. Plenty of people knew her from working at her aunt's store. If someone saw her with Gavin and Sean and told her mom...Alex shook her head. She would have to cross that bridge when she came to it. There was more at stake here than the possibility of getting grounded.

Gavin and Sean were sitting at a table in the foyer of the hotel. They both jumped up when they saw Alex. Gavin grabbed her in a grandfatherly hug that made Alex feel as though everything was going to be okay. Sean simply shook her hand.

Alex filled the men in on the call she received from Max Poder.

Gavin put his hands over his face. "This certainly changes things."

"Is there any way to stop myself from going?" Alex asked.

Gavin shook his head. "Sean has tried, believe me. Once Stygian goes back in time, you will be compelled to go to the nearest mirror or reflective surface."

"What if I was somewhere where there wasn't a reflective surface? Like Antarctica or the Sahara Desert or something?" Alex asked desperately.

Sean sighed. "I have tried it all. When I first learned I was a Traveler, I locked myself in a room with no mirrors and no windows. Gavin was so angry." He looked at his Master sheepishly. "Anyway, when the urge came, I simply left the room and went into one with a window and ended up traveling anyway."

Alex nodded miserably. She had felt fear during her other trips back in time but this one was different. Poder had her in a corner. Her stomach knotted and bile rose in her throat.

"If I can't stop myself from Traveling, then what do I do? Poder will know if I stop Stygian and then he'll kill my uncle. I can't let that happen."

Gavin took her hand. "There's more at stake here than one man's life, Alex."

Alex jerked her hand away. "How can you say that? Haven't I done enough? Isn't it time for someone else to take over and save the damn world?"

Alex barely noticed her voice was getting louder. Jenn's kick under the table brought her back to her senses.

"Why can't Sean go in my place? Stygian won't be expecting a guy." She looked at the pair of men hopefully.

"It doesn't work that way. It's only blind luck that the pair of you were in Egypt at the same time. Sean has his own destiny and his own time periods to visit," Gavin said.

"It's not fair," Alex said miserably.

"You've had a terrible burden placed on your shoulders. But if you fail in your duty, the whole world could suffer. Your uncle is a soldier and understands about putting the needs of the greater good above your own."

Alex sighed. "Looks like I don't have choice, do I? No matter what I chose to do, I don't think I'll come back from this one," she whispered as tears fell down her cheeks.

"Don't say that! You've beaten that bastard every time. You'll do it again," Jenn said as she rubbed Alex's back.

"Jennifer is right. There's no reason to think he will beat you this time," Gavin said.

"All he has to do is come here and kill me. He doesn't have to lure me back in time. Besides, that doesn't change the fact that my uncle will die if I stop Stygian," Alex said.

"There is still a chance Stygian will come here for you. Especially if he fails in his task to change the past in Germany," Gavin said.

"That's not very reassuring."

"I'm sorry but at this point, reassuring won't keep you alive. Sean and I are here until this thing is settled. You can count on that."

"Thanks. I'm glad you guys are here. I just wish I knew when Stygian was planning on traveling. Waiting for him to make the first move is driving me crazy."

"I have a feeling it will be soon. Maybe even tonight. Is there any way Jennifer can stay with you for the next couple days?"

"Not until the weekend and that's two days away."

"What about you staying home from school then? It would be best to have you travel in a controlled environment like your home rather than in a public place where someone may see you."

"I think I can manage to play sick for a couple days."

"Excellent. It's the best we can do. If you succeed in stopping Stygian, we will figure out what to do at that point. It might mean getting you and your mom out of the country for awhile."

"Leave the country? Mom would never go for it."

"We will have to convince her. Stygian won't stop until you are dead and to do that he will kill anyone in his way. He's already killed many Travelers and their Masters. The world can't lose someone of your special talents."

"I need to try to get a message to my uncle," Alex said.

"That may be difficult. He won't be allowed outside phone calls until he has been cleared of the charges."

"Great. So he's in danger and there's no way to tell him," Alex said as she flopped back in her chair.

"Why can't she travel into someone on her uncle's base?" Jenn asked.

"Unless a woman could gain access to your uncle in his cell, it wouldn't do any good. And might put another person in danger," Gavin said.

"Yeah, I already got someone killed. And probably my uncle," Alex said.

"Sorry, Alex, guess I didn't think —"

"It's okay, Jenn. Just don't want to have to make a decision that will mean my uncle dies, even if it *is* to save the world."

"I wish things were different," Gavin said.

"We should get going, Alex. I have to babysit this afternoon," Jenn said after checking her watch.

"Keep us in the loop. Have Jennifer stay with you this weekend," Gavin said.

"I will watch out for her. I won't let her near any mirrors or windows without me being right by her side," Jenn said.

Gavin smiled and squeezed her shoulder. "Alex is lucky to have a friend like you. Keep her safe."

The girls left the hotel. Each step they took away from Sean and Gavin, the more afraid Alex became. She wished she was eighteen and lived on her own. She could have Sean and Gavin stay at her apartment, she wouldn't have to worry about school, and she wouldn't have to worry about her mom finding out that she had been meeting with two strange men.

"I'll talk to my mom about staying at your house this weekend. Say we have some project due or rehearsing or something," Jenn said.

"I'll ask mom tonight too. I hope I don't travel until you're there. I am going to be scared out of my mind when I get near a mirror until then," Alex said.

"Try not to think about. School will keep you busy until then."

Alex said goodbye and waved to Jenn as she pulled out of the driveway. Her mom wasn't home from the store yet, so Alex went to her room and got started on her homework. It was difficult to focus. The house was too quiet and her imagination was just too active for her to concentrate. Her bladder twinged and Alex bit her lip. The doorway into the bathroom took on a sinister air. *What if the reflection in the mirror changes?* Alex knew there would be no way to stop if Stygian decided to travel back in time. But she wanted to avoid mirrors all the same.

When her bladder couldn't be ignored, Alex forced herself to enter her bathroom. She kept her eyes glued to the floor and didn't turn on the light. When she was done she raced from the bathroom and jumped on her bed, breaking out into hysterical giggles.

Get a grip, Alex!

She needed to think clearly. Her mom would be home any minute and she needed to work on her acting skills. If she was going to play sick for the next few days, she would have to be convincing. Alex thought her mom would believe her. She rarely missed school so there wouldn't be any reason for her mom to doubt her story.

When she heard the key in the door, she snuggled under the covers, covered her laptop, and turned away from the door. She could hear her mom walk down the hallway and into her own room.

"Alex! Are you home?"

She stayed quiet, feigning sleep. She ignored the soft knocking at her door. After a few minutes she heard the knob open. The light from the hallway spilled across her carpet. Soft footsteps came closer to her bed.

"Alex? Are you okay, honey?"

Alex groaned and rolled over. "Hey, Mom. Just don't feel good."

Her mom put a hand to her head. "You don't feel hot. Is it your stomach or more like a cold?"

"My stomach. I felt tired all day. I threw up a couple of times when I got home. Maybe it was just something I ate at the cafeteria."

"There's something going around. Several customers have kids out sick. Maybe you should stay home tomorrow. No sense in spreading your germs around. Do feel up to some soup?"

Alex was starving but she had to keep up the act. "Not right now. Maybe later?"

"Okay. I'll check on you in a bit."

As soon as the door closed, Alex grabbed her laptop from under the blankets. She sent an email to Gavin telling him she would be home tomorrow. Jenn was on Facebook so she filled her in. When Jenn sent a message asking if it was okay that she spend the night, Alex told her that it would have to wait another day. Her mom would say no if Alex asked now.

--I'll ask after I'm "better"

--My mom said it was fine. Want me to come by tomorrow?

--I'll be okay. If you get caught, we're both in trouble

--I just hate leaving you alone

--If I'm gonna travel, I'd rather be here than at school

--I hear ya

The girls chatted for a few more minutes. Alex didn't want to spend too much time on the computer. If her mom came in and caught her, Alex wouldn't be able to play the sick card.

As Alex lay in bed, watching the moonlight creating shapes on her carpet, she tried to form a plan of action, something to make her feel as though she was in control of her life. She hadn't been in control of much of anything since her father left, and that had been just prior to her freshman year. Being forced to travel through time at the whim of a mad man was almost too much to bear. Her stomach clenched and Alex laughed at the irony that her fear and anxiety were causing her to be truly sick.

To calm her nerves, Alex thought about Chandon and the look in his eyes as she left him standing in the hallway. As tempting as it was to spill her guts about her secret, she knew she couldn't tell him about traveling back in time. He would probably never believe her in the first place but even if he did, Alex didn't want to put him in danger. She felt bad enough knowing that Jenn's life and those of her mother and even her aunt were in danger from Stygian and Poder. Not to mention that her uncle would die if she managed to stop Stygian at his game.

I just want all this to be over.

Chapter 29

ALEX SNUGGLED under the blankets, putting on her best sick face in case her mom came in to check on her before she left for work. When she heard the garage door open, she jumped out of bed, trotted down the hall to the living room, and peeked through the decorative glass window next to the door. She just barely caught the back end of the Blazer as it sped down the street.

After a quick breakfast, Alex sent a text to Jenn to let her know that all was well and that she hadn't traveled back to World War II Germany yet.

--Chandon asked about you

--What did you tell him?

--That you were sick. Don't think he believed me

--Leave the notebook in your backpack. Can't have him seeing it

--Until you go back in time again, I have nothing to write about anyway

Alex promised to stay away from mirrors, even though she knew it wouldn't do any good. If Stygian decided to go back in time, she would soon follow. But she didn't want Jenn to worry.

None of her friends were on Facebook so she wasted some time on various other websites. Driven by boredom, she went out to the living room to watch television. Alex flipped through channels, finally stopping on a show about puppies and kittens.

She jumped when her phone vibrated on the end table. It was from Jenn. Alex sent her a message back, assuring her that all was still well. While she had her phone out, Alex sent a quick email to Gavin to let him know that she hadn't traveled as of yet.

Alex tried to focus on the program on TV but couldn't sit still. She tingled with nervous energy. She also thought part of her problem was boredom. Unlike many students her age, she actually enjoyed school. She couldn't imagine staying at home all day long watching TV.

Even though she wasn't really hungry, Alex thought making lunch would kill some time. It was too cold to eat outside so she took her plate back into the living room to watch more TV. The hands on the clock crawled along as she flicked through more channels. Nothing held her interest. She supposed it was because most things seemed pretty boring in comparison to what she was dealing with in real life.

She grabbed her laptop from her room and came back into the living room, propping the computer on her lap with her feet up on the coffee table. She hoped someone remotely interesting would be on Facebook. Alex needed distraction.

Her breath caught in her throat when she saw a friend request awaiting her response.

Chandon Rose.

When they had met the first time, Chandon didn't give his last name. Alex thought it was dreamy, sounding like something from a romance novel. She hesitated with her finger hovering over the accept button. The last time they had spoken, he had overheard her and Jen talking and had nearly learned about her secret. He knew Alex was in danger but didn't know any details. Alex didn't want him to question her about it and yet she wanted a deeper look into his life.

With a deep breath, she accepted the request and prepared herself for the barrage of questions she was sure would come. Alex went to his profile to see if she could learn more about the mysterious new boy at Grand Junction High.

He had just moved to town from Oregon, he liked much of the same music she did, was a fan of tough guy movies, didn't seem to like any books as far as she could see, came from a rather large family, and didn't appear to be very happy to be moved his senior year of high school.

A chat window opened from Chandon.

--Noticed you weren't here today

Alex put her hands over her mouth to cover her giggles. She knew she should be worried that he was keeping tabs on her but all she could feel was thrilled and flattered that he noticed she wasn't at school.

--Not feeling so hot

--Is that really it? Or are you avoiding me?

--Why would I avoid you?

--Because I was butting in where I didn't belong

Alex closed her eyes against a wash of emotions flooding through her. She had hurt his feelings. But it had been for his own good. She fought the urge to tell him everything. Alex didn't know where the strong yearning to tell this strange boy about the danger she faced came from. She knew he would put his arms around her and promise to protect her. And more than anything, she needed that.

--I really am sick. Ask Jenn

--I did.

Alex didn't know what else to type into the chat box. He seemed so short and angry, although it was nearly impossible to tell from words on a screen what someone was feeling.

A chat box from Jenn popped up and Alex spent the next few minutes chatting with her about Chandon. Jenn thought it was quite adorable that the new boy in school was taken with Alex after seeing her only once.

--I bet he asks you out

Alex bit her bottom lip. –That would be so awesome

--You could always ask him ya know

--Not even

--I gotta run. Class starting in a few

Alex wished she was in school rather than being stuck at home. She sighed in disappointment when she noticed that Chandon hadn't typed anything else in the chat box. She sent a quick email to Gavin to let him know that she was still okay.

She heard the familiar popping sound that occurred when someone had sent her a chat message on Facebook. With shaking hands, she opened the tab with her Facebook profile and nearly squealed when she saw that Chandon had sent her a new message.

--Are you still there?

--Yeah, just chatting with Jenn

--So would you want to go out sometime?

Alex couldn't believe her eyes. She stared at the chat box for a moment to gather her thoughts. She wanted to go out with him so badly and yet what if she was out on a date and Stygian decided at that moment to go back in time? He could find out her secret and he'd probably never want to see her again.

Maybe I should wait until I beat Stygian.

If she turned him down, he might not ask her again. Her heart raced and tears built up behind her eyes as her anxiety rose. He was important to her, had been with her in the past no matter which time period she had visited. Alex knew in the depths of her soul that they were meant to be together. What right did she have to keep this secret from him?

Get a grip, Alex!

If she stopped everything in her life because of this gift of time travel, it would mean that Stygian and Poder won, even if she managed to foil their plans. Unless both men were killed, she would live in fear for the rest of her life. Even if they weren't killed, she would still live in fear. What if someone else came along who wanted to use time travel for nefarious purposes? She might never be able to live a normal life.

Unless she made a stand and refused to hide.

Alex typed her response into the chat box. --I'd love to

--You took so long getting back to me, I thought you were going to say no

--No, just checking my email

--Would you like to do something tomorrow night?

Alex had to keep up the sick routine. –I doubt I'll feel better by tomorrow. But maybe Saturday?

--We can do dinner and a movie. Or just dinner. Or just a movie

Alex laughed at his quick responses. It made her feel better that he was obviously nervous.

--I'll have to ask my mom but I'm pretty sure she'll let me

The two chatted about what they would like to see and settled on an action movie that started at eight o'clock, giving them plenty of time for dinner. She typed her address and promised to ask her mom as soon as she got home from work.

Alex knew that if she were going to go on a date, she would have to go to school tomorrow. Her mother would never let her go out with Chandon if she thought Alex was sick. It made Alex feel empowered, not allowing the bad guys to run her life. And yet she was nervous about going against Gavin's wishes.

I can take care of myself.

She knew she had survived thus far and even though she was scared of Stygian, she thought she could handle him if he traveled back in time. The ability to sense when he was near would help her stay one step ahead.

Guilt gnawed at her belly. Here she was planning a date when her uncle could be dead soon. *It's just not fair.* She got back on Facebook and chatted with Jenn, asking what she should do.

--If it was me, I'd go

--Really? You don't think it's horrid of me to go out on a date when my uncle's life is in danger?

--Your uncle is a bad ass, Alex. He can handle those guys. And if he's in jail, then it's not like just anyone can sneak up on him

Alex began to feel a little better. Her uncle *was* a bad ass. --I guess you're right

--Of course I am. Now I gotta go. Dinner's almost ready. Back on later

Alex couldn't help but laugh. When her mom walked through the door, Alex accosted her before she had time to set her purse on the end table.

"Alex, slow down and let me at least get out of my coat," Patricia said.

"There's a new boy at school and he asked me out to a movie Saturday night. I'm feeling better and was planning on going to school tomorrow." Alex bounced on the balls of her feet and smiled as big as she could just to prove how much better she was feeling.

"Were you feeling good before or after this boy asked you out?" Patricia asked with a raised eyebrow.

Alex rolled her eyes. "Before. I ate lunch and everything stayed down. He didn't ask me out until just before you got home. So can I go? Can I? Please?"

"Only if he comes to get you and I can meet him. You know the rules."

"Of course, that's fine. Thanks, Mom!" Alex hugged her mom and bolted back down the hallway to her room.

She sent a message to Chandon and waited for him to reply. While she waited, she sent a quick email to Gavin, hoping that he wouldn't answer it until after she had already gone to bed. The last thing she wanted was to get into an argument about her leaving the house. Alex had nearly died of boredom staying home for one day. She couldn't imagine being stuck at home until Stygian decided to travel. Gavin was sure it would be soon but what if it was a week away? Alex couldn't play sick for that long.

Alex and Chandon chatted, settling on a time for him to come pick her up the following evening. With a racing heart, Alex sent a message to Jenn, barely able to contain the euphoric giggling threatening to erupt. The girls chatted about the possibility of having a double date sometime, Jenn demanding Alex to tell her every detail of the date, what Alex should wear, and how she should style her hair.

For the first time in a long time, Alex felt like a normal teenage girl. She hoped Stygian would hold off his traveling long enough for her to enjoy it.

Chapter 30

ALEX NEARLY SCREAMED in frustration as she stood in front of her mirror. She peeled off her shirt and threw it on the bed atop dozens of other shirts and jeans. Tears filled her eyes and threatened to spill down her cheeks.

Get a grip, Alex!

Chandon would be there in half an hour and she had yet to find an outfit that she even remotely wanted to wear. She wished she had a thousand dollars to blow on new clothes. *I can't impress him with these old things.* Alex shoved a mass of clothes off the bed and onto the floor. She only felt a little guilty at acting like a child. This was a first date, after all, and she couldn't be expected to wear just any old clothes on a first date.

She glanced at her alarm clock and moaned in frustration. She was wasting so much time trying to find an outfit that she would barely have time to put her make-up on before Chandon arrived. Alex hurriedly grabbed a pair of dark denim jeans and a long-sleeved sweater. It was too cold to wear anything else. She thought other girls were silly when they ran around in the freezing cold weather in clothing that was meant for warmer temperatures, and shivered, turned blue, and complained about being cold.

Alex grabbed a pair of knee-high boots and sat on the edge of the bed to pull them on. She avoided looking at herself in the mirror so that she wouldn't be tempted to change clothes for the hundredth time. She hurried to the bathroom to put on her make-up.

As she was putting mascara on her last eye, the reflection in the mirror changed to the nurse from World War II Germany.

"No! Not now, not now!" Alex made a futile attempt to back away from the bathroom counter but her legs wouldn't budge.

She strained against the urge to touch the mirror with a strength she didn't know she possessed. Cords stood out on her neck and she tried to force her leaden legs to move.

Tears fell from her eyes as her hand moved of its own accord to reach up and touch the mirror. The familiar pain shot up her arm as her finger touched the mirror which was now the consistency of thick pudding.

Alex's mouth opened in a silent scream as her essence left her body.

Chapter 31

ALEX AWOKE on the floor. She groaned. Every part of her body hurt. She opened her eyes and noticed a chair lying on its side.

Guess that's why I'm so sore.

She stood slowly, holding on to the edge of the vanity to steady herself. She grabbed the chair and righted it, sitting down to gather her thoughts. It didn't take long to figure out the woman's name and a few other useful things about her. Her name was Agnes and she was a nurse who worked in Hitler's army. She had just come off a double shift but was expected to return to the tents in a few short hours.

Alex studied the woman's face in the mirror. She had pale skin, blonde hair, and the biggest blue eyes Alex had ever seen. The woman's eyes were shrouded in shadows that spoke of the long hours she was forced to work treating injured soldiers.

Whatever Stygian plans to do, it obviously has something to do with Hitler.

She wondered if Stygian was going to try to help Hitler win the war. It seemed like an impossible task to her. There were many allied armies that fought against the German armies. Alex didn't know how Stygian was going to turn the tide. But she vowed to stop him. A world where Hitler and his armies won the war was something Alex didn't want to see.

Would I even exist?

As she got dressed, Alex pondered that question. If Stygian had managed to alter the past in any of the times he had visited, would the world Alex knew still be there? Would *she* still be here? The thought made her sick to her stomach. Alex couldn't help but wonder if it would hurt to just wink out of existence.

She pushed those morbid thoughts to the back of her mind. They wouldn't help her stop Stygian from whatever it was he was planning. Alex was sure it must be big if he and Poder had to get her uncle out of the way first. She hoped Mark wasn't still stuck in the brig. Mostly because she hated the thought of her uncle behind bars. But there was also the possibility that if he was free, he would find a way to stop Stygian, maybe wake him up before he could finish his mission. It had been so nice to have an adult on her side, someone who knew her secret and *believed* her.

She finished tying the strings to her white pinafore over her light blue dress. It took a little longer to get the hair pins just right to hold her hat in place. Alex smoothed her skirt, grabbed the lunch pail that Agnes had already prepared from the small wooden table in the even tinier kitchen, and headed out of the small apartment.

Using the other girl's memories, Alex made her way to the hospital. The German armies had taken some casualties and Agnes had barely had enough time to catch a few hours of sleep and a quick bite before having to return. The thought of dealing with sick and injured people made Alex want to throw up. She took a deep breath and opened the door to the hospital

The smell hit her first. It was a mixture of antiseptic, blood, unwashed bodies, and something underneath all that that smelled foul, disgusting, sickly. Like death. Alex nearly gagged.

But the sounds were worse than the smells. Moaning, crying, wailing, men screaming for their mothers, snipping of scissors, shouting of doctors and nurses, wet, squelchy noises as wounds were sutured, the buzzing of saws as limbs were cut off. Alex wanted to cover her ears and walk right back out of the hospital.

"Nurse! I need you."

Alex turned at a shout from a nearby table. A doctor stood hovering over a soldier with a gaping chest wound. The Agnes part of Alex's brain knew it was hopeless, that the man would never survive. And yet the doctor was doing everything in his power to save the man.

Relying on Agnes' knowledge, Alex moved by reflex. She ran to the table, grabbed a packet of gauze bandages, and applied pressure to his chest wound. It soaked through in a matter of minutes.

"Start an infusion while I try to find the artery to clamp it!"

Alex ran to a nearby refrigerator and grabbed a bag of plasma, tubing, and a needle to start an IV. It was so surreal watching herself expertly shove the needle into the man's vein, although it took a minute to find one since the man had lost so much blood.

She turned to the doctor, who had his hands shoved into the soldier's abdomen. The dying man screamed hoarsely, his upper body coming off the table. Alex was surprised he had the strength to yell.

"Shall I give him some morphine?" The guttural German accent coming from Agnes' throat almost made Alex laugh.

"Not yet. He's already had a dose. Another with this much blood loss could kill him."

He's going to die anyway.

Alex hoped the voice in her head was wrong. She absently checked the IV to make sure fluid was flowing and watched helplessly while the doctor futilely tried to stop the bleeding. The soldier's movements slowed, and then stopped as the bleeding slowed. Not because of the heroic efforts of the doctor, but because his heart was stopping.

"You can stop the IV now, nurse," the doctor said as he stared down at the dead soldier.

Alex worked quickly. The plasma was a precious resource that couldn't be wasted. The doctor peeled off his bloody gloves and threw them violently into a trashcan.

"Take a good look, nurse. We can expect more of that as the war continues," the doctor said as he gestured to the dead soldier.

"Der Fuehrer will win this war very soon." Alex said the words she knew Agnes would say.

"Maybe. As long as the United States doesn't get involved."

"If they are stupid enough to join the fighting, they will fall to our armies." Alex gritted her teeth as she spoke the words. She knew how things really turned out and it took all of her will power not to tell the doctor that Hitler would lose the war.

The doctor did not respond. He walked away slowly, peeling off his bloody gown as he made his way to the back to his office.

Alex knew Agnes had many other patients to visit during her rounds. The hospital was full, but not with soldiers. The war was in its infancy so most of the patients were normal every day citizens dealing with a variety of ailments. Alex spent the next several hours changing bed pans, sheets, soiled clothing, giving baths, dispensing medications, giving what comfort she could.

Her lunch break was short and spent alone. According to Agnes' memories, she always ate alone. And lived alone and pretty much spent all of her time alone. There had been a man once. Long ago. He promised her the world, swore his undying love for her. Agnes fell hard and fast, certain she had finally found "the one", that elusive other half she had always heard the other girls speak of. They were wed after a short engagement.

Several affairs left Agnes with a shattered heart and untrusting spirit. When her husband left after a few short years, Agnes shut herself off from the world, preferring to be alone rather than open her heart to anyone.

Alex wanted to weep for this lonely beautiful girl. The emotions tucked into Agnes' brain were familiar. Alex felt the same way about her father. A stab of guilt shot through her when she thought of her behavior toward her mom's new boyfriend. Her mom didn't seem scared to open her heart. *Why am I so scared?*

The thought of what it would do to her mom if Bruce left made Alex cringe. They had just gotten their lives together, had their own house, her mom was coming into her own helping her sister run the stores. The last thing either of them needed was to have their lives upheaved again.

Suddenly, the face of Chandon Rose flashed through her mind. Alex stood in a panic, forgetting up to now that she was standing in her bathroom back in her own time waiting to go out on a date with Chandon. The initial disorientation of waking up in Germany in 1939, trying to save the soldier's life, and working Agnes' shift had made her completely forget about her date.

She tried to remember what time it had been just before she had traveled back in time. The last thing she could recall was having a difficult time finding anything to wear. Alex sat back down and put her hand over her face. She knew she needed to focus on finding Stygian and stopping him from whatever his plan might be but all she could think about was her mom walking in on her while she was traveling. There was no way she could come up with a lie to explain why she was ice cold and standing in front of the mirror in a trance. Worse, if her mom broke the connection, Alex wasn't sure if she could make it back to stop

Stygian. She tried to remember if Gavin or Sean had ever mentioned what would happen in a scenario like this.

Get a grip, Alex!

Her mind was running in circles and she needed to focus. There was nothing she could do about her mom or Chandon. What she *could* do was find Stygian, stop him from changing history, and get back home so she could out on a date with the hottest guy in school.

Alex finished her lunch and got back to Agnes' rounds. She didn't know how the woman did it. With all the work she was doing, Alex thought for sure she should be falling down exhausted but Agnes' body just kept going and going and going. Alex giggled at the picture of a pink bunny with a German accent that flashed through her mind.

The sun had long since set when Alex clocked out for the day. Agnes' body was finally feeling the effects of the long shift. Part of it was the hard work, but part was knowing she would repeat it all tomorrow. And the next day. And the day after that. Alex knew that the woman's days would be more grueling as the war continued and the injured and dying piled up.

Alex couldn't help but wonder if Adolf Hitler was here or off somewhere with his troops. Since it was 1939, Alex knew Hitler could be in Poland. She couldn't remember exactly when he invaded Poland but she knew it was sometime in 1939. And her instincts told her that wherever Hitler was, Stygian was sure to be.

If Stygian was in Poland, then I'd be there too.

Alex shook her head as she walked back to Agnes' small apartment. Of course Stygian was here in Germany. Either her skills were slipping or she was more distracted by the date with Chandon. She mentally kicked herself. If she was going to beat Stygian and stay alive in the process, she'd have to do a lot better than she had thus far.

Chapter 32

ALEX YAWNED SO HARD her cheeks creaked and her eyes watered. It had been difficult to sleep. The noises were unfamiliar and she woke at every creaking of the apartment and voices coming through the paper-thin walls. In a daze she went through Agnes' morning routine. She looked all over for some coffee but didn't see any in the apartment. It was probably considered a luxury item in this time period. Alex didn't see how she was going to make it through another busy day without some caffeine.

After nearly leaving without grabbing her lunch, Alex considered calling in sick to the hospital. She would probably end up killing someone. There was nothing in Agnes' mind pertaining to sick days or time off. Considering where she was now, Alex figured there was no such thing. Rather than get Agnes fired, Alex trudged to the hospital, trying to stay awake enough to avoid being hit by passing cars.

This day went much like the last except for the bleeding, dying soldier part. Agnes would find it routine, boring even. Alex found it equal parts scary and exciting. Someone's life was in her hands. Nothing like this had ever happened before. The only thing that came close was tutoring the students this semester. True, it wasn't life or death in a literal sense but Alex knew that most of them were counting on scholarships to go to college. Failing high school wouldn't exactly help those goals.

After cleaning up after a particularly bloody surgery, Alex was glad she had never considered going into the medical field. Dealing with body fluids had never been her thing. Being the curator of a museum was a cleaner line of work.

Suddenly, her skin tingled with an all-too-familiar crawling sensation that started at her toes and ended at her scalp. She fought the urge to turn around when she heard the murmur of voices in the hall. Alex continued checking the patient, hands shaking so badly she feared missing the vein as she tried to inject the elderly gentleman with his medication. She strained her ears, hoping to overhear what the men were saying, but they were speaking too quietly.

The voices faded as the men moved past the door and continued down the hall. Alex finally chanced turning around but the men were already out of sight. She bit her lip, unsure how to proceed. She needed to find out what Stygian was up to and at the same time, she had to remain out of danger long enough to stop him.

You gotta follow them, Alex.

Alex groaned at the sound of her uncle's voice in her head. The last thing she wanted to do was follow Stygian. He knew more about traveling than she did and could probably kill her easily. Alex cringed as she remembered the time she had nearly lost her life. She could almost feel the pillow over her face, the sound of the blood in her ears as her body fought for air. Then she was floating in a black void and she had somehow managed to find her way back to her body. Gavin seemed to think this was part of her being some sort of special Traveler. Alex didn't want to bet her life on being able to do it a second time.

Besides, if she stopped Stygian, her uncle was dead. But if she didn't stop him, then her uncle and a lot of other people would probably die. She didn't have a choice. She couldn't allow Stygian to alter history.

Mustering her courage, Alex walked out into the hallway, trying to act as though she belonged there.

You're a nurse, you idiot, of course you belong here!

That sarcastic voice that sounded a lot like Jenn didn't do much to slow her galloping heart or stop her palms from sweating. Alex knew Agnes had patients down the wing the men had taken so she simply walked as though she was merely doing her rounds.

When she spotted the four doctors walking she slowed her steps, unwilling to get closer. She didn't want Stygian to suspect anything. She was too far way to hear what they were saying but all four men were gesturing wildly and had their heads together. They clearly didn't want to be overheard.

Alex wasn't sure which one was Stygian. But she knew he was one of them. Her stomach roiled as though she would vomit any moment and her skin pebbled in goose pimples. Every instinct told her to run the other direction but the fate of the world rested on her finding out what Stygian had planned and stop him.

The men stopped just short of the room that belonged to Agnes' patient down this hallway. Alex knew if she turned away, it could draw unwanted attention. But walking up to the men who had their backs turned could also get her in trouble. She found herself in a situation that called for a decision to be made in a split second. Another step and the men would be able to hear the squeak of her shoes on the linoleum floor.

Alex put on her best bland face and continued down the hall, steps quick and hurried like the other nurses would do while on rounds. She nodded to the men as she passed and continued on as though she couldn't care less who they were or what they had been whispering about. Alex kept an even pace but it was difficult not to trot past them. She didn't see how the men could stand the smell of the evil Traveler in their midst. The odor made her almost gag.

She entered the room of Agnes' patient and did her job. She did nothing that would raise any eyebrows. Quick and efficient, giving a kind word to the lady lying in the bed propped on several pillows. Try as she might, Alex couldn't hear anything the men were saying, even this close. As soon as she was done, Alex left the room exactly like she entered, mind on the next patient on her rounds and not on the men standing outside the room.

Alex could feel his eyes on her as she walked down the hall and she sent up a silent prayer that the men would not even notice her. Most doctors ignored the nursing staff unless there was an emergency. Her shoulders wanted to droop under the weight of the terror.

The next patient was in another hallway, which would take her out of earshot but there was no help for it. Hesitating or walking back would raise Stygian's suspicions. He would already be on the look-out for her. Alex couldn't give him any reason to suspect that she was the same Traveler who had thwarted every plan he'd had for the last few years.

"Oh, nurse. Could you come back here a moment please?"

Alex nearly fainted. A voice—*his voice*— echoed down the empty hallway. Her breath caught in her throat. Did she run and hide? Go back the way she came and try to convince Stygian that she was only a German nurse and not the spirit of a 21st century girl?

"Yes, my dear, I'm talking to you. Come here this instant."

Alex froze in place. She had rounded the corner so it was impossible for Stygian to actually see her. She held her breath and waited for the voice to say something else.

"What is it, doctor?" a timid voice answered.

"I need you to come with me."

"Of course, doctor." The voice sounded terrified.

Alex tiptoed to the corner and peeked around. Only one man stood in the hallway and he was beckoning to a tiny blonde nurse. Her hands were full of fresh linens. She glanced around as though looking for somewhere to deposit the sheets.

Or looking for somewhere to run.

Even from down the hall, Alex could see her trembling from head to foot. She wanted to do something to help the girl but she couldn't risk bringing attention to herself. Tears threatened to fall as Alex battled within herself. An innocent girl was in danger and yet if Alex failed at stopping him, the whole world would be in danger.

Stygian pushed the linens out of the woman's hands and onto the floor. He grabbed her arm and forced her down the hall and into a room next to the one Agnes' female patient was in.

Alex trotted down the hallway toward the room Stygian and the nurse entered. She had to hear what was said, even if it put her life at risk. The only sound she heard was the distant footfalls of someone in an adjacent hallway and raised voices coming from the room.

"I asked you a question. Why were you following me?"

The woman yelped in fright. "I wasn't following, not exactly. Please, Doctor, I wasn't eavesdropping or anything if that's what you think. I couldn't hear anything you said."

"Then what were you doing hiding in the supply closet?"

The woman sobbed for a few minutes and said something that Alex couldn't make out over the crying.

"Let me see if I understand. You were hiding in the closet because you had stolen some narcotics and were scared that we were on to you, is that right?"

"My mom's real sick and needs the medicine for the pain. It's the only way I can get it. Please don't fire me! If I lose this job, we'll starve."

Stygian laughed. "I should fire you but I won't. But I will be watching you and there will be no more stealing of medicine meant for the patients in the hospital. We'll need it for our soldiers. Now get out of my sight."

The woman's footsteps drew closer and Alex realized that she had nowhere to hide. She ran to the sheets on the floor and began picking them up as though she had just come across them lying in the middle of the floor. Pulling on all the acting skills she possessed, Alex mumbled under her breath, clearly angry at having to clean up someone else's mess.

Alex turned to the nurse as she emerged from the room. "Did you leave this here?" She shook the wrinkled linens at the distraught nurse.

The nurse nodded her head and walked over to Alex. "It was an a...aaa...accident."

"What's all the crying about? Did you lose another one? You're not to let your emotions get in the way of—" Alex stopped short as Stygian came out of the room.

"It wasn't entirely her fault, nurse. I admit I startled her when I came out of a room behind her."

Alex forced herself to meet the man's eyes. She must be every inch the part of Agnes, irritated nurse. "I don't see how a little scare has her all worked up." She turned back to the nurse. "You better get yourself together. You have rounds to finish I presume?" When the woman nodded, Alex handed her the sheets. "I am at the end of a twelve hour shift and don't fancy having to cover yours. Pull yourself together and be about your duties."

The nurse nodded and moved quickly down the hall and disappeared into a room. Alex turned to face Stygian but the man was already moving away down the hallway in the opposite direction of the poor frightened nurse.

Heaving a sigh of relief, Alex left to finish with her last patient. Even though she had no idea what Stygian was up to, she may have saved an innocent woman's life. Alex had no idea how many people Stygian had already killed but she guessed it was probably a lot.

Her last patient, a little boy being treated for leukemia, was fast asleep when she arrived at his room. Alex checked his IV bag and bit her lip to hold back tears. He looked so tiny and fragile in the bed. Alex wished she could bring something modern back to treat him. His chances weren't good with the medicines available back in 1939. The name on the IV bag said Fowler's solution. Alex didn't know what that was but she didn't think it would be as good at fighting the cancer as chemotherapy drugs.

She smoothed his hair back from his face and walked toward the door with a heavy heart. Alex stopped dead in her tracks at the sound of voices. One of them sounded like Stygian but she couldn't be sure without getting closer. She crept forward on the balls of her feet so her shoes wouldn't squeak on the floor.

It's him!

According to Agnes' knowledge of the layout of the hospital, the voices sounded like they were coming from a lounge area just for the physicians. Alex took up a position behind the door and tried to slow her breathing.

"Are you sure we're alone?" a deep voice asked.

"No one is around. We're safe. Now, did you have a chance to look over the notes I gave you?" Stygian asked.

Alex heard the shuffling of paper then a high-pitched voice say, "Yes, and we're quite impressed. You've never demonstrated any interest in pharmacology before. And all of a sudden you come to us with a new compound that you claim can help Adolf Hitler?" The man laughed haughtily. "We weren't aware that there was anything wrong with him."

"I am privy to information that you are not. I'm telling you, Der Fuehrer is ill and will require this medication to win the war."

More laughter and a third strange voice. "What war? No one is strong enough to stand against us. Our armies will wash over the world like a green tide."

"You are fools if you think the United States will stay out of the fighting. They will come against us and we will fail," Stygian said.

"I will not stand here and tolerate such words against Der Fuehrer." A chair falling backwards and hitting the floor made Alex jump.

"If you want to win this war you will listen to me. Der Fuehrer has an illness of the brain. It's in the early stages so the symptoms haven't manifested as of yet. Do you want him going into battle without his full faculties?" Stygian asked.

"What is this brain illness? And why haven't we heard anything about it?" asked the first man who spoke, the one with the deep voice.

"Are you mad? What do you think would happen to his support if the people knew he had a mental illness?"

"I see your point," said the deep-voiced man.

"Do you have what you need to make the drug?" Stygian asked.

Shuffling papers. "Yes, we have everything we need." A pause. "I have never heard of anything with these items. What is this medication called?"

"I call it L-DOPA. Now, you mustn't tell anyone about this. Make the drug as soon as possible and give the finished product to me."

"Wait. What manner of illness does Hitler have?" asked high-pitched voice man.

"His doctors think he has Parkinson's disease," Stygian said.

"I've heard of this. Are the doctors certain?" asked deep voice.

"The symptoms are subtle and Der Fuehrer takes pains to hide them but the signs are there. And this drug should hold the symptoms at bay so he can win the war."

Alex bit the soft part of her thumb to keep from squealing out loud. She had read about this strange theory about Hitler last year in AP history class. She hadn't thought there was much to it at the time since there was only circumstantial evidence but with what Stygian just said she wondered if it was true.

Does Stygian know for certain?

She didn't know how he could possibly know the real truth. Coming back in time for a hunch didn't seem like Stygian's style or Poder's. They had to have some sort of proof. Alex wished she had some way to get in touch with Gavin or her uncle. She couldn't say why, but she felt it with every bone in her body that this was an important piece to the puzzle as to why Stygian had been traveling back in time.

*   *   *

Max Poder stood in front of the shelf that held the photos of his family. He reached out a shaking hand toward one of the pictures. Poder growled and shoved his hand behind his back. The picture that held his gaze looked so much like Hitler that Poder kept the picture purposefully hidden behind other nondescript pictures that wouldn't raise an eyebrow.

It wasn't Hitler, of course. Only a relative, Leo Rudolf Raubal Jr., who looked so much like the real Hitler that he would stand in as the Nazi leader's double. Max Poder could trace his lineage to Leo, though his family kept it a secret. Poder had found out as a kid and didn't understand why his family had changed their name and pretended like they were just ordinary citizens like everyone else. They had a legacy, a heritage, something that should be passed down proudly.

He had studied his ancestors, learned their proud moments and not so proud moments. The idea to restore how he felt history should have unfolded came about the same time he realized his gift, his calling. When he found out that he would train time Travelers, Max Poder knew what he had to do: search for someone who would follow his every order and embrace his ultimate plan to change history.

When Poder found Lane Stygian, who preferred to be called Drifter, he knew it would only be a matter of time before his family legacy would be restored to its previous glory.

The one thing he hadn't counted on was a meddling time traveler and a specially gifted Traveler at that. He had been so sure Drifter had taken care of most of the Masters and their Travelers but he had obviously missed one very important one.

At least the girl's uncle can't interfere.

Poder wanted to throw something when he thought of the girl being almost under his nose this whole time. What were the chances that she lived in the current time rather than in the future or the past? He shook his head, trying to shove down the anger. And just when his plans were about to come to fruition, the girl managed to find out where he and Drifter were and told her uncle everything.

Max wanted to remain angry with Drifter for murdering the girl in her barracks. It had brought unwanted attention that he couldn't afford right now. But framing Mark had been brilliant. The perfect thing to get the meddling Captain out of the way. The charges wouldn't stick of course but if Drifter was successful back in 1939 Germany, it wouldn't matter.

And his phone call to the meddling niece meant that his plan would come to fruition.

Poder chuckled and walked slowly back to his desk to take his medication. The tremor in his hands made it difficult to open the bottle of Sinemet, a drug combination to treat Parkinson's disease. The disease ran in his family: father, uncles, cousins, as far back as they could remember. All the way back to Hitler.

Chapter 33

ALEX DIDN'T THINK she was going to make it through her shift the next day. She had experienced what she thought was exhaustion. Today, she realized that she in fact had not. Not even close. Alex didn't think she had even slept an hour the previous night. Thoughts of Stygian giving Hitler medication to prevent the symptoms of Parkinson's disease plagued her. Alex remembered her AP History teacher telling the class that some folks thought it was Parkinson's that caused Hitler to lose the war, that he wasn't listening to his Generals, countermanding orders, making mistakes. She had always thought that was oversimplifying things, but this latest development with Stygian had her wondering if Hitler did indeed have Parkinson's.

She supposed it didn't matter. It was her duty to stop Stygian no matter what he was planning. And that was the hard part. When she had traveled in the past, she had never had to worry about anyone else when she came up against Stygian. Now that her uncle was in danger, she wasn't sure how to proceed. It was so tempting to let Stygian do whatever he wanted and claim that he got the best of her. No one would ever know.

Except her.

Alex sighed and rubbed her grainy eyes. She imagined this was what it felt like to be drunk. She had barely caught herself giving patients the wrong medicine. She'd never forgive herself if someone died because of her.

Uncle Mark is going to.

Tears filled her eyes and she forced them back by sheer force of will. She couldn't afford to be distracted by her tears. The fate of the world rested on her young shoulders and like it or not, she had to stop Stygian. Her uncle would want her to do her duty.

As she had lain in bed, tossing and turning, she had realized that the only way to stop Stygian would be to use the magic spell she and Sean had used when they had traveled back to Egypt. Alex practiced it throughout the night just to make sure she wouldn't forget the words. She put her hands in the pockets of her pinafore and touched the small hand mirror she'd taken from Agnes' dresser. When she thought of confronting the evil Traveler alone, her stomach twisted into knots. Alex had no idea how she was going to restrain the man in order to recite the spell.

Maybe you can kill him.

Alex refused to listen to that voice. It was madness. She couldn't kill Stygian. She'd only be killing the man whose body he inhabited. She couldn't possibly do it, not even if it meant saving the world. She knew she'd have to find some other way.

Even though she was tired and wanted nothing more than to end her shift, she was also hoping the time would slow just a little. Agnes was due in the trauma ward that afternoon and Alex didn't want to listen to any more dying soldiers begging for death. Though their numbers had dwindled, it was still more than Alex could bear.

As she walked to the lunch room, she heard a squeaking behind her. She turned and gasped as warmth flowed through her body all the way to her extremities. A handsome young man was pushing a mop bucket down the hall, heading right for her. He had cropped hair so blonde it appeared silver under the glare of the fluorescent lights. He kept his head down so Alex couldn't see any more of his features.

It was difficult to filter through Agnes' memories of this boy. His name was Christoph and he had been working at the hospital since before Agnes was hired on. He had tried unsuccessfully to engage Agnes in conversation but she rebuffed his advances, politely at first, but becoming more insistent as he grew more persistent. Agnes had tried desperately to make Christoph understand that she would never be able to date another boy again. The thought of going through the motions of getting to know someone else and putting her trust in them just seemed too exhausting and futile. Agnes convinced herself that all men were alike and that there was no man in the world that could ever remain truly faithful.

Alex knew that Agnes was drawn to Christoph on a level so much deeper than she had ever had with her ex-husband, but Agnes was unwilling to take a chance. For her it was easier to be alone.

Alex wanted to cry as she watched Christoph walk by, head down, refusing to even look at her. Part of her wanted to reach out, touch this man, speak to him, spend time with him, show Agnes what she was missing. But when Agnes returned to her body, she would only spurn Christoph once again. Alex couldn't do that to the poor boy.

Her lunch break flew by. As she walked to the trauma ward, Alex steeled herself for the agonizing moans and shrieks, the smell of rotten flesh and death. She didn't know how Agnes did it day after day. Most of her patients were on the brink of death. Alex could see the work being more rewarding if more people survived. Searching through Agnes' mind revealed the answers. The woman actually enjoyed this ward. Most nurses did everything they could to be reassigned. Not Agnes. There was a peace here that she couldn't sense on any other ward. Agnes had overheard doctors speaking about her calm nature and how it seemed to sooth the patients. Agnes knew she had a gift of bringing others comfort. She only wished she could do the same for herself.

Alex shook her head. It was so strange knowing that her name was Alex, that she was from the future, and yet to *feel* like she was Agnes, a nurse from 1939 Germany. Both lives seemed real.

Lucky for Alex, there weren't many soldiers in trauma this afternoon. She met with the head doctor to see which patients needed care, if there were any surgeries she would be assisting with. As she stood receiving her instructions, she felt her skin crawl and a familiar voice came from over her right shoulder.

Alex held her breath. *Does he know who I am?* Panic crawled through her guts.

"Please excuse us. I must speak with the doctor alone."

She tried not to jump at the sound of Stygian's voice addressing her. Using all of the acting skills in her arsenal, she forced herself to meet his eyes, nod in agreement, and move to the first of her patients she would treat for the rest of the afternoon. Alex couldn't believe her stroke of good luck. The two men began speaking with her still within earshot.

"Were you successful in creating the medicine?" Stygian asked.

"We followed the instructions you gave to the letter. But without being able to test it, we don't know that it will work," the doctor said.

"If you followed the protocol, it will work," Stygian said confidently. "How much were you able to make?"

"More than enough for your needs. And we have the supplies on hand to make more."

"Very good. I trust that you've spoken to no one of this?"

"Only the other doctors involved."

"I expect you to keep your word. Tell no one of this."

"Of course." The doctor sounded unsure.

"I'll be back in a few hours to collect the L-DOPA. Have it ready for me."

Alex had to move away from the two men. She wanted to hear more but she had lingered too long already. Her frustration grew as she saw to her other patients. She still had no idea how to stop Stygian from giving Hitler the medication.

She felt rather than saw Stygian leave the trauma ward. Alex watched the doctor for a time. The man saw to several patients, all while checking the clock.

When he left the ward, Alex followed him, unable to believe what she was doing. She walked on the balls of her feet, ready to duck into a doorway if the doctor turned around. He pushed through a door and into a laboratory. Alex peeked through the window before following. She glanced at a table and grabbed a large glass beaker, holding it in her hands like a baseball bat. Her arms shook as she made her way to the back of the dimly lit room. Alex had no idea what she planned on doing with the beaker but it felt good to have a weapon.

The doctor was standing with his back to her. She tiptoed closer until she could see what he was doing. There were several bottles of white pills on the counter. The doctor was packing them into a black patent leather bag.

Acting on instinct, Alex swung the beaker as hard as she could, aiming for the back of his head. The doctor gave a muffled grunt and fell to the floor. With shaking hands, Alex grabbed the bottles and took them to a nearby lavatory. She opened the bottled and dumped the contents into the toilet, smiling grimly as the pills swirled and were carried away. Before going back to her duties, Alex checked the doctor, relieved to find him still breathing.

She hurried back to the trauma ward, sending up a prayer of thanks that she passed no one in the hallways. Alex resumed her duties, smoothing her hair, checking her uniform for anything that would give her away when Stygian came looking for the doctor.

When Stygian returned, she was arm deep in aiding another doctor with a critically injured patient. She refused to acknowledge Stygian when he walked up, keeping her eyes on her work.

"Where is Doctor Haussen?" Stygian demanded.

"I haven't seen him. But I've only just arrived," the doctor answered without looking up from the patient.

"Nurse, you were here earlier. Where is Doctor Haussen?"

Alex kept her voice steady. "I haven't seen him since you ordered me to leave the two of you alone. As you can see, this ward is very busy and I can barely keep track of my patients let alone the doctors." She, too, kept her eyes on her work.

She watched Stygian walk away out of the corner of her eye. Alex couldn't help but breathe a sigh of relief. Her relief was sort lived when she saw that he was heading right for the laboratory. Alex hoped her deed wouldn't be discovered until she was already home for the evening.

When Stygian's roar of rage echoed through the trauma ward, Alex jumped in terror.

Stygian ran back into the ward. "Someone get in here now! Haussen's been injured!"

A doctor and several nurses ran after Stygian. Alex stayed where she was. The doctor she was helping was in the middle of a critical procedure and it was her job to assist him. Agnes had enough training to ignore anything but the patient at hand. Nurses and doctors couldn't afford to get distracted.

By the time the others arrived carrying Haussen, Alex was finished with her current patient. There were several people surrounding the unconscious doctor. Alex knew she couldn't go near the man without arousing suspicions. She went about her duties and left when her shift was over. It drove her mad to have to leave but it was the only thing she could do. Alex was careful to ignore what was happening with Doctor Haussen and left with the others that had also come to the end of their shift.

As she passed, one of the nurses who had been treating Haussen left his side and came closer to Alex.

"Is Doctor Haussen going to be okay?" Alex asked.

"Just a nasty bump on the head. He'll come around soon," the nurse said. "Sad thing, though, doctors getting attacked in the hospital."

Alex's widened her eyes and put her hands over her mouth. "He was attacked? Are we safe?" She looked around as though someone was going to come at her any moment.

"If you're off shift, best head home. Security is organizing a search for the one responsible. Hopefully Doctor Haussen can tell us more when he wakes up," the nurse said as she walked away.

Alex made her way to the exit doors she usually took on her way out. There was more activity in the halls than she had ever noticed before. Several security officers dressed in pressed uniforms were systematically searching every room and asking to see identification badges of all staff they saw. She showed them her badge and the man told her to be careful going home and to report any strange activity immediately.

A group of nurses ahead of Alex were whispering about the attack on Doctor Haussen. One was convinced it was a family member seeking revenge for the death of a loved one at Doctor Haussen's hands. Another thought it was a disgruntled employee, maybe a janitor.

Alex kept her head down and refused to look at anyone, sure they would somehow know that it had been her. The walk home was a blur. The mixture of exhaustion, excitement, and fear made her mind a whirlwind. She wished she could contact Gavin and let him know about what she'd done.

At least Stygian can't contact Poder.

That gave her some small measure of comfort. Until she defeated Stygian and she returned home, her uncle would be safe.

*   *   *

Drifter wanted to put a bullet in Doctor Haussen's head. It took every ounce of will power not to strangle the man.

"I was standing at the counter ready to put the medicine in the bag and someone hit me. I never saw him. Never even heard him," Doctor Haussen said, wincing as he rubbed the back of his head.

"The bottles were found next to the toilet so I can only assume that they were flushed down," Drifter said.

"I take full responsibility. The others and I will get started on a new batch right away."

"I will be assigning extra security to the laboratory. No one goes in or out except for you, me, and the other two doctors. What I wouldn't give for some security cameras," he muttered to himself.

"Security cameras? What are you talking about?"

Drifter spun around. "I expect you to get to work on more medicine as soon as you leave here. Do not fail me again."

"Now see here, I don't take orders from you—"

Drifter grabbed the man by the throat and squeezed. Doctor Haussen flailed futilely at Drifters hands, face turning red as he struggled for air.

"You will follow my orders or I shall kill you. It's as simple as that. Do I make myself clear?"

Doctor Haussen managed to nod. Drifter released the man, turned on his heel, and walked out of the room. He made his way to his office and closed the door.

With a roar of frustration, he swiped everything off the desk. Drifter paced the small space, pulling his hair as he tried to grapple with what had happened.

He knew it had to be the girl. Poder said she wouldn't be a problem and yet *someone* had stopped him. Drifter knew it had to be here. He tried to remember any women he'd come into contact with the last several days. The only one that stood out in his mind was the nurse he'd caught lurking about and confronted. But she had claimed to be stealing medicine for her sick mother.

Of course she did. The girl isn't going to admit who she is.

Drifter wished he could go to a shooting range. He could barely resist the urge to wreak havoc on a paper silhouette. But that wouldn't satiate his hunger. Deep down, he wanted to do far worse than shoot at a target.

He smiled as he walked out of his office, closing the door softly behind him.

Chapter 34

AGNES HAD THE NEXT couple of days off work. Alex knew there was no way she could go to the hospital without arousing suspicions.

Alex wandered around, getting to know Agnes a little better. Her apartment was small but cozy. Nearly every surface was covered with crocheted doilies that Agnes had made herself over the years. The walls were decorated with various landscape paintings. Agnes loved the outdoors. She didn't get outside enough so she brought the outdoors into her living space. Various plants sat on tables and bookshelves.

It didn't take long for Alex to explore the space. She tried reading but her nerves wouldn't allow her to sit long enough to get through more than a page or two.

Alex spied a hand mirror on Agnes' small vanity. Desperate to contact Gavin or Jenn, she tried to force the mirror to change to her own reflection. No matter how hard she tried or how long she stared at the mirror, only Agnes's face stared back. It seemed as though she was stuck here until she completed her task.

She had no idea what people did to alleviate boredom back in the 1930's. All she wanted to do was watch TV or get on her laptop. Alex sighed and decided to go for a walk and burn off some of her nervous energy. She grabbed a shawl and walked out into the warm afternoon air. Alex wished she could wear less clothing. It was hot outside and the long dress coupled with the shawl was stifling. But it wouldn't be proper to walk about outdoors without being covered.

Following a route Agnes walked often, Alex let her mind wander. She tried to pay attention to the buildings and their wonderful architecture but she just couldn't make herself care. Life as she knew it would probably end if she didn't stop Stygian. And if she did manage to foil his plans, her uncle would pay the price.

Tears slipped down her cheeks. Alex brushed them away. Crying wouldn't help her stop Stygian. She wanted to be surprised by her decision to perform her duty but she wasn't. The moment she destroyed the medicine for Hitler, she had made the decision to stop Stygian. She couldn't let people die, even to save her uncle.

Alex hoped that whatever Stygian had planned would occur while she was at work. If he was in the middle of making new L-DOPA, it would still take him a few days until he could replenish his supply. That meant that Alex would indeed be back at the hospital. She doubted it would be as easy to destroy the medicine this time around. Stygian would be watching for her. She'd have to be very careful unless she wanted to get caught.

She wished there was someone in this time she could trust, someone she could turn to for guidance or help. Beating Stygian with Sean while back in Egypt had seemed easy compared to the time she had had to face Stygian alone. Alex shuddered and pulled her shawl closer despite the heat of the day. She had nearly lost her life to Stygian once. She didn't want to tempt fate and try to survive the void again. Best to find a way to beat Stygian without revealing her true identity.

Alex turned around and began the walk back to Agnes' apartment. She stopped by a market that was a favorite of Agnes' to get some food for dinner. Alex knew that Agnes enjoyed cooking but didn't do much since she lived alone. That was part of what she missed most about being married. Her ex-husband may have treated her horridly in every other aspect of their marriage but he had always loved her cooking. It had made Agnes feel special to hear her husband speak of her cooking skills to others.

Hot anger burned through Alex. She couldn't believe a man would cheat on someone as sweet as Agnes. The woman was as nice as could be, smart, great at taking care of the home. Alex wondered if any marriage would ever work. It seemed an impossibility from where she stood. Her own parents couldn't even make it work.

Alex thought of her mom and Bruce and wondered how her mom could date again, even though it had been years since Gary had left. Alex didn't think she would ever be ready to open her heart to someone if she had suffered what her mom had.

Aren't you willing to go on a date with a boy knowing you may not survive to date him a second time?

She couldn't help but chuckle at the sound of Jenn's voice in her head. The voice was right, of course. Alex wasn't willing to put her life on hold just because she had a duty to save the world. She sort of understood why her mom was willing to open her heart to another man. Alex just hoped that Bruce wouldn't ask her mom to marry him for a while yet. She wasn't ready to have a step-father, no matter how nice he was.

Alex wasn't any closer to solving the dilemma of how to stop Stygian by the time she arrived home. She hoped the mindless task of cooking dinner would leave her mind free to come up with some possibilities. It was Agnes who knew how to cook. Alex was lucky if she didn't scorch the pan while trying to boil water. She was learning but no one would say her cooking was anything but mediocre.

As she chopped and sliced, she let her mind wander. She would have to try to destroy any more medicine Stygian made. She couldn't allow him to give it to Hitler. Even if it meant her life, she would somehow have to stop Stygian.

*   *   *

Alex was ready to go back to the hospital after only two days in Agnes' apartment. Though she didn't think it was possible to die of boredom, Alex thought she had come pretty close. Agnes' taste in books did not match with Alex's. They were long and flowery and convoluted. Alex found herself re-reading paragraph after paragraph and ended up tossing the book on the floor in frustration. She spent much of her time staring out the window, thinking of Chandon, wondering if he was thinking of her, hoping time was passing very slowly back in her time so that she wouldn't be discovered by her mom.

She was due in the trauma ward all day so she mentally prepared herself. While treating the patients came from Agnes' skill, Alex still had to deal with the blood, the dying, and the screaming. She had to fight tears with nearly every patient. Agnes was a seasoned nurse and would never allow tears to fall where others could see her. If Alex cried, it might cause suspicion.

Alex went about her duties, keeping an eye out for Stygian and yet trying to look like she wasn't trying to look for someone. The man never made an appearance.

When she left the ward to eat lunch, Alex thought she could use a few minutes to snoop around without getting caught. She made her way slowly back to the laboratory, pretending that she had every right to be walking down that particular hallway. Her skin prickled as her senses stretched out for any sign of Stygian.

She stopped short of turning down the final hallway. With her back against the wall, Alex moved to the corner and peered around the edge.

There were two guards on either side of the doors to the laboratory. Both carried wicked looking rifles and looked they would have no problems shooting her down if she stepped into their view. At the very least, they wouldn't let her get anywhere near the lab.

Alex turned and walked to the lunchroom, feeling disappointment and relief at not being able to get near the laboratory. As she ate her meal, she debated her next move. She couldn't force her way into the lab; that much was clear.

Maybe there's another way in.

That thought filled her with excitement at first but she soon came back to reality. Stygian wasn't a fool. If there were multiple ways into the lab, he'd have them all covered. Especially after losing one batch of the medicine.

Alex was no nearer a solution after lunch than before. She made her way back to the trauma ward to finish her afternoon shift. Each minute that passed brought elevated anxiety. Stygian would have more L-DOPA made soon and then he would take it to Hitler. Alex had to stop him, somehow.

As she finished helping a doctor with a patient, she felt the familiar skin crawling and nausea that signaled Stygian's approach. He was walking with two of the doctors who were helping to make the drug. Their heads were close together and they barely spoke above a whisper; Alex couldn't hear a word they were saying. All three headed down the hallway leading to the lab.

Her work in the trauma ward, finished, Alex took a deep breath and followed the three men. On the way, she snatched a head mirror off a small table, a plan buried in the back of her mind. The idea was ludicrous, dangerous, and necessary. Alex knew she was nearly out of time.

She walked down the hall like she had every right to be there, hoping the men wouldn't turn around. The door to the lab was guarded by the same two men as before. Alex turned down a different hallway just as Stygian and the two other doctors pushed their way through the doors. She had held out a small hope that the doors would be unguarded. She cursed her bad luck and wondered how she was going to get into the lab and get Stygian alone.

Alex tiptoed to the corner and peeked around, sending up a prayer that the two burly guards would be magically gone. She rolled her eyes when she saw them still standing on either side of the doors, guns at the ready.

"What are you doing?"

Alex squealed and spun around.

"What are you doing sneaking up on me, Christoph?" Alex put her hand over her belly, trying to catch her breath.

"Why are you acting like you don't want someone to see you?" Christoph asked. "And why are you carrying around a head mirror?"

"I was just curious about the laboratory. Aren't you wondering what's going on in there?"

"It's none of my business. The guards are there to keep the doctors safe. I, for one, am glad they are here. Someone in this hospital attacked a doctor. And it has something to do with what's in that lab." Christoph frowned at her. "Do you know something?"

"No, why would you even ask that?"

"I can tell when you're lying to me. Did you see something? You have to tell someone," Christoph reached for Alex's arm, but she moved back, looking to the left and right, hoping no one was noticing the scene.

"I don't know anything! I told you, I was just curious about the guards," Alex whispered fiercely.

"The guards are not a secret. You can speak to them if you wish; I have seen them conversing with many nurses. You were acting like you didn't want them to see you."

"Don't be ridiculous."

"You must tell someone what you know. If you won't do it, I'll give them your name and let them question you."

"Why are you doing this to me? Is this because Ag—" Alex took a deep breath to steady her nerves. "Is this because I won't allow you to take me out?"

Christoph's eyes widened and he backed up a few steps. "Of course not! This has to do with someone in this hospital being attacked, something to do with the laboratory, something bad enough that guards are necessary. I want the person caught and punished. What if he attacks someone else? Maybe even one of the nurses?" Christoph moved toward Alex and she was mesmerized by the naked worry and desire in his eyes. "Don't you see? If this man attacks you, I couldn't bear it. Please, if you know something, you have to tell someone."

Alex turned away and put her hands over her face. This was a development she definitely didn't need. She needed to find a way into that laboratory so she could get rid of Stygian. She couldn't afford the distraction of this handsome young man. Her shoulder blades itched. She could almost feel his eyes boring into her back, willing her to turn around.

"I sense there is something different about you. I can't put my finger on it."

The blood rushed from Alex's face. She turned slowly. "What do you mean? I'm the same as I've always been."

Christoph was standing so close Alex could feel his breath on her face. "You look the same, smell the same, dress the same. But there is something..." He reached up to gently stroke her face.

Alex wanted to melt into this man's arms and tell him everything. Fighting a mad man alone was no job for a teenage girl. It would be such a relief to spill her guts and acquire his help.

"You can tell me. I see something in your eyes." Christoph smiled crookedly, attempting to lighten the mood. "If you don't tell me what's going on, you'll never be rid of me."

Despite Agnes' obvious objections to opening her heart to this young man, Alex didn't think she had a choice. She was running out of time. If Stygian had more of the drug for Hitler, he could be packing it up right this moment and on his way.

"I'll tell you what I can but you have to accept the information I give and not seek more. And you can't speak of this to another person," Alex said.

"I promise."

"Several of the doctors have been working on a medicine for Hitler. His physicians think he has Parkinson's Disease and this drug is supposed to make him better. The person who attacked Doctor Haussen poured the drug down the commode."

"Why would they do such a thing? If Der Fuehrer is truly ill, and the medicine can make him better, why would someone throw it out?" Christoph's eyes widened. "Are you saying we have a spy in our midst?"

Alex sighed and hung her head. She hadn't expected this level of fervor.

What am I going to do?

"It's more than that. I can't tell you everything, but you have to believe me that throwing away the medicine is the best thing that can happen." Alex felt a rush as an idea came to her. "The medicine isn't safe. Don't you see? If this doctor manages to get more of the drug made and gives it to Hitler, it will make him sicker."

Alex hated saying the words. She wished she could tell Christoph the truth about the coming war, make him see reason. But he believed in Hitler and she would never gain his help if she spoke out against the German leader.

"So the culprit is actually trying to help Hitler? What does this have to do with you?"

"I found out about the drug. I can't tell you how. But I have to stop the doctor from making more of the drug and giving it to Hitler."

"Have you told anyone else about this?"

"I was sworn to secrecy. I can get in trouble by telling you."

Christoph pulled Alex close. "I will die before telling your secret."

She felt a little guilty about using Christoph but she didn't have any other choice. There was more at stake than the feelings of this one person. She hoped Agnes wouldn't go back to ignoring him after all this. The more Alex thought about what she had just done, the worse she felt. Not to mention the fact that she wasn't even sure if Agnes was aware of anything going on or whether she would remember any of this. If Christoph started talking to her about their plot to stop the production of medicine for Hitler, she would think Christoph was insane.

Oh my God, was what I thinking?

Alex wanted to go back in time and take back her stupid decision to tell Christoph anything. By opening her big mouth, she had probably made things worse.

Get a grip, Alex!

It was too late to worry about it now. The damage had been done. She would have to trust that Christoph and Agnes would be fine after she returned to her own time.

"What do we do to stop these men?" Christoph asked.

Alex pulled back. "I need to get into the lab."

"Don't you mean we need to get into the lab?" Christoph said with his adorable crooked grin.

"Okay, we need to get into the laboratory. After that, what needs to be done I have to do alone." Alex reached up and put her hand over his mouth just as he opened it to protest. "Remember, you promised."

Christoph frowned and nodded sharply. "Fine. But if your life is in danger, our agreement is off."

Alex didn't argue. There was so much that could go wrong and probably would that she almost considered giving up the whole thing and just letting Stygian win. *Maybe life won't be so different.*

She shook her head, shutting up the voice. She had a job to do and she would see it done.

"Question is, how do we get in there? Those guards are there all the time as far as I can tell," Alex said, getting back to the first obstacle that was in their path.

Christoph looked deep into Alex's eyes. "Oh, didn't I mention it before? I know of a back way in."

Chapter 35

"YOU WHAT?"

Christoph stood with his hands on his hips. "I know of another way in."

Alex blinked a few times and fought to keep her voice steady. "And why did you fail to mention this until now?"

"I was too busy trying to absorb what you told me about Hitler's life being in danger."

"Well, I'm sure there will be guards on that one too," Alex said, unwilling to get her hopes up.

"Not likely. It's kind of a secret entrance."

Alex crossed her arms over her chest and raised an eyebrow. "Secret entrance?"

"Sort of. It's an old hallway that got closed off after the renovations. Me and a bunch of the other custodians found it in a broom closet years ago. We sneak in there to smoke while we're on duty."

"And this hallway goes from this closet into the laboratory?"

"It opens behind a set of metal cabinets. We'd have to push them out of the way but that shouldn't be too hard."

"The noise alone would alert them," Alex said.

"It's in a back store room that's full of boxes and cabinets of old notebooks. It doesn't get used much. If we're careful, we can get in undetected."

It seemed too good to be true. But Alex didn't see any other option. "Let's go."

She followed Christoph as he led the way. Alex gripped the head mirror, hoping that she would have the opportunity to use it. If things didn't go smoothly, she would have tipped her hand to Stygian and

Agnes' life would be in danger and she would never get another chance to get anywhere near him.

The pair passed several nurses and doctors in the hallways but no one paid them any mind. Alex was nervous that some doctor would demand her aid with a patient and she would miss Stygian. She already pictured him on his way to see Hitler, medicine in hand.

Christoph looked both ways before opening the small broom closet. He ushered Alex inside and closed the door. It was a tight fit. Alex was aware of his body pressed against hers. Christoph grabbed her shoulders and switched places with her so he could have easier access to the back wall.

In a few moments, part of the wall moved aside, revealing a dark hallway. Christoph grabbed a flashlight from his belt and led the way.

"Why did they cover this up? Is it dangerous?" Alex asked.

"There are a lot of these around. Me and the other guys think they are some sort of emergency escape in case of attack. Then again, they could just be nothing."

"If there's more than one, I doubt they're nothing. Do any of them lead outside?"

"Most of them do, yeah."

"Maybe they are a way for the elite to gain access to the hospital without the general public knowing about it."

"That makes sense."

"Do you know which ones lead outside the hospital?" Alex asked.

"I know several, yes. Why? Are you thinking we will need to make a run for it?"

"We have to plan for that possibility."

"If it comes to that, I can get us out. Don't worry."

Their footsteps kicked up dust but not as much as Alex expected for the hallway being abandoned. It seemed to lend weight to her idea of the hallways being used, even if it was infrequently.

Christoph bent nearly double and hid the light from the flashlight. Alex followed, walking on the balls of her feet to make as little noise as possible. Christoph pulled back on another section of wall. Instead of open space, Alex saw a metal wall.

"Ready?" Christoph whispered as he turned off the light and hung it back on his belt.

Alex nodded and placed her hands against the cold metal. Christoph held his fingers and did a countdown to three. They pushed. Alex gritted her teeth as the cabinet squealed against the floor but she admitted it wasn't nearly as loud as she was expecting. They pushed the cabinet only as far as they needed. Alex followed Christoph, squeezing between the cabinet and the wall.

Christoph was right about the room. A thick layer of dust covered a dozen or more tall filing cabinets and even more boxes. Alex breathed through her mouth to avoid getting dust in her nose. The last thing she needed was to sneeze just when she was about to sneak up on Stygian.

Just before they reached the door, Alex pulled on Christoph's arm, pulling him up short.

"The doctor behind this, he's very dangerous. He's killed people and won't hesitate to do the same to us. I have a way to stop him that will seem ridiculous and crazy to you but you have to trust me."

"A plan involving that?" he asked with a smile.

Alex looked down at the head mirror. "Yes, involving this. Please, I know this is hard. But I can't tell you more. When I spot the doctor, I'll point him out."

"What do you need me to do?"

"We'll need to take out the other two doctors before I face the one in charge. I'll need you to hold him down while I do what I need to do. And you can't let go no matter what."

Christoph looked around the room and grabbed an old fire extinguisher off the wall. Alex looked around for a weapon she could use. She found an old piece of metal that looked like it used to be a table leg. She swung it a few times to get the feel for it, then nodded at Christoph to take the lead.

He slowly opened the door and peered around. When she saw him gesture to follow, Alex made her way through the door, heart racing. She strained her ears for the slightest sound but all she could hear was the blood pounding through her head.

Christoph made his way through the unused lab area toward the populated areas. Alex had no idea the laboratory was this big. She had only seen part of it when she had attacked Doctor Haussen and assumed it wasn't much bigger than that. But comparing what she knew of the layout of the hospital and where they were at now in relation to the room directly behind the guarded doors, the laboratory must be many times the size of that one room she had seen.

Christoph moved in the general direction of the main room behind the guarded doors. Alex smiled, loving how smart he was. All of the men she had encountered in the past had been not only handsome, but also smart, which was something Alex knew she wanted in that special someone in her life.

She cringed when she thought of how much she had crushed on Beau Johnson. She had been so attracted to his looks and had overlooked his personality. At first, his arrogance had been daring and she had thought he was so hot, but over the years, she had come to know his true colors and he had grown uglier with each passing day. She hadn't even missed him much when he had walked out of her tutoring class.

I have someone better.

Alex didn't know anything about Chandon other than the fact that she knew him better than she knew herself. He was like the men from the past so Alex figured he would be kind and smart, just like they had been.

Thinking about Chandon made her worry about how long this latest excursion was taking. Days would pass here but only minutes would pass back in her time. She only hoped that trend would hold true. The last thing she needed was her mom walking in on her while she was traveling.

If all goes well, I will be home very soon.

She was so caught up thinking about Chandon that she nearly ran into Christoph's back. He had stopped, head cocked to the side. Alex was about to ask him why he stopped when she caught the sound of voices ahead.

She gripped her metal rod tighter, worried that her sweaty hands would lose their grip. There was so much that could go wrong with this plan. Alex wanted to back out, rethink things, maybe give up all together.

Get a grip, Alex!

Christoph had his ear pressed up against the door. Alex wished there was a window so she could see where the man were and what they were doing. The plan depended on taking the men by surprise. Christoph and Alex couldn't do that if they couldn't see where the men were.

The voices moved away and silence soon followed. Without hesitation, Christoph pushed the door open and threw his body behind a desk. Alex followed, nearly tripping over her feet. She kept the metal rod close to her body, knowing that if she dropped it, the men would hear it and she and Christoph would be killed.

Christoph motioned for her to stay where she was and crawled from behind the desk. Alex wanted to follow but she knew she would just be in the way. She smiled when she remembered what it had been like being in the body of Arachidamia. The woman had been strong and fierce. Alex could use a little of that right about now.

When Christoph appeared on her left, she nearly squealed in fright.

"The men are in the next room. There's a window so we can see exactly where they are."

Alex followed Christoph, hoping Stygian and the two doctors would stay where they were and not come back to this room. They crouched low and stayed underneath the bottom sill of the window. The voices were too low for Alex to be able to hear anything. She took a risk and peeked over the edge of the sill.

She spotted Stygian right away. He was standing behind the two doctors while they worked at a bench. As far as Alex could see, there were only the three men in the room.

And they had their backs to her and Christoph.

"The man standing behind the other two is the one I need."

"Okay. If we are quiet enough, we should be able to sneak up behind them and dispatch them fairly easily. Do you need this one particular man alive?"

Alex hesitated. If Stygian was dead, all her troubles would be over. But the man that Stygian was inside of would also die. And she didn't want to be responsible for his death.

"Alive is better," Alex said.

"I'll do my best. I will take out the man you need, then go after the man on the left. You go for the one on the right. We need to do this quickly so hit him on the back of the head. If they make noise, the guards will come in. This won't do much good against guns." Christoph pointed to the extinguisher.

Alex nodded.

Christoph moved through the door so quickly that Alex didn't have time to rethink her plan. She rushed after him, panic moving her forward. She wanted to keep her eyes on Stygian but the man she was supposed to dispatch was already turning to face her and Christoph.

Alex swung the heavy metal bar, eyes squeezing closed as it connected with the side of his face with a dull thwack. She hadn't swung very hard, only wanting to knock him unconscious. The man dropped like a sack of potatoes. Christoph was next to her and swinging the fire extinguisher at the other doctor. Alex winced as the extinguisher connected with much more force than she was comfortable with. But she didn't have time to worry.

She turned and was relieved to see Stygian on the floor, blood staining his white-blonde hair. Just as she reached him, he groaned and reached a feeble hand up to his head.

"Christoph, I need you!" Alex said breathlessly.

Christoph knelt next to her and used his body to keep Stygian on the floor.

"Whas going on?" Stygian's speech was slurred.

With shaking hands, Alex placed the head mirror in front of Stygian's eyes. She didn't want to recite the strange words that would send Stygian back into his own body until the other man's eyes could stay open for longer than a few seconds. Her stomach roiled and she swallowed hard. The stench coming off the man was worse than she imagined death would be.

"What are you doing with that?" Christoph asked.

"I can't tell you. But I promise you that Der Fuehrer will be safe very soon," Alex said.

She gasped as Stygian's eyes flew open and stared into her own. Pure rage and hate were all she could see in their icy blue depths. Head wound forgotten, Stygian bucked and twisted his body in a desperate attempt to throw Christoph.

"You think this is over? Do you?" Stygian snarled. "The second I get back your uncle is a dead man! And you will follow soon thereafter."

Alex closed her eyes and bit back a sob. She wished she could tell her uncle Mark that she was sorry she'd gotten him involved. She wasn't even worried about herself, at least not yet. All she could picture was her Aunt Karen's face when she was told her husband was dead. She knew Max Poder could do it and make it look like an accident. No one would ever know the truth.

I'll know.

Anger like she'd never felt flooded her veins. She wanted to punch Stygian's face until it and her hands were bloody and torn. This man had ruined her life, was threatening her family. He'd put the entire world at risk for some selfish plan and didn't care who he killed to accomplish it.

"I have friends that you can't even possibly imagine. They know about you and they know about Max Poder. If you lay a *finger* on my uncle, you will regret it." Alex leaned forward and smiled a little as she saw Stygian almost imperceptibly try to move away. "And just try to come after me. I dare you. My friends and I already have a plan."

Alex had no idea why she said what she did. She had no idea what Sean and Gavin would or could do if her uncle was killed. Probably nothing. And she had no idea what she could do to protect herself from Stygian. But the look of doubt that flickered across his eyes gave her confidence.

She held up the hand mirror and began the chant. Stygian tried to close his eyes but the minute she spoke the words, his eyes flew open.

"*Falvetch inksashekbum!*"

Alex was surprised she remembered the words. She had only used the incantation once back in Egypt, the first time she had met Sean. He had explained that it was possible to force a Traveler from a body using those words and a mirror or other reflective surface.

Stygian howled in fury. Christoph shouted in dismay as it appeared that Stygian was about to succeed in shoving Christoph to the side. But the doctor's body went limp as Stygian's spirit departed.

"Agnes, what in the world was all that about?" Christoph said as he slowly lifted himself off the now unconscious doctor.

"I can't explain. I'm sorry, Christoph."

Alex's voice sounded like it was coming from far away. Her arm came up of its own accord and the head mirror filled her vision. With a sigh, she reached out with her other hand and touched the mirror.

*   *   *

Drifter awoke in his own bed, fear and rage burning through him. He couldn't believe the girl had managed to stop him yet again. He remembered her face from encounters in the hospital and yet he never suspected her. She had managed to walk around right under his nose and he hadn't suspected a thing.

He stood and threw on some clothes. He was dreading the visit to Master. Poder would be most displeased that his pupil had failed again. The plan to restore his family name was everything to Poder. That dream slipping away would drive his Master mad.

He would have to break the news to Master. Putting it off would only make things worse. All Drifter wanted to do was find Mark Reynolds and wrap his hands around the man's throat, to feel it disintegrate beneath his grip. But unless the man was out of the brig, Drifter knew he'd never get close enough to choke the life out of Mark.

Drifter made his way to Poder's quarters knowing his commanding officer would be at home in bed at this hour of the night. *He's got to let me go after the girl, now.* The one person he wanted dead more than Mark Reynolds was the man's meddling niece, the girl who had thwarted his plans at every turn. It would be a sweet sensation, taking her life. He knocked loudly and waited for Poder to open the door.

He stepped back in shock when the door opened almost immediately. Poder was still in uniform and looked like he hadn't slept in days.

"Get in here." Poder moved to a small desk with a decanter of scotch and two glasses on top. He poured himself one, not bothering to offer one to Drifter. "Mark will be out of the brig in a few short hours. The authorities want to question you about the death of Lance Corporal Jensen. They will want a handwriting sample and that alone will prove your guilt. I suggest you leave the base immediately."

Drifter waited for Poder to mention his failure in WWII Germany. "Where shall I go?"

"Go? Does it matter?"

"I want the girl."

"You may do whatever you wish." Poder gulped down a second glass of scotch. "You need to leave immediately."

"If the CID wants me for questioning, I can't simply walk off the base."

"Then I suggest you put your skills to work and leave undetected."

"What about you?"

"Oh, I'll be fine. Now go before the MPs come looking for you."

Drifter left the house, guilt forcing his shoulders to slump. He had failed his Master miserably. Poder had never looked or sounded so dejected. Drifter considered going back inside, to offer to try again. He couldn't go back to the exact time and place he had traveled before, but he could go back to a sooner time point, try again.

You can't do anything unless the girl is out of the way.

With a renewed sense of purpose, Drifter made for a deserted part of the base to make good his escape.

Chapter 36

ALEX AWOKE standing in front of the sink in her own bathroom. She gasped and hung on, fighting the nausea that threatened to unhinge her knees.

"Alexis Davenport! If you don't open this door this instant, I'll break it down!"

Thinking quickly, Alex opened the toilet lid and seat. She fumbled with the door lock and flung open the door. Keeping up the pretense that she was ill, Alex knelt down next to the toilet.

"Why didn't you answer me?" her mom asked.

"Sorry, Mom. Having my head buried in the toilet makes it kind of difficult to talk."

"Chandon is here and waiting for you. I suppose I'll have to tell him you can't make it."

"No, I'll tell him."

Her mom nodded, then left, closing the door.

Alex cursed the timing of her return. A few more minutes and she wouldn't have had to play sick to keep her mom from breaking down the door. She had been looking forward to the date with Chandon for so long. Now she had another reason to hate Stygian.

Stygian.

She very nearly vomited for real when the realization hit her that she may be dead very soon and wouldn't be going on any dates with anyone. Ever.

Alex hurried to the living room and she nearly wept when she saw Chandon Rose standing there talking to her mom. He looked completely at ease. When he spotted her, his eyes held nothing but concern.

"Guess you're not over the stomach bug, huh?" he asked.

Alex held her hands over her stomach and shook her head. "I'm really sorry. Maybe some other time?"

As Alex stood there, the impact of what she had done hit her like a bolt of lightning. Her legs started shaking and her vision narrowed. *I think I might faint.* She almost laughed at the calm voice. Her legs buckled and she pitched forward, right into Chandon's arms.

"Let me help you to the couch."

Alex barely heard his voice and was too distracted by the terror threatening to choke her to register that she was in his arms. She needed to get rid of him and get back to her room so she could email Gavin and text Jenn. And she had to somehow find a way to contact her uncle to warn him.

"Alex, do we need to go to the hospital?"

Her mom's suggestions broke through her fear. The last thing she needed was to be in a hospital room away from her computer and phone.

"I'm okay. Just weak I think. Haven't been able to eat much the last few days," she said.

"Are you sure? You could have something worse than just a stomach bug," her mom said.

"Mom, don't overreact. I have been puking for days. It's a wonder I didn't pass out sooner than this."

"There's been some stuff going around school," Chandon said.

Alex could have kissed him. Her mom glanced at Chandon and nodded. "Well, it's off to bed with you, young lady. And if you aren't showing signs of improvement by tomorrow, I'll take you in to see the doctor."

Alex nodded, eager to be back in her room. She regretted not being able to go on a date but her life was in danger. She didn't have time to waste indulging in a romantic evening out.

She got off the couch slowly, still acting the part, but moving more confidently than she had before. "See? I don't feel faint anymore. I'm fine," she said as her mom reached out to her.

"I'll see you Monday at school," Chandon said as he made his way to the front door.

"I'm so sorry about this,' Alex said.

"It's no big. We'll plan something for next weekend."

If I'm even alive next weekend. "Sure thing!" Alex said a little too cheerfully, trying to beat down the morbid thought threatening to unhinge her legs again.

Her heart hurt as she watched Chandon walk out the front door. The unfairness of it all made her want to scream and throw something. All she wanted was to go out on a date and be a normal girl for the first time since she had found out she could travel back in time. She didn't think it was too much to ask for. Apparently, the universe had other plans.

"Off to bed with you."

Alex nodded to her mom and walked slowly back to her room, fighting the urge to sprint. Every second counted. For all she knew, Stygian was on some military jet on his way to kill her right now. And Alex knew it wasn't a very long flight from Camp Pendleton to Grand Junction.

She grabbed her phone off the desk and carried it to her bed. Her fingers shook so badly she could barely dial Gavin's number. Tears filled her eyes, blurring her vision.

"Alex! Is everything okay?"

At hearing Gavin's voice, she finally gave in to her emotions. She somehow managed to tell Gavin about Stygian's plan, his defeat, and his threat. She hoped her mom couldn't hear her through the closed door.

"What do I do? He's going to come here and kill me. How can I fight a guy that's military trained?" Alex asked.

"You can't. You don't fight, Alex. You run."

"Run where? And what about mom and Karen? My friends? Do I bring them all with me?"

"There's no plan yet, Alex. I need time to think—"

"I don't *have* time! For all I know he could be on his way here right now."

Alex fought the urge to throw her phone against the wall. She had hoped Gavin would tell her exactly what to do. A mad man was coming for her, had probably already killed her uncle, and the one man she counted on to help her had no idea what to do.

"I know, Alex and I'm sorry. I wish I had an answer. My first instinct is to have you come with Sean and I to Scotland. He'll never find you there. But you don't have a passport and we can't wait for you to get one." Gavin sighed loudly. "You're right about your family and friends.

Do they all come? And for how long? And what do we tell them? The truth? A lie? What if they suggest calling the police? I doubt we could convince them of your ability to travel through time."

Alex lay back against the headboard, the enormity of what she faced weighing on her shoulders. Gavin was right. There was no easy answer. She had been so focused on how Stygian was going to ruin her life that she hadn't considered the implications to those around her and that there was no easy answer.

"I don't know. I hadn't thought of all that. All I can think about is my uncle lying dead in a jail cell."

"This is all so unfair. A girl your age should never have to deal with this. But you are not alone, Alex. Do you hear me? You are *not alone*! Stygian will have to get through Sean and I before he gets to you. I'll die before I let him touch you."

His words brought another fresh onslaught of tears. Some of the terror left with the conviction in his voice and she felt a little better.

"Is there any way for me to contact my uncle?" she asked.

"I don't think so. I will look into it and see what I can find but unless he's out of the brig, I doubt he can have phone calls."

Alex sighed miserably. "I thought so."

"Try to get some rest and I'll call you in the morning. I doubt Stygian can come after you tonight. People can't just up and leave a military base whenever they feel like it. It will take a little time for Stygian and Poder to come up with a plan that won't arouse suspicions."

"I guess so. But being in the military didn't stop them from killing someone and framing my uncle."

"I promise that I will have a plan by tomorrow."

They said their good-byes and Alex hung up. She called Jenn next.

"Oh my God, Alex, what are you going to do? Are you really going to wait for tomorrow? I know Gavin is old and wise and all but I wouldn't put it past this Stygian guy to say 'screw it' to military protocol," Jenn said.

"I agree. But what do I do? I had to play sick so it's not like I can leave the house."

"Alex, you may have to leave anyway. You can deal with being grounded after this guy is stopped."

"How do I stop him? Let's face it. The only way this will be over is if Stygian and Poder are dead. Are you going to be the one to do it?" Alex asked.

"If it was my life on the line, I think I could, yeah," Jenn said hesitantly.

"And how do I go up against two grown men with all that military training? Stygian could probably kill me without me even seeing him."

"You gotta tell your mom, Alex. Seriously. You guys all have to get the hell out."

"If we *do* manage to kill them, what then? You think we can just walk away and live life happily ever after? We'll go to jail, Jenn," Alex's voice broke.

"I don't know. Maybe your uncle can help once he's free—"

"My uncle is probably dead already!" Alex sobbed.

"Oh, Alex, I don't know what to do or how to help. Do you want me to sneak over? Run away with you? Say the word and it's done."

Alex chuckled through her tears. "Thanks, Jenn."

"I'm serious about running away. You can't stay there and hope that someone else figures things out. He could be on his way right now."

"I know. But running away?" Alex bit her lip, fear clenching her abdominal muscles and making her feel queasy.

"You travel back in time and you worry about packing a bag and taking off?" Jenn asked.

"Where would we go?"

"I don't know. Maybe Amy's house?"

"I guess so. But that could put her at risk. And what do I do about mom? I bet he would kill her too."

Jenn sighed. "This is why you just need to fess up. It's the only way to keep her safe."

"I'd have to tell Karen too. If he knows where I live, he'll know where Mark and Karen live."

"If only we could call your uncle and see if Stygian is still on base," Jenn said.

Alex sat up. "I can't call my uncle but I can damn sure travel and try to find out."

"Don't you end up back in the past somewhere? How will that help us? You need to know if he's there *now*."

"I have to do *something*! Maybe I can try to focus on traveling back only a few hours or something."

"Yeah, I guess. Just seems like a waste of time."

Alex wanted to push the idea but she knew Jenn was right. She was putting off the decision to tell her mom her secret and putting off leaving home to run for their lives.

She sat back against her bed and closed her eyes. She hated to admit it, but she had to come up with a decision on her own. No one was going to come swooping in to save the day. It was all on her shoulders. Alex glanced out the window at the deepening shadows and decided to wait until the next day to make a decision about what she was going to do.

*   *   *

Chandon walked dejectedly to his car. He had been looking forward to his date with Alex and having to cancel bummed him out.

There was something about Alex he couldn't quite put his finger on. He had felt it the moment he laid eyes on her. It was like he'd known her his whole life, that he knew all her deepest secrets. Every fiber of his being wanted to be near her.

His instincts screamed that there was something going on that didn't add up. It was perfectly believable that Alex had a stomach bug and was not feeling well enough to go out. Her demeanor seemed to suggest that as well.

Yet he didn't believe her. And he didn't know why.

As he sat in the car gazing at Alex's front door, he thought there was another explanation for her "symptoms." And even though he couldn't prove it, he knew that he was right.

Alex hadn't been ill; she'd been terrified.

*   *   *

Mark stared at Matt Schmidt, his lawyer, unable to believe his ears.

"Did you hear what I just said? You're a free man."

"How? I thought it was going to take a while to get through the evidence."

SHAY WEST

"All they needed was to compare handwriting and your hand size to the bruises on the Lance Corporal Jensen's throat. That alone is enough to prove you didn't kill her. There isn't enough evidence to hold you."

Mark sat in the interview room, the same one he sat in when he had first been arrested. He knew he would be found innocent, he just didn't think it would be this quick.

"What about Lane Stygian? Did you check on him?" Mark asked.

Matt rubbed the back of his head and looked uncomfortable. "It appears he has gone AWOL. The MPs are searching the base but no one has seen him for hours."

Mark jumped up. "I have to get out of here. My niece is in danger."

Matt gave Mark a sideways look. "Why would your niece be in danger?"

"I can't explain. You would take me and lock me up in a loony bin. But trust me when I say that Stygian is going after my niece." Mark paced the small room.

"You are free to leave any time you want. If Lane Stygian presents a danger to your niece, then you need to call the local authorities."

Mark nodded. "Thanks for everything. And don't forget what I told you about Max Poder. He's behind all of this. Someone needs to keep an eye on him."

"I don't see how we can do anything without direct evidence linking him to Lance Corporal Jensen's death," Matt said.

"Then we'll have to find some," Mark said as he walked out if the interview room.

It seemed to take hours to get his possessions back and to make his way back to his quarters. It seemed as though everyone he passed had heard about his release and wanted to offer their congratulations. By the time Mark reached his home, he was nearly ready to scream at the next person that tried to stop him.

He dialed Alex's number, praying he wasn't too late.

Chapter 37

ALEX GRABBED her ringing phone and nearly flung it back on the bed when the number showed up as one she didn't recognize. But something stopped her. She gripped the phone and swiped her finger across the screen.

"Hello?"

"Alex! Alex, it's me!"

Alex cried out and put her hand over her mouth. She couldn't believe she was hearing his voice.

"Uncle Mark! Is that really you?"

"Yes, it's me. Alex, I don't have time. You have to get out of there, leave town. Stygian has been missing since yesterday. He could be in Grand Junction already."

Alex couldn't breathe. Her mouth opened and closed but nothing came out.

"Alex? Did you hear what I said?"

She nodded, blissfully unaware that her uncle was hundreds of miles away and couldn't see her. She knew she should be feeling something, but her body was completely numb. Her heart was steadily beating, her breathing was even, and her mind was completely at ease. It didn't make sense. She should be gibbering in terror and running for her life. Yet here she sat.

"Say something! Are you still there?"

The fear in her uncle's voice broke through the fog.

"I'm here. What do I do, Uncle Mark?"

"I don't know! But you need to leave town. Stygian knows where you live."

"How can he know where mom and I live?"

"Alex, listen to me. Even if he doesn't know exactly where your house is, he can find it. Trust me on this."

"What about Karen and mom? I can't leave them here. Stygian would hurt them just to get to me."

"I hadn't thought about that." The phone went silent for a few minutes. "Alex, you may have to tell them both what's going on."

"They'll never believe me," Alex said miserably.

"Wait, I think I have an idea. What if I told them that the guy that killed Lance Corporal Jensen is angry at me for some reason and told me that he was coming after all of you? Karen and your mom would believe that and your secret would still be safe."

"That might work. Can you call them? They're at the stores. I'm supposed to be heading that way in a few hours."

"No, you need to get out and get out now. Call Jenn and have her come get you. I'll call your mom and Karen."

"Sean and Gavin are here too."

"Then call them and leave Jenn out of it. I'd feel better knowing you're with two adults."

"Okay. Where do I go?" Alex glanced around her room wondering what she should take with her.

"I don't know. Anywhere but in Grand Junction. Maybe head west, Utah or something. I'll send word to the local authorities to be on the look-out for Stygian. Hopefully someone will spot him and he'll be arrested before he can get anywhere near you."

Alex didn't think her uncle sounded very hopeful about that. "Where can I reach you?"

Mark rattled off his number. "I want to hear from you at least three times a day. Call your mom as soon as you are heading out of town. Now, pack a bag and hurry! He could already be in Grand Junction and it won't take him long to find you."

Alex stared at the phone. Her pulse pounded in her ears and her stomach was clenched so tight Alex feared she would vomit. Despite her uncle's advice, she dialed Jenn, voice shaking as she filled her in.

"Pack your stuff. I'm on my way."

"Your mom is never going to let you just up and leave town," Alex said.

"I don't really think we need to be concerned with getting in trouble. I'll gladly serve my punishment when this is all over."

"Jenn, I.... I mean, I just..." Alex couldn't get the words out.

"It's okay. I know. Now get moving. And call Sean and Gavin!"

Alex dialed Gavin's number and told him everything her uncle had said.

"Jenn's on her way right now," Alex finished breathlessly.

"That's good. Listen, why don't you two meet us at the hotel, and we can get on the interstate from there?"

"Okay. We'll see you soon."

Alex jumped off her bed, the full impact of what her uncle told her hitting her like a physical blow. She slumped to the ground and sobbed, terror stealing any desire to move. She knew moving meant saving her life but her muscles wouldn't obey what her mind was trying to tell her. Exhaustion threatened to overwhelm her. She hadn't slept at all the night before. Every creak and sigh of the wind kept her awake, certain that each noise meant certain danger.

Get a grip, Alex!

The voice in her head sounded like her uncle. She reached under her bed for the small suitcase and jammed it as full of clothes as she possibly could. She had no idea how long she would be gone or where she would be going so she packed some warm clothing and some for chilly days and nights.

She lugged the suitcase out to the living room and sat it by the front door. Alex grabbed her purse and hastily counted how much cash she had. *I'll have to run to an ATM before we head out of town.*

Nervous energy coursing through her veins kept her from sitting for longer than a few seconds at a time. Alex paced the living room, debating on whether or not she should call her mom. Mark said he would take care of it and Alex wasn't sure she could handle hearing her mom's voice while in this fragile state. It would likely send her into another fit of hysterics and she had to remain focused. *Time to fall apart later.*

Her phone rang and she jumped and squealed in fright. *It's probably just Jenn or mom.*

She swiped her finger across the screen without paying attention to the number calling her, wondering what she was going to say if her mom was on the other end.

"Hello?"

A stealthy chuckle. "So... I get to hear your voice at last."

Chapter 38

"**WHAT'S WRONG?** Cat got your tongue?" More laughter.

Alex wanted to hang up, refuse to listen, but her arm was locked in place, with the phone covering her ear.

"You don't have to speak. Just listen. I have been waiting a long time for this." Delighted sounding sigh. "I am coming for you. Just got into town, as a matter of fact." Diabolical laughter. "And if you think I don't know where you live, think again." Voice hard as nails. "Killing you will be such a sweet treat. I have dreamed of snapping your neck with my bare hands. Looks like I'll finally get the chance." More laughter. "See you soon."

The phone dropped from Alex's hand. She didn't even flinch when it hit the floor. Part of her knew she needed to leave, get out of the house, but her body seemed incapable of moving. She couldn't even feel her chest rise and fall with each breath. *Can people really die from not breathing when they are terrified?*

Get a grip, Alex!

The voice brought her to her feet, though her knees wobbled so badly she could barely move. She grabbed her phone out of her purse and dialed Jenn's number with shaking hands.

"Jenn! Where are you?"

"I haven't finished packing yet. Alex, what's wrong?"

"He called me! Stygian called me and said he's coming, he's in town and he's on his way, Jenn, he could be at my house right now. Why aren't you here, why did you take so long to pack?" Alex paced the living room and ran her hands through her hair.

"I'll leave right now. It's okay, it's going to be okay—"

"No, no, no, there's no time," Alex mumbled, shaking her head. "He's on his way, he said he was. I have to get out now, hide somewhere."

"Alex, where are you going to hide?"

"Don't know, don't know, but I have to go right now. Yes, I have to leave and hide so he can't find me..."

"Alex," Jenn said slowly. "You need to calm down. I am in my car and turning it on. I'll drive faster than I've ever driven before. Do you hear me? Stay where you are. Call Sean and Gavin. Alex? Alex!"

"Can't stay, have to leave. Right now." Alex hung up the phone.

Her mind was in a fog. The only coherent thought blaring through her head was to leave, hide, run. The thought of staying was out of the question. Alex grabbed her purse, and shoved her phone inside, completely forgetting Jenn's sensible orders to call Gavin.

She ran out the front door, with no idea at all where she was going. Alex spun in a circle, hoping some brilliant idea would come to her. Several people were walking their dogs. On her right, a neighbor was putting his trash can out on the curb. On her left a little girl and boy were riding their bikes down the sidewalk, her in a pink helmet, him in one made to look like Iron Man. Their giggles echoed in the relative quiet of the neighborhood. The nice, normal neighborhood. No one knew her secret. No one knew what was coming for her. Alex saw all the people on her street and had never felt so alone.

The sun was crawling behind the Colorado National Monument, bathing the area in warm golds and pinks. Alex wondered if this was going to be her last sunset. Tears fell down her cheeks. She wanted to run to the nearest adult and beg them to help her. A murdering maniac was coming for her and the only thing she could think of was to stand in the street and stare at the normal things going on around her.

Alex turned back around to stare at the mountains behind her and an idea blossomed in her mind like a growing fire. It probably wasn't the best plan but it was all she had at the moment. Without giving herself time to change her mind, Alex took off running the couple of blocks to her aunt's house.

I hope I can remember where to find it.

* * *

Drifter steered the stolen truck down toward Alex's neighborhood. It was the third vehicle he had taken since running away from the Marine base. His skills made stealing money and vehicles easy. The drunk outside the bar that owned the truck didn't even know what hit him. Drifter didn't regret killing the man. But it had taken time and had been messy. Two things Drifter didn't like. But he didn't really care. All he cared about was killing Alex.

He had stolen another vehicle just outside of Grand Junction that had an extra bonus: a working cell phone in the glove box. Drifter took the slip of paper out of his pocket that had the girl's home address and cell phone number on it. This time he thanked his access to information that made getting the numbers and addresses all too easy. Calling the girl to torment her had been almost as sweet as killing Lance Corporal Jensen.

Drifter checked his map again and turned, almost hitting another vehicle when he spotted his quarry running up the street. He shook his head, unable to believe his good fortune. Rather than scaring her off, Drifter turned onto a side street and made a U-turn. He grinned when he saw where Alex was going.

Surely she should know Auntie isn't home.

*   *   *

Chandon drove to Alex's house. He hadn't been able to stop thinking about her since he had left yesterday. He had her number on his phone but he hesitated with his thumb over the little green phone icon that would actually dial it. If he asked Alex what was wrong she would only lie and say nothing. The only way for him to get the truth from her was to see her face-to-face. He was sick with worry for her and he couldn't even put his finger on why. But with each passing moment, he feared he would lose her.

Suddenly, he spotted her trotting around the side of a house, heading up into the Monument. The car lurched to a stop as he stomped on the brakes. Chandon rolled down the window, ready to shout for her but he closed his mouth when he saw she wasn't alone. Chandon grabbed his cell phone off the passenger seat.

Who is that guy following her?

Chapter 39

ALEX RAN UNTIL her breath came in gasps. She slowed down as she got near her aunt's house. She would have to save her strength for climbing up into the mountains. Just as she rounded the corner of her aunt's house, she thought she heard someone calling her name. Alex shook her head, certain she was hearing things.

She wondered if Mark had been able to reach her aunt and her mom at the stores. Alex hoped Stygian wouldn't go anywhere near downtown. She didn't think she could take it if he did anything to her aunt or her mom.

Alex stopped and stared at the familiar path she had walked so many times with her friends. She wished more than anything they were here with her now. Simon with his ready jokes would ease the stress of the moment. Paul, with his imposing height, would make her feel safe. And Amy's quiet presence would ease her mind.

And Jenn. The one who actually knew her secret. She was the one Alex wished was with her right now. Terror stole her breath and threatened to overwhelm her as she walked up the dirt path, hoping and praying that she could remember the way to the secret cave Paul had shown the group years ago.

She grabbed her phone out of her purse and dialed Gavin's number. Alex looked to the left and right, certain she could feel Stygian's eyes on her.

"Alex? Where are you? Jenn just called and told me what happened."

"I'm heading up into the mountains." Her breath came in gasps as she climbed higher. "Paul showed us this secret cave. If I can get there and hide, Stygian can't find me."

"And what then? How are any of us supposed to find you?"

"Call Jenn and have Paul bring you guys to the cave to come get me. We can sneak out when it's dark and leave."

"I'm not sure I like this plan, Alex."

"It's a little late for that since I'm already on my way to the cave." Alex didn't dare mention that she wasn't certain she could find it after all this time.

"I'll call Jenn and we'll come to get you."

"Wait until it's dark! And don't come from anywhere near my house or Aunt Karen's. He could be watching and he'll just follow you. Paul will know how to get to the cave from a spot Stygian won't be watching."

"It won't be full dark for hours yet. Are you sure you'll be okay?"

Alex's eyes teared up at the worry in his voice. "I'll be fine. There's no way Stygian will ever guess I'm up here. I'll see you guys soon."

* * *

Drifter followed Alex through the mountains on silent feet. His tread barely disturbed the dirt as he made his way up into the mountains. He had no idea where the girl was going but he couldn't have picked a better place to kill her than the solitude of the sandstone hills surrounding them. She had gone off the trail and was making her way deeper into the mountains, stopping every so often to check landmarks and glance around like she was lost.

Curiosity kept Drifter from killing the girl. He wanted to know where she was going. Alex didn't act like she was just running scared; she acted like she was looking for something, or some place. The further they got from the houses below the more excited Drifter became. He could kill her, hide her body in one of a thousand crevasses, and she would never be found. He would finally pay her back for ruining his Master's plans.

Chapter 40

ALEX PAUSED and glanced around at the terrain. Her heart sank. Nothing looked familiar. The sun would be all the way down soon and then she would be out here in the wilderness in the dark. Where there were wild animals ready to devour or envenom her.

She wanted to sit down and cry but she forced her feet to keep walking, certain that something would look familiar. Suddenly, her skin crawled in a familiar sensation and she felt nauseous. A sound like falling rocks came from behind her. Alex whirled.

It can't be!

* * *

Drifter smiled at the look of terror on the girl's face. It sent his blood racing through his veins. His hands clenched, eager to squeeze the life out of her. He had hoped to confront her further along but as it was almost dark, he thought it was fortuitous that he had slipped on the sandstone rocks underfoot. He wanted to look into her eyes when life faded from them.

* * *

Alex looked around, praying that there would be someone, anyone close by but she and Stygian were alone. The way he walked, it was like a predator. His eyes never left hers. Stygian came closer and Alex couldn't do anything but stand there and stare into his eyes. She wanted to run, to scream, but her body was in such a state of terror that she had lost complete control.

She wondered if Gavin, Jenn, and Paul were in the area. *You aren't anywhere close to the hidden cave.* That thought made her shoulders slump. Paul would lead Gavin and Jenn right to his secret cave and Stygian would kill her in this spot and no one would ever find her. Alex knew that line of thinking should send her into hysterics but her body still seemed incapable of responding in a normal fashion.

When Stygian was only a few steps away her body finally decided to move. But it was too late. At the same time she took a step back, Stygian swept her legs out from under her. She landed with a thud that forced the air from her lungs. Her purse went flying. She could hear the contents spilling on the rocks.

"I am going to enjoy this," Drifter said as he straddled her middle.

Alex tried to fight him off but he was too strong. He knelt on her arms, scraping the skin off. She managed to scream once before his hands closed around her throat. With the man on her arms, she couldn't fight.

Suddenly, she was back in Agy's body. Only instead of a pillow stealing her breath it was hands wrapped around her throat. She twisted side-to-side, bucking her body, trying to throw him off. All he did was laugh. Spots danced in front of her eyes as Stygian cut off her air supply. Terror worse than she had felt when she was Agy filled her. There would be no coming back from this. There would be no void, no body to return to. Stygian was going to kill her and she would be gone forever.

Alex was surprised at how angry she was despite the fear of dying. It wasn't fair. She had never been asked if she wanted to have the gift of time travel, to save the world, to have her life turned upside down. All she wanted was to be a normal girl, finish high school, go to prom, get her driver's license, go on dates, go to college, meet the man of her dreams, become the curator of the Smithsonian, and live to a ripe old age.

She would never have the chance.

*   *   *

Alex's eyes widened as she saw something come at Stygian from behind. *It can't be him!* The boy she was supposed to have a date with appeared like some hero out of a fairy tale. Chandon swung something at Stygian and the man fell backward with a cry.

Alex choked and gagged, sucking in the sweet air through a bruised throat. She rolled to the side and coughed into the dirt. The relief at being able to draw a breath pushed all other thoughts aside.

"Alex, are you okay?"

She let his arms pick her up. It hurt so bad to breathe! *I just need to rest.*

"It's me. Open your eyes."

Alex forced her eyes open. *It's not possible!* She tried to speak but her throat was too raw. She swallowed a few times but that only seemed to make it worse.

"Chandon?" she managed to croak.

"Yeah, it's me. Can you stand? We gotta get you down the mountain and to a doctor."

Alex managed to gain her feet with Chandon's help but the motion made her cough so badly she nearly passed out. When she spotted Stygian lying on the ground, she cried out in a guttural, hoarse cry and nearly fell over trying to get away.

"It's okay, he's not going anywhere."

Alex nodded and let Chandon lead her away. Before they got a few steps, she stopped and pointed toward where her purse lay on the ground. Chandon nodded. Alex watched as he gathered what he could find and bring it to her. She checked her phone and wilted when she noticed she didn't have a signal.

"We can call when we get down a little ways," Chandon said.

Alex stumbled down the mountain, throat so raw she wondered if it was bleeding. It was hard to fight the urge to swallow every five seconds but swallowing made her want to pass out. She peered behind them certain Stygian would be coming after them.

"You don't happen to have a flashlight do you?" Chandon asked.

Alex shook her head. It was full dark and the moon wasn't bright enough to light their way. The Monument, so beautiful during the day, was treacherous at night. One wrong step and both of them would end up with broken bones or cracked skulls.

"It's not a flashlight, but I guess it'll do in a pinch." Chandon held out his phone.

The cell phone provided barely enough light to see. Alex checked her phone and as soon as she had a single bar, she dialed Jenn's number and gave the phone to Chandon.

"Wait, what do I say?" Chandon asked.

Alex pointed to her throat and back up the trail. She tried to speak but doubled over in a fit of coughing.

"Hello? Hello, this is...no, my name isn't...if you'd let me explain..." Chandon looked at Alex helplessly.

She could hear Jenn's voice screeching through her cell phone but she couldn't hear what she was saying. It would be funny if she wasn't sitting on this rock coughing so badly she was about to pass out. Alex motioned for Chandon to give her the phone. She grabbed it and hung up on Jenn, then quickly sent a text telling Jenn that Chandon was the one that called because she couldn't talk.

When Chandon called back, the conversation went a little more smoothly although Chandon didn't know some of the answers to Jenn's questions and Alex wasn't able to answer.

I wish I would have brought some water with me.

"Alex, are you close to Paul's hidden cave?" Chandon asked.

Alex shrugged.

"She doesn't know." He paused and nodded. "That would be great except neither one of us has a flashlight." Chandon rolled his eyes and pulled the phone away from his ear as Jenn yelled. "I wasn't planning on a trip into the mountains at night. If you want to yell at someone for not bringing a flashlight, yell at Alex."

Alex croaked laughter and fought down the coughing fit about to ensue.

"Oh great, so if you guys have a flashlight, why don't *you* shine it up into the air instead of yelling about us not having one?" Chandon said.

Chandon walked a little ways off and stood on a large rock, getting a better view of the surrounding area. She could barely make him out in the darkness. Alex hoped she wasn't too far off course. She needed to find her friends and get off this mountain.

"Hey, *hey!* I see them!" Chandon waved his arms, jumped off the rock, and trotted off in the direction of the light that Alex could barely see off to the left. In a few minutes, she heard familiar voices. Jenn was at the front, running so fast Alex feared the girl would trip and break her head open. Jenn threw herself at Alex, her tears wetting the side of Alex's neck.

Alex held Jenn and sobbed, though it hurt like hell. The sobs tore from her ravaged throat but there was nothing Alex could do to stop it. A vision of Stygian lying on the ground, his face bloody and torn made her cry all the harder. She wondered if he was dead or if he was on his way to them right now to finish the job.

"It's okay, don't try to talk," Jenn said.

Alex shook her head and forced the words out. "Stygian, up trail." Alex pointed in the direction she and Chandon had come from.

"Gavin has already been in contact with the police," Jenn glanced at where Gavin stood with Paul and Chandon. "For now, he wants us to keep up the crazy Marine on the loose act and keep quiet about the time travel thing. Cops wouldn't believe it anyway," Jenn whispered.

"Cops, coming here?" Alex said.

"I think so. Gavin is having Paul explain to them how to get up here. He's got his fancy GPS thingy. Thank God, or else we could be up here all night."

Gavin ran up to the girls. "Alex, thank God you're all right. Chandon is going to take me to where he thinks Stygian is. If he hit the man as hard as he said he did, he's probably still up there and unconscious. But I don't want to take the chance that Stygian will leave before the cops get here."

Alex nodded. "Careful," she croaked.

"We will be. Stay here and try not to talk. Jenn, help her drink some water."

Alex wanted to gulp the water but her throat felt like it was the size of a straw and would only allow a tiny bit past the injury. After she sipped a little, Alex put the bottle against her throat. The cold eased the throbbing a little.

"What in the heck is going on here, Alex? Why would some Marine come after you?"

Alex glanced up at Paul. His face was lit by the GPS unit he held in his hand.

"Don't know. But he killed a girl and framed my uncle." Alex was relieved that it was easier to speak. It still hurt but at least she was able to say a few words without coughing.

Paul shook his head. "It's so bizarre, like something out of a movie. Hey, maybe Simon and I can write a screenplay!"

Alex chuckled at his enthusiasm. Part of her wanted to come clean and tell Paul everything but it had become so much easier to keep the secret.

"What about mom?" Alex asked.

"Gavin told her and your aunt that he was on his way to get you and for them to wait at your house in case Stygian got away," Jenn said.

"I should call, let her know I'm okay."

Alex called her mom and had to fight the tears at the fear in her mother's voice. She assured her that everything was fine, that Chandon had come in like a knight in shining armor and saved her from the bad guy.

"I still can't believe this guy came after you. Why would he do something like that?" Patricia asked.

Alex thought quickly, something she was getting used to. "While he had me down, he said he was coming after you and Karen too, that there was nowhere you could hide."

"It's terrifying is what it is. And who's this Gavin character? Mark says he's a friend of his but Karen doesn't recall ever hearing his name before."

"I don't know where they know each other either. But I'm glad Uncle Mark has such good friends." Alex was glad her uncle was as good at coming up with lies as she herself was.

"Yeah, me too."

Her mom didn't sound convinced so Alex changed the subject. "I think the cops are here so I gotta go. I'll let you know which hospital they take me to so you and Karen can come down, okay?"

"I can't believe it. This guy nearly chokes the life out of you and you are the one that's all calm and collected while I'm a complete mess. When did you grow up?"

Alex smiled. "I guess it's the shock. See you soon."

Alex couldn't tell her mom that she had survived death several times already so she was sort of used to it. If she did spill her guts, her mom wouldn't let her leave the house until she was forty.

"I know it's probably too soon but I am so excited to get back home so I can write all this down. As soon as you're up for it I plan on picking your brain for every last detail of your flight into the mountains." Jenn glanced at Alex. "How do you feel now that it's over?"

Alex opened her mouth but shut it before answering. *Over. Could it really be?* She had wanted that for so long, to be free of time travel so she could live a normal life. Now that it looked like that might happen

Alex didn't know how to feel about it. Time travel had become such a big part of her life that it would be strange to be able to look into a mirror without the fear of traveling back in time and facing Stygian hanging over her shoulder.

She looked up at Jenn. "To be honest, Jenn, I don't know how I feel."

Chapter 41

"LOOKS LIKE SOME deep bruising in the neck and arms but no broken bones or cartilage. You're one lucky young lady," the doctor said.

Alex sat on the hospital bed, her mom on one side, Jenn and Chandon on the other. Alex gave her statement to the police, though it hurt her throat to talk so much. The cops thanked her and said they would be in touch at a later date.

"Where is Stygian?" Alex asked.

The doctor smiled sympathetically. "You don't have to worry about him. He's unconscious and will be for quite some time. The Marine base is sending some men to guard him and they should be here later today."

"But what if he escapes? He got away from a base that had a lot more men than just a few guards." A vision of Stygian prowling around her house made her skin crawl.

"Trust me. Stygian isn't going anywhere. Your friend there," the doctor pointed to Chandon, "hurt him pretty badly."

"How badly?" Alex asked.

"I'm sorry but I'm not allowed to discuss that. Against the privacy rules. I'll be back shortly to check on you." The doctor left.

"Hey mom, we could really use some snacks. Would you mind?" Alex asked.

"Sure. I'll go see what they have in the cafeteria."

Alex waited until her mom was out of earshot. "I need to know what's wrong with Stygian."

"You heard the doctor. There's no way to find out," Jenn said.

"He only said he couldn't tell me. But if Stygian is here, we can try to get a look in his room, maybe his chart or something."

"How are we going to do that if he's under guard?" Chandon asked.

"There are no guards yet. And mom will be back so we don't have much time."

Alex hopped off the bed and the trio walked to the door. "By the way, where are Paul and Gavin?"

"Down at the police station. I guess they have your uncle and some guys at the base chatting through a computer about Stygian and the girl he killed. Gavin said he would text me as soon as they were done," Jenn said.

"So which direction do we go?" Chandon asked.

"I have no idea."

Actually, Alex *did* have an idea but she couldn't tell Chandon about it. She was going to follow her instincts, that strange feeling she got whenever she was close to Stygian, and let them lead her to the evil Traveler.

Jenn and Chandon followed her without a word. Whether by divine intervention or just plain luck, no one stopped them as they wandered the hallway. It helped that Alex walked with a confident air, the tight feeling in her belly growing with every step she took toward Stygian.

She stopped in front of a closed door and peeked through the window. She could see Stygian on the bed. At least, she thought it was him. Between the gauze and enormous amount of tubes, she couldn't see his face.

"It's him, it's on the chart," Jenn said.

"What else does it say?" Alex asked, unable to look away from the window.

"It's all technical. Something about deep lacerations to the eyes, fracturing of the supraorbital ridge, nasal bones, lacrimal bones, zygomatic process, occipital bone...I don't even know what all that is."

"His eyes, front of his face, side of his face, and back of his head are damaged," Alex said.

"How do you know all that?" Jenn asked.

"I took anatomy, remember?"

"It also says something about medically induced coma, swelling of the occipital lobe, and blindness."

That last part made Alex turn around. "Blindness? Are you sure?"

"That's what it says."

"Do you know what this means?" Alex asked excitedly.

Jenn stared at her, eyes darting to the right where Chandon stood. "Yeah, it means the guy's blind."

"That's right. Which is exactly what he deserves." Alex mentally chided herself.

Chandon squinted. "What's going on? Alex, you were way too excited at the thought that this guy might be blind. I know he hurt you and I don't necessarily regret whacking him upside the head but even my stomach feels queasy thinking about what I did. How can it not bother you?"

"Because it's not the first time he's come after me!" Alex snapped.

"What do you mean it's not the first time? You need to let the cops know so they can put him away for even longer."

Alex turned and walked away from Stygian's room. This was not a conversation she wanted to be having but she'd spoken out of anger and frustration. Chandon had no idea what she'd been through.

She stopped short when Chandon grabbed her arm. "I risked my neck coming after you and I am the one who did that damage to Stygian. I think I have a right to know what's going on. It's way more complicated than him being some rogue Marine out for a joy ride to come kill you, isn't it?"

Alex tried to look away but the concern in his brown eyes rooted her to the spot.

"You'd never believe me even if I told you," she said.

"Try me."

"Look, we're attracting an audience. Let's go back to the room and wait for your mom," Jenn suggested, pointing to the nurses taking notice of the trio.

Alex walked back to her room, rehearsing what she would tell Chandon in her head. No matter how she tried it, she feared he would laugh at her and walk away. And she'd never see him again.

But if I don't tell him he may walk away.

She breathed a sigh of relief when her mom walked into the room just moments after they returned.

"Thanks for the snacks, Mom."

"The doctor said you can go home just as soon as I fill out some more paperwork. I'll be right back, okay?"

Once her mom was gone, Chandon turned on her.

"Out with it. I mean it, Alex. I deserve to know what's going on."

Alex looked and Jenn, who only shrugged.

"Okay, but you have to promise me that whatever you hear you don't say one word to anyone, even if you don't believe me. Got it?"

Chandon nodded and sat in the chair, and didn't say a word. Alex took a deep breath and began to tell her story.

Chapter 42

ALEX TOOK A DRINK of water. She had hurried the story of her ability to time travel as she didn't want her mom to walk in right in the middle of it. She searched Chandon's eyes for any sign that he believed her or if he thought she was crazy but the expression on his face never changed.

"So that guy Stygian was the one coming after you in time?" Chandon asked, speaking for the first time since they entered Alex's hospital room.

"Yes, but he has a Master, someone who he was taking orders from. He's someone very high up in the Marines," Alex said.

"Won't he come after you?"

"I don't know. In all the rush to get away from Stygian, I never thought to ask Uncle Mark about Max Poder." Alex met Chandon's eyes. "You're not running away screaming or rushing off to tell people I'm nuts."

"Well, you *are* nuts. Mainly for keeping this a secret for so long. Stygian could have killed you and you chose to face him alone. I'd say that's pretty nuts."

"I'm not alone. I have Jenn, and Sean and Gavin. Besides, most people would never believe me. Why is it you do?"

"I don't know exactly. I just do. It's like that feeling I get that I have known you forever. Which isn't possible because I only just moved here. I can't explain why I believe you any more than I can explain why I know you, you know?"

Alex laughed. "I do know, yes."

"So what do we do now?"

"Go home and sleep for a week. After that..." Alex shrugged.

"I vote sleeping for two weeks," Jenn said, her jaws creaking as she yawned.

"The whole blindness thing totally makes sense now," Chandon said.

"Without being able to see, Alex won't have to worry about traveling back in time anymore," Jenn said.

Alex's mom returned with the doctor.

"You're free to go but I want to see you back here in a few weeks. And I also recommend that you talk to someone. A trauma like this can come back to haunt you," the doctor said.

Alex nodded absently, having no intention of talking to anyone about this but the people who already knew her secret. They would help her through what was to come.

She said goodbye to her friends and followed her mom to the car. Everything looked strange to Alex. The sky was the same blue, the mountains still surrounded the valley, the cars still made their way on the same roads, the air smelled the same and yet it was all different. Alex felt as though she was an intruder and that the world was grinding along, hoping to shake itself free of her presence.

The world's not different. I am.

"Your uncle's friends left for their hotel room but wanted to talk to you as soon as you were released," her mom said.

"I'll call when I get home."

"Maybe you should wait until tomorrow. The doctor said you have to rest your voice."

"If I feel fine later I'll give them a quick call."

"All of this is still so strange, like it's happening in a movie or something."

"Tell me about it." Alex reached up and rubbed her throat, certain she could feel Stygian's handprints pressed into her skin.

"You're lucky Chandon was there. If he hadn't been, I don't..."

Alex reached out and patted her mom's arm. "But he was, so let's not even think like that."

"You're right. You're fine, Chandon is fine, and that guy is most definitely not. What do you say we call Karen, C.C., and Bruce and have them over for my famous spaghetti dinner?"

"Sounds good to me."

Alex retreated to her room as soon as she and her mom got home. She could tell her mom wanted to talk, or perhaps just keep Alex close but Alex needed to be alone to process what happened. And she needed to call Gavin, despite her mother's warnings to wait until tomorrow.

"Alex! I still can't believe what's happened. It's a miracle that Chandon was there."

"If he hadn't have come to see me and followed us, Stygian would have killed me."

It was the first time she had said the words aloud and they terrified her. She reached up to her neck and tried to hold back the flood of tears threatening to fall but they would not be denied. Gavin said nothing as she sobbed into the phone, trying hard to be as quiet as she could so her mom wouldn't hear.

She apologized to Gavin when she regained control. Alex told him what she had read on Stygian's patient chart.

Gavin whooped into the phone so loudly Alex had to hold the phone away from her ear.

"That's the best news I've heard all day. You're free, Alex. You can finally put all of this behind you."

"Can I really? What if his sight returns and he starts traveling again or what if he just pays someone to come after me?"

"He will be in prison a long time so I don't think you have to worry about him being able to pay someone to come get you. From what your uncle says, he was a loner and only spent time with Max Poder."

The mention of that name sent a shiver down Alex's spine. "What's to stop him from training someone else? Maybe the connection isn't between me and Poder, but between me and whoever Poder trains."

"You won't have to worry about him either."

*   *   *

Max Poder stood staring at the pictures of his ancestors, hand reaching out to gently caress the glass. When he'd received word that Stygian had fled the base and that he was wanted for murdering a man in the civilian world, he knew it was only a matter of time before his own involvement would be questioned.

He walked calmly to his desk, opened the bottom drawer on the left hand side, and grabbed his firearm. Poder fixed his eyes on the pictures as he cocked the gun and pulled the trigger.

Chapter 43

ALEX DID HER BEST to ignore the whispering and stares as she walked down the hall. She had hoped the months since the attack would lessen the attention but it seemed like it her attack on the Monument was still the talk of the town. Or at least the school.

Why couldn't he have attacked me after school was done?

She buried herself in school work, glad there were only a few months left to go until the end of the year. Her mind wandered as the teacher began the lesson. Chandon had asked her to prom earlier that day and she was imagining the dress she would wear.

Alex gazed out the window at the perfect spring day. The sky was brilliant blue, as only the sky in the desert can be. She had nearly completed her driving practice requirements and would be allowed to get her license at the beginning of summer. She had an amazing boyfriend, one she was able to share everything with, and a best friend who had stuck by her side through the worst of times. Things should have been as perfect as the beautiful day outside.

Yet a shadow still enclosed Alex's heart. She had hoped the nightmares would only last a few nights but they persisted for weeks and then months. Her mom wanted Alex to see someone but the only people Alex needed to talk to already knew about her ability to travel back in time and knew the truth of who Lane Stygian was. Alex knew Gavin was worried for her even though he always had a cheerful tone of voice when they spoke on the phone. Alex knew she needed time to believe that the nightmare was finally over. As each day passed with no changing of the reflection in the mirror, the more she began to believe that she may yet have a normal life.

It was still hard to believe that Stygian's Master had killed himself. She had called her uncle just to make sure Gavin had told her the truth.

"It's true, Alex. I saw them wheel him out of his office. Didn't leave a note but the powers that be are already linking him with Stygian. Since he killed a civilian, he is going to be left in the hospital and tried in a civilian court rather than being transferred back here to base. Our prisons aren't exactly the place for someone in Stygian's condition," Mark said.

"So he's really blind and still in a coma?" Alex asked.

"Yes, and likely to be there for some time. Doctors say there is no sign of him waking up any time soon. But when he does, he'll be tried for murder and theft and will be put in prison for the rest of his life. He will *never* be able to hurt you again."

That conversation had made her feel so much better. She'd only woken up from a nightmare once that night.

Maybe it really is *over.*

After her last class, Alex met Jenn and Chandon in the parking lot. Her heart skipped a beat when his eyes locked onto hers. It was like he could see right through her. When his arms wrapped around her, the worry about the future melted away. Chandon broke the hug and he stroked her face with one hand. When his lips met hers, the whole world fell away. Alex didn't even notice Amy, Paul, Simon and his new girlfriend arrive.

"Break it up you two. Us girls got some serious shopping to do," Jenn said as she poked Alex in the side.

Alex laughed and mumbled hello to her friends.

"Where's James?" Alex asked, just now noticed Jenn's boyfriend was absent.

"He's at work but said he'd meet us later tonight. We're still on for skating, right?"

"Sure, as long as you girls don't take all evening to find your prom dresses," Simon said, giving his girlfriend, Jasmine, a hug.

"Just be lucky we aren't dragging you with us," she teased.

"The last thing you want is boys cramping your style."

Alex basked in the warmth of her friends, both the ones she had met when she first moved to Grand Junction and the new ones she'd met along the way. Her life had been anything but normal since she had first spotted Aine in the mirror in the fast food restaurant restroom but she had prevailed, she had beaten the bad guys and lived to tell about it.

And in a few short months, she would be going to her junior prom.

Just like a normal girl.

Epilogue

DRIFTER TRIED TO OPEN his eyes. Something was dreadfully wrong. Every instinct screamed that something very bad had happened but he couldn't remember. Memories flitted through his mind with no coherence, no time line.

His arms wouldn't move either. Strange.

"He's moving around. Get a doctor," a strange voice said.

Obviously in the hospital. He could hear footsteps leaving and after a moment, several sets of footsteps returning. Hands touched him, checking God knows what. Part of his brain started to panic. *Why can't I remember?*

"Nurse, monitor his vitals and increase fluids. Officers, I want the Marine base notified immediately."

"Yes, doctor," a voice said.

Officers? Marine base?

One set of footsteps left the room. Drifter couldn't say how long he lay there in the darkness, uncertain of who he was or how he had gotten here. The officers spoke in whispers as the nurse moved about the room, eventually leaving after she was finished.

Small bits began coming back to him. His name, his rank, and soon after that, the face of Max Poder. It all came back, his time traveling gift, the girl, the mountains...

His muscles clenched when he remembered someone hitting him with something heavy across the face. *My eyes!* He strained against the restraints, wanting desperately to touch his face.

"Easy there, you're not going anywhere. Best rest easy so you don't hurt yourself." The gruff voice spoke on his right.

Drifter forced himself to relax, but the fear was still there. He opened his mouth to speak and his lips brushed against something that felt like gauze. He cried out, desperate for answers, more afraid of this darkness than he had ever been of anything in his whole life, including his drunken father on one of his rampages.

"Are you trying to say something?" the voice on his right asked.

"Help me, please."

"Sounded like he said help me," the voice on the left replied.

"Nothing we can do for you, son. That kid did a number on your face, and the back of your head took a beating as well. You're lucky to be alive," right voice said.

"What's on my face? Take it off so I can see."

"Sorry, pal, but even if we did, you'd never see anything. Docs had to remove your eyes right after they brought you in."

My eyes?

"Why? Why would they do that?"

"The kid hit you with an old fence post covered in barbed wire. Busted up your face pretty bad and the wire shredded your eyes. They couldn't leave them in or risk you getting an infection."

My eyes.

"I see. How long have I been asleep?"

"Let's see, I think pretty close to 6 months or so, give or take."

"Six months? Why am I still here? Why aren't I on base?"

"Your base has turned you over to the civvies. See, you killed a man and that means you'll be tried in a civilian court and put in a civilian prison. Guess the Marines are too worried about having you in a military prison in your condition."

"I think they want to forget he even exists. I mean, look what Major Poder went and did. The military is good at covering up embarrassments," left voice said.

"Master? What did he do, what happened?"

"Shot himself right there in his office. Master? Never heard anyone use that term for a CO before," right voice said.

Poder's dead?

Drifter knew it was over, the girl had won. It seemed impossible. He had killed so many Masters and yet one girl on her own, with no Master to guide her, managed to stop him? He wanted to throw something or hit something or shoot something but since he was tied down and couldn't see, he would just have to settle for grinding his teeth and planning his revenge.

ALSO BY SHAY WEST

The Chosen (Book One of the Portals of Destiny) (Fantasy) To each of the four planets are sent four Guardians, with one mission: to protect and serve the Chosen, those who alone can save the galaxy from the terrifying Meekon. An epic story of life throughout the galaxy, and the common purpose that brings them together.

Shattered Destiny (Book Two of The Portals of Destiny) (Fantasy) In the second book of The Portals of Destiny series, the Chosen of prophecy must work together against the universe-threatening Mekans.

Resigned Fate (Book Three of The Portals of Destiny)(Fantasy) The Mekans come, bringing death and destruction. Only the Chosen can save those who call this galaxy home.

The Mad Lord Lucian (A Portals of Destiny Novella) (Fantasy) A young magician is at risk of being corrupted by dark magic, a magic more powerful and dangerous than any he has ever known. Will an old story of a lord, a dark magician, and the man who dared to stand up to the Mad Lord Lucian be enough to change his path?

MORE GREAT READS FROM BOOKTROPE

The Unintentional Time Traveler by **Everett Maroon** (Young Adult Fiction) Jack Inman's seizures aren't good for anything. Except time travel. Once he's caught in a strange place and time, falling in love is the last thing on his mind. But it may be the key to getting home.

Schasm by **Shari J. Ryan** (Young Adult Romance) A young woman finds herself lost between what is real and what is imagined, but a chance encounter with a man brings new hope for the future.

Discover more books and learn about our
new approach to publishing at **booktrope.com**.